The Trial of
Goody Gilbert

by

Suzanne Ress

The Trial of Goody Gilbert

ISBN 978-0-615-66226-8

Cover design by Rickhardt Capidamonte

Print book layout by eBooks by Barb for booknook.biz

CONTENTS

For my great-grandmother

Lena Gilbert

The Trial of Goody Gilbert

Author's Note

Few facts are known about the life of my ancestor Lydia Gilbert, upon whom this work of fiction is based. It is believed that she was probably born in Yardley, England, as Lydia Ballett. Records show that she was living in Windsor, Connecticut with her husband, Thomas Gilbert, in the mid 1650's, and that in 1651 the Gilberts took on Henry Stiles as a boarder. Henry Stiles was killed on a musket day in the fall during his stay at the Gilberts' house, by a stray bullet that issued from Tommy Allyn's rifle. Tommy Allyn was charged with the accidental crime, his father paid a fine, and the young man was stripped of his right to bear arms for one year. Three years later, in the month of November, 1654, Lydia Gilbert, having been accused of witchcraft, was charged with the death of Henry Stiles, and sentenced to death.

The rest of what I have written, after doing much research into how colonial American society, government and law functioned at that time, came to me in a waking dream. Although many real historical characters appear in my story, the parts they played in the life of Lydia Gilbert and her family are of my own invention.

CHAPTER ONE

FROM THE JAIL door to the meeting house steps was only a short distance, no longer than twenty-five or thirty yards, but the frail old figure, slowly making its way from one to the other, seemed hardly able to hold up the weight of its own body. Although this person was clothed in a woman's dress, it had no hair and was so thin and lacking in form that it appeared to be an old man. Its eyes were closed tightly against the bright glare of the snow, and two large brutish men, known by the townspeople as the jailers, pushed the puny individual roughly onward along the icy footpath. Its hands were bound behind it with a rope, and it tripped and fell down twice, one time hitting its head so hard that it made a loud clunk upon the ice, but the jailers dragged the body up again roughly by the armpits.

At the bottom of the meeting house steps the little bald person faltered, and, looking up through the open slit of one eyelid, seemed to take in its surroundings for the first time. All around, and at the top of the steps, and by the door, lingered the townspeople. They emanated a greedy curiosity. All eyes were upon the prisoner, as if it were a strange new animal, and not human like themselves.

They whispered, "Poor thing! Look what's become of her!"

"Her state is dreadful."

"It is hard to believe that's her…"

"I can smell her from here!"

She fell again upon the steps, and then, because she had lost consciousness, was dragged by the jailers into the meetinghouse, where she was slapped upon the face and given several whiffs of spirit of harts' horn until she roused.

When she opened her eyes she found herself standing at the front of the court meeting house surrounded by seven persons unknown to her, all but one of them male.

Except for one of these men, who was thin and angular with a sallow skin and long yellow fingernails that continually scratched at his chin and jowls, they were well-fed and pink-faced, likely having come from a hearty breakfast together. These were the men of the jury, and they were from other towns in the Commonwealth. The woman who stood among them was less well dressed than they were, about thirty years of age, and would not meet the eyes of the prisoner with her own, but chewed and bit at her chapped lips, and appeared to be uncomfortable.

Although it was late November, the unheated meetinghouse was already becoming warm with the crowd of human bodies inside. Every place on the wood hewn benches was taken up with prattling people, and agitated children forced to sit still upon adults' laps. There was barely room enough for one more person to stand. No Sunday meeting had ever drawn such a noisy and excited crowd as this.

The prisoner, whose hands were still bound, had been looking out at all of the people, seemingly searching for some face she recognized, but now she turned her gaze downward toward the floor.

There were few trials in Windsor, and what made this one particularly spectacular was that the accused person was neither a wanderer nor a madwoman, but a lady of middle age known to many, married to a wealthy ship owner and former magistrate, and well respected in her community as a healer.

Not very long ago this same lady had hosted the Governor as a regular guest in her home. He, the Governor, was a former associate and fellow magistrate of her husband, and he now sat before all of the others in the meetinghouse to judge her. Though she herself had never trusted nor been keen on this man, despite her husband's good words about him, she had served him at her table with her finest home made ale and food, and had never outwardly revealed any disloyalty to her

husband's opinions, nor to the rules of the Commonwealth of Connecticut, nor to the laws of God.

She turned her gaze toward the Governor, who was standing at the
doorway, in conversation with several townspeople, before making his
entrance. He was in his early sixties, and wore a wooden denture that
sometimes slipped. Built stoutly, he was also well padded with a layer
of sagging fat. He looked briefly toward her, and with a gesture she had
become too familiar with, he stuck his index finger into and out of his
nostril, as if to say, "Thou shall be fucked, and I care not a whit,"
before looking away again.

During the long weeks she had spent alone in the lightless town
jail, which was more like an underground dungeon, she had thought
carefully and often of the events leading up to her first accusation and
then to her unexpected imprisonment. Allyn, the Governor, was not a
man to be trusted; he seemed to be motivated by nothing so much as an
ungodly desire for power. She was certain he knew the trial to be a
farce, and yet he would go on with it, and she would be the victim of it.

Now the warmth and excitement of being amongst so many
familiar fellows, whether they be friend or foe, began to bring the blood
back into her countenance. She pinned her gaze on a rough-looking
man seated in the front row, as if she were trying to remember who he
was, or what relation he might possibly have to her, but when she
caught the Governor's eye upon her she quickly looked away, down
again at the wide wooden floorboards she stood on, for, in truth she
knew very well that that man was her neighbor, Daniel Wescott. Beside
him sat his grown son Josiah, disheveled and dirty as ever she had seen
him. She, too, was rank now with bad odor and filth, so she should not
judge him badly on his appearance.

She was thinking on what law, according to the Code of Laws, she
had broken that anyone had been witness to. What felonious crime had
she committed that she should have been imprisoned unfairly for so
long, and now brought to public trial?

Lydia wondered if her husband were here now in the meeting

house, and she felt that he must be, for surely it had been he that had insisted with the Governor that she be taken from the jail and given a trial by jury. She looked for him in the sea of jabbering faces, but could not find him. He was a silver haired gentleman, good-looking and strong. He had been away in England for the better part of a year now, and she had given up on receiving any letter from him. He used to tell her that she was beautiful, even at the age of forty-two years. Remembering this now she felt ashamed for her appearance in the light of day, before everyone, and hoped that, if he were present, his view of her might be blocked by someone in front of him.

She was sorry for the sourness between her husband and herself just before he'd gone away. So much had changed unexpectedly for the worse during the course of these months, and so quickly. She had not admitted it, but she had missed his solidity and his support. An image came into her mind, a happy time with him soon before he'd left for England.

One evening after having lain together, he had remained in her embrace, dozing off to sleep.

The wind howled around outside the house like a river rushing downstream, and she heard the heavy trunk of a tree hit the earth with a sullen thud somewhere in the nearby woods.

"My Lord," he mumbled, half asleep already.

"A tree fell," she said.

She stroked his back, underneath his shirt, softly.

"I'll chop it tomorrow…when the rain stops," he uttered.

Then he began to snore quietly.

"Who are ye?" she whispered close to his ear.

"Thomas," said he, sleeping now.

She let some moments pass and then she said,

"Who am I?"

He snored.

She asked again, "Who am I?"

He opened his eyes a crack, and she could see he was not awake, but was dreaming, and she wondered what he saw.

"Your majesty," said he.

A sensation of prickling spread over her face and head when she remembered him saying those words, for she realized his esteem for her had increased over the years and he was able to see her for the strong person she had felt herself to be.

And yet, she was not being truthful, even to herself, for she had not been strong enough to resist breaking one of God's laws, and in doing so, perhaps she no longer deserved her husband's love. Was it for this crime that she was being tried?

There, near the central aisle dividing men from women, and not far from the front, was James Stiles, the Reverend's cousin. He was a fine-looking gentleman in his late forties, his hair still dark, and his carriage upright and springy. He did not live in Windsor, but in New Haven, and she wondered at his briskness in travel to be seated at her trial now when she believed its date had only been decided the previous day.

He was a lawyer, and well spoken, and, for reasons she did not understand, he had held a misdirected grudge against her for many years concerning the accidental death of his brother Henry.

Next to him sat his cousin, the Reverend Stiles, and she wondered if his wife, Judith were here, too.

Scanning the left, the women's, side of the court house, she found her friend, dressed in a new crimson cloak, with her daughter Mercy, and with her own daughter Reliance, one on either side of her. When she saw Reliance, tears filled her eyes, but her youngest daughter did not look at her, for she was conversing with Judith and Mercy. For some time, she watched her daughter speaking, and she thought, if she did not know her, she would believe her to be an ordinary pretty girl of seventeen. She wished to meet her eyes, but Reliance would not look at her.

She had not realized that all the time she was trying to get her daughter's attention, a lady seated just behind had been intensely staring at her. When she saw this angular-faced lady's glare, her brow furrowed but she refused to be intimidated, and did not look away. It was Susanna Fuller, the wheelwright's thornback sister. She wondered what evidence Susanna had to testify against her, for she and the wheelwright had been careful in their affection for each other. Finally, the spinster disengaged her stare, frightened perhaps of Lydia's evil eye.

Sitting beside the spinster was the wheelwright's wife, Humility, whose face looked peaceful, and rounder than when she had last seen her, for now she was about half the way through her pregnancy. It made Lydia glad to see that her cures had worked to help get this good woman with child after so many years of barrenness, but she also thought that it would be better if Humility had not come to the trial, for she did not have a strong constitution, and there could likely be unhealthy vapors in a place so crowded with people.

Closer to the front she saw Daniel Wescott's slovenly wife Elizabeth. Her greying head was hatless, and she was chattering wide-mouthed with her remaining daughter Mariah, also without a hat. She tried to block out the image that began to come into her mind of the Wescotts' other daughter, Mehetabel, now deceased, thinking critically instead on her neighbors' appearance. Then she remembered again that she herself had neither hat nor hair, and she looked down at the floor, humbled.

Again she turned her eyes to the men's side, which was directly in front of her, and found her husband's manservant standing at the back of the courthouse, alone and tall, his bald head higher than the heads of those people before him. He was not speaking, and he was looking at her. For some moments she met his gaze, and by his look she knew that he intended to protect her. This made her worry, for he knew things that no one else did, and he could only harm himself by saying them.

Governor Allyn was making his way, with difficulty because of the number of bodies standing in the way, down the central aisle toward the front of the courthouse.

He passed her son-in-law, prim-looking with his little spectacles, seated at the end of a row in the middle, and saluted him by patting his shoulder. He was a surgeon, and a friend of the Governor, and she would not worry for him, for defending her he surely risked nothing, he was too important a man. Still, she wondered what effect his defense could have on the outcome.

She looked around furtively for the wheelwright, but could not find him. There were many other craftsmen and shopkeepers present, and she wondered whether the wheelwright was present but merely out of her sight, or had he stayed away? In any case, it mattered little to her now, for she was afraid there were to be many accusations against her, and she would not be judged kindly.

Governor Allyn took his place behind the stand where she, and the rest of the church-going townspeople, was used to seeing Reverend Stiles stand to preach. He took off his hat and gloves, and, without removing his greatcoat, lifted the Bible in his two hands, to the level of his chest. With one great whack of it upon the top of the oak stand, he called order to the courthouse. All of the chattering came to a sudden halt, and the only noise was the settling shifting of tightly seated bodies on wood, and a child's sneeze.

CHAPTER TWO

TO THE TOWNSPEOPLE, Governor Allyn in his black great coat, standing one step higher than the woman on trial, seemed enormous, and when he had slammed the Bible upon the stand he had done it with such violence that certain of the weaker people present had suffered heart palpitations. Having everyone's full attention, the Governor loudly cleared his throat, and announced the charges against the defendant.

"Lydia Gilbert, thou standest here indicted by your name of Lydia Gilbert of Windsor as being guilty of witchcraft for, not having the fear of God before thine eyes, you have been familiar with Satan, the grand enemy of God and mankind, and by his help have done things beyond and beside the ordinary course of nature, and have thereby hurt the bodies of divers of the subjects of our sovereign Lord the King, for which, by the law of God and of this corporation, thou must be punished."

Several townspeople coughed, but no one spoke, not even a whisper, for all in attendance, having previously known the charges, were settling in, prepared for an entertaining spectacle.

Governor Allyn paused for some moments, gazing out arrogantly at the sea of faces before him. He had lain the Bible down on the dais, and, touching his nose briefly with the fingers of one hand, turned his attention to Goodwife Lydia Gilbert, who stood, shrunken and ugly, her hands tied behind her, in front of a wooden stool.

"Lydia Gilbert, how do you plea?"

She made no answer, but insolently stared at her neighbor, Elizabeth Wescott, who sat near the front, and was looking not at her, but at the Governor.

Again, the Governor inquired, "Lydia Gilbert, how do you plea?"

The courthouse was so silent that when the child again sneezed, it made some persons jump in their seats.

Goodwife Gilbert did not answer, but now turned her gaze to the Governor.

After some moments, he looked down at the Bible and then, addressing the audience, said,

"Being mute of malice, Lydia Gilbert, by the name of Lydia Gilbert of Windsor, shall be considered pled not guilty and referred to a trial by the jury present."

The men of the jury were seated upon a long bench against the wall behind Lydia Gilbert. When the Governor turned toward them, they all stood.

To them Governor Allyn said,

"You do swear by the great and dreadful name of the ever-living God that you will well and truly try to give just verdict and make true deliverance between our sovereign Lord the King and such prisoner according to the evidence given in court and the laws, so help you God in our Lord Jesus?"

"Aye," all of the men agreed.

When the Governor turned away from them, they sat down.

"Lydia Gilbert, you may be seated," he said to her.

She remained standing.

He spoke again, "You may be seated."

She did not sit, and refused to take her eyes from him.

Governor Allyn switched his attention to the audience.

"We shall proceed with the first testimony. Elizabeth Goodwife Wescott, step forward."

From the left side of the courthouse a lanky grey-haired woman stood and made her way through the crowd to the front. She had not washed nor changed her clothes since the start of the previous summer, and Lydia Gilbert, catching a whiff of her familiar foul odor of tobacco smoke and rot, looked on her now as she reached the front, but not, as she once would have, with disdain and disgust at her physical appearance. She knew herself to be as filthy and stenchful, if not more so, than her neighbor was.

Without so much as a glance toward Lydia, Goody Wescott stood before Governor Allyn, who thrust the Bible out toward her in both of his hands.

He said, "Do you give oath to the truth of the following testimony in the name of our lord God?"

She pressed her right hand on the cover of the book, and her left upon her heart, and gave her oath.

"Elizabeth Goodwife Wescott of Windsor, you may give your testimony," said the Governor.

She began speaking, looking out at all of the people before her, apparently enjoying being, for the first and only time in her life, the center of their attention.

"Ever since my husband and I have lived near the Gilberts as neighbors, our fortunes have dwindled and we seem unable to make good of anything. I have seen Lydia Gilbert looking at our house, my children, my husband and myself, and I saw her looking at our cow with her evil eye a couple of days before it run off into the woods and died."

"Goody Wescott, your own husband broke down our fence to let your cow into our cornfield to graze!" Lydia blurted at the back of her neighbor's head.

Elizabeth Wescott trembled visibly on hearing Lydia Gilbert's voice, but did not turn to acknowledge her.

"You were too lazy to bring that poor cow to a public green or pasture!" Lydia continued.

"I heard your husband breaking down our fence early one morning, and then William found the cow there, and had to chase her out to fix the fence!"

Without turning around to look at her, Elizabeth Wescott answered, her voice wavering,

"Your manservant chased her off into the woods and beat her so bad with a plank of wood that he made her lame, and when night fell the lynx ate her for his supper."

"He chased her out with an ordinary stick, and you did not go looking for her until after nightfall, so certainly the lynx got her!"

The Governor had returned to his position behind the stand, and, after allowing the two women a few minutes' argument, he lifted the Bible in one hand, and, again using it as a gavel, slammed it down upon the wood before him, and said,

"That's enough from you, Lydia Gilbert. We will hear Elizabeth Wescott's testimony in its entirety, and, not until she has finished will you question her or make comment. You shall be seated."

Lydia said nothing, but smiled at the Governor and remained standing before the wooden stool.

"Continue your testimony, Goody Wescott."

He nodded in Goodwife Wescott's direction, and she, who had turned her head to look at him, faced the audience again.

"I understood that my neighbor Goody Gilbert was not a God fearing woman the time my daughter Mariah came home from that woman's house with some butter and a pitcher of milk, and told me that she had offered her a cake of magic soap and a ride on her witch's broomstick."

The sound of quickly sucked in breaths from the townspeople encouraged Goody Wescott to continue in a slightly louder and more animated voice.

"When my daughter told me this I was afeared, and warned her to stay away from that house. Whatever dealings we had with the Gilberts after that I took care of myself, or else sent my son Josiah, who is strong in body.

"Why should Goody Gilbert's gardens, fields, livestock and family prosper whilst ours wither? Tis a simple rule of nature that, with the aid of her master, the Devil, she has taken away all of our good fortune and used it as her own. I am not one to initiate trouble where it lay not all ready, but in such a case as this, and for the good and well fare of my family, I can not but see what she is and how daily she sucks the life blood from us and thinks to repay it with an occasional crock of butter and half a pail of milk.

"Thinking back over it, twas some years ago that our worst misfortunes began, starting with my now deceased daughter's affliction."

At the mention of her daughter, Goody Wescott's voice became choked with sorrow. She paused a few moments to regain her composure.

"One day my husband brought home a cat from the woods, a big black tom with orange eyes. It took so long to strangle and it clawed at him so whilst he did it that I knew twas no normal cat, that one. For this cat, having previously been an ordinary earthly cat, had taken up living in the Gilberts' barn for the better part of the winter, where I now know that Goody Gilbert met with him each morning, and called the evil spirit of Satan into the cat's body. When my husband had finally managed to kill it, his arms and face were full of scratches, but not ordinary scratches such as any other cat would make: these were writing upon my husband's skin, and though none of us knew what the words said, I was certain twas not a good auspice. For those words were a hex, written into my husband's flesh by the dark Lord's servant. My husband, not knowing that he carried the hex, then touched my elder daughter Mehetabel, who was about thirteen years of age at the time, on the hand, and twas that very evening that she suffered her first spell. After the first spell, she became afflicted, having fits more and more frequently, and ever stronger.

"During one of her fits, Mehetabel began crying for no good reason. She wept uncontrollably, the tears coming so fast that I had to stand beside her and wipe them off her countenance with my petticoat. When I looked outside through the window hole, I saw Goody Gilbert pouring water from a bucket into a vessel by her doorstep. Only after she'd taken the vessel into the house and some time had passed did Mehetabel stop her weeping."

The townspeople had been listening carefully, and, presented with this image, some of them could not help but utter little cries of astonishment.

Behind Elizabeth Wescott, Lydia, still standing, lowered her chin to her chest and smiled, showing her few remaining teeth. Her eyes caught those of Elizabeth's husband, who sat before her. His face reddened, and he looked down into his lap, and placed his hand over his nose and mouth.

Goody Wescott continued,

"One morning, I'd got up late from the bed in a sweat, for the air in the house was stifling hot. I'd been wakened by the sound of Goody Gilbert, singing outdoors in a loud voice some version of the devil's dictum, for the words were all a garble and I could make not sense from them.

"My husband was still abed, and he rolled over onto his other side as I went to the window hole and looked out.

"My neighbor was standing amongst the flowering herbs in her flourishing garden, singing to the plants. She opened up her arms as though to take flight, and upon one hand there landed a great bird, the color of blood, and with eyes like burning brimstone, but instead of feathers, it had the scales and fins of a fish! She sang to the bird and then stopped singing and spoke to it with her face up close to its sharply pointed black beak. I watched, mortified with fear, as my neighbor then unfastened her bodice and took the great fish bird into her arms and let it suckle at her teat."

At these words some of the women in the courthouse cried out in alarm, and looked around at each other with expressions of pained shock, as if they, too, were nursing pointy-beaked birds.

Goody Wescott's tale, however untrue it might have been, was suspenseful, and welcome entertainment.

She went on,

"I called out to my husband who roused himself from the bed and came to the window.

"At that moment, perhaps because she had heard me cry out, she turned toward my house and looked directly at my husband and myself at the window hole. My husband's member then grew inexplicably so large and hard that twas equal to his legs in length, and it burnt and stung him so that he grabbed it with both his hands and tried to bring himself some relief. Twas the Witch's evil eye that did this to my husband, I have no doubt."

A few of the younger men stifled guffaws which they quickly transformed into coughs.

"She had a great crimson fish bird suckling at her teat, Daniel," said I to my husband.

"But she's fastened up her waist now. And where's the bird?" he asked me.

"Twas that which you held in your hands a moment ago, between your own two legs," said I.

As she re-enacted this entertaining conversation between herself and her husband, Goody Wescott swiveled her body from left, to represent herself, to right, to represent her husband.

"She sent it here, and now the vapors and fluids of its essence are all that remain."

"Clean it up then, woman," my husband said.

"I went to find a rag but there was not a clean one about. You see, my son, Josiah, had taken the habit of using the rags for cleaning his nether end after he shat, as he said he had blood leaking out of there and the dried husks and leaves hurt him. Surely this, too, was a curse put upon my son by the woman's evil eye."

At the mention of his name, Josiah, sitting next to his father, lifted his head proudly, and looked around, with a serious, injured expression.

"About two months ago, Goody Gilbert came to my door quite early. I'd been beating out the mattress and just lay down on it a minute to get my wind back—"

The Searcher looked at Lydia. Their eyes met and Lydia saw that the younger woman, despite her tough outward appearance, was terrified, and she looked away.

Goody Wescott said, "She came into my house, and to the foot of my bed, and was dressed in red crimson—"

She faltered and looked to Governor Allyn, who nodded quietly, urging her to continue.

"When she spake to me, from her mouth stretched out a black and double tongue, so long she could have licked her own backside with it."

This indeed was a vile picture. Several terrified gasps were heard from the crowd, and one young woman swooned.

"She pricked my feet and legs with pins and said that if I got out of bed she would tear me to pieces with her teeth and nails. Her teeth were all pointed, like a she wolf's, and they dripped with blood and bits of flesh, as if she had just finished a killing, and in place of human fingernails she had black claws like a bear's. When she turned to leave I saw she had a tail, its pointed end shew from beneath her skirts."

The woman who had swooned now fainted and fell upon her mother-in-law beside her, who, not wanting to miss a single detail of the story, very quietly slapped at the young woman's face with her gloved fingers.

Governor Allyn spoke,

"Goodwife Wescott, what was the reason for Goodwife Gilbert's visit that morning?"

"She left behind four blocks of her cursed soap, to bring me and the rest of my family misfortune and ill luck. Later, after she'd gone, I dug a hole in her hops field and buried that soap, and tried to burn it, for it frightened me, but the evil had been done. If we had ever had a chance for prosperity, her maledictions dwindled it down to nothing."

Goody Wescott stopped speaking and hung her head woefully. Several tear drops fell from her eyes to the floor. She lifted her apron and made a great show of blowing her nose and dabbing at her eyes. This scene made more than several of the townspeople's eyes burn, and even the Searcher had to blink hard to keep herself from crying.

From the crowd there was a low murmuring of outrage.

Lydia heard various words and phrases.

"Devil worship!"

"Danger to the community!"

"Witch!"

After some moments Governor Allyn said,

"Goodwife Wescott, have you any more evidence for the jury?"

Lydia Gilbert focused all of her attention upon her neighbor. Behind her back she clenched her bound hands into two tight fists.

Goody Wescott let her apron drop down, and, looking quickly at the Governor, began again.

"Ever since her husband disappeared mysteriously last spring, the Gilberts' holdings have prospered more than is natural for them to do. I look at my own empty field, where the earth is as dust and not even a burdock will take root, and then I look to the Gilberts' field of maize—great stalks twice as high as I am, and each one holds at least ten ears. There is not a yard of space with nothing growing on it, for between the stalks are hearty pumpkin vines, and climbing up them are beans so large and plump they nearly burst their pods.

"The manservant cleared all the rocks from Goodman Wood-mason's field last winter and planted rye grass, and I've seen him carrying sacks of rye to the millers for flour. For as many years as my husband and I have been on this land, Goodman Mason kept that field fallow and there was a reason for it and that was because twas no good for crops. Only the Devil himself could make rye grow from that field.

"I've seen, too, that with the stones he took out of the field, the manservant built an altar to the underworld, and I think tis where he and Goody Gilbert go at night, for inside there is a staircase that descends to hell, and he made the altar tall because when the door to hell is opened the flames rise so high they would otherwise be seen as far as New Haven."

"My Lord, protect us!" shouted a woman.

Several other voices agreed, saying, "Aye, Aye! Protect us!"

Elizabeth Wescott now aimed her glance toward William, although she would not look directly at him. He still stood in the same place at the back of the courthouse, but everyone had moved away from him, so he stood alone, in a wide open space.

Even from such a distance, Lydia noticed the pained expression on his face.

"He's a clever one, that manservant. I knew from the start that he was the lover of Mister Gilbert's wife, for the Magistrate was oft times away on board one of his ships, and his wife was left home with the manservant, whom, twas known, had never married and had no other woman. I believe the Magistrate and the Devil each loved a different half of the same woman; the one loved the light side and the other the dark. And her youngest daughter is not from the Magistrate, but from the Devil, for she is the strangest girl I have ever known and I can make no sense of her, and my husband and children are in accordance with this."

There arose an undertone of shocked voices, and Lydia shouted,

"Goody Wescott, do not dare bring my daughter's good name into this trial!"

Despite her weakened state, she was filled with indignation at the profane words her neighbor spoke aloud before so many people regarding Reliance.

"Be silent! No more outbursts from you, Goody Gilbert!" said Governor Allyn.

"Or you will have your mouth bound."

He looked to the Searcher as he pronounced these last words.

Lydia was steaming, and she glared at the Governor, who leered back at her.

"Silence in the court! Continue with your testimony, Goodwife Wescott," he said.

Elizabeth Wescott would not look at Lydia's daughter Reliance, but pinned her stare upon the farthest people, those standing at the back against the door in the meetinghouse.

She continued.

"One day, my husband was at the river, trying to get a fish, and he saw the girl sitting alone on a rock, but her back was to him. He, keeping very still, did not disturb her, for he heard she was chanting some blasphemous rhyme from the devil's book. As he stood there in the river, hypnotized by the sing-song tone of her girly voice, not one, but two great trout jumped up out of the river and into his arms.

"He minded this not, and was, at first, glad to have something to bring home to me besides another cat. But after some moments the fish became so hot in his arms that he could hold onto them no longer, and they jumped back into the river.

"With all the noise of splashing about, the girl turned to see what was going on, and got off the rock and walked some steps closer to the riverbank, a little distance upstream from my husband. She stared at my husband, who was staring back at her, until he remembered his manners and said,

"Good Day, Gilbert girl. What ye be doing down here all alone?"

"Said she to my husband, "I shall get you a fish."

"And without ado, she lifted up her skirt and waded into the water, to her waist, and within moments plunged both her hands into the river and brought out a very fine big fish.

"My husband was astonished by this, and frightened, too, for we had all ready many suspicions against this weird family.

"Take it," she said to my husband.

"She walked toward him, holding the squirming fish.

"But Daniel was certain twas a cursed fish, or else a trick upon his senses, and he refused it.

"Suit yourself," the girl then said, and she let the fish go.

"But instead of jumping down into the water, the fish went flying into the sky like a bird, and it traveled away out of sight, red gills and scales and fins and all."

Lydia had been keeping a steady watch on her daughter's face, which remained calm throughout Goody Wescott's testimony. Reliance did not look at her mother at all, but carefully studied the reactions on the faces of the six jurymen.

"Whilst Mister Gilbert was amongst them, the evil ones of the lot were mostly of an ordinary comportment, but I say mostly for there were exceptions, and many was the time the hairs on my head prickled up in knowledge of the presence of Satan, for she carried that all ways with her. Knowing this, I should not have trusted her to heal my eldest daughter when she was nearing her time of birthing pains, and in a bad fit. Perhaps twas Satan himself who blinded me in that time of need, and even he who'd set the fit upon my daughter all for the purpose of having my neighbor end my girl's life in the most gruesome of ways. That is a picture inside my mind that shall not be gone until my own death."

Once more Goody Wescott fell to weeping, and this time many more persons in the audience felt their throats choke with emotion, for most of them had heard gossip and rumors about the Wescott girl's tragic death.

"Goodwife Wescott, you spoke of the Gilbert's manservant being associated with Satan. Have you any other words of evidence on this subject?"

Lydia narrowed her eyes and opened her lips in a wide grimace to show the audience that she held her tongue between her teeth to prevent herself from speaking.

"Yes," she sniffed.

"My son had all ready told me that the Gilberts' manservant had yellow eyes like the devil, and Goodwife Gilbert slept with him whilst her husband was abroad, and she had entered in secret compact with him, Satan, because she is possessed of the evil eye.

"Late one afternoon my son Josiah returned home from Wethersfield, where he'd gone the day before to sell at market a pig he had found in the woods.

"He came home with rum and tobaccy, and injun meal enough for a fortnight, but I smelt also that there was rum upon his breath, and I saw that he looked affected from liquor. I knew he had been at the tavern in Wethersfield, drinking up a portion of that pig, and when he came near me I struck his face and all about his ears, and told him, "You are a rotten bastard of a son, wasting what you got at the tavern. I told you not to go drinking in there—what are we to eat when this meal runs out? The cow is gone and my cucumbers make us no fruit!"

"He hanged down his head but spake not, just took out the Indian meal and rum and tobacco from his sack, and I looked at it and went to get my pipe, for I'd not had any smoke for ten days—only dried corn hair and it wasn't good.

"My husband was down at the brook fishing, and my girls were not about, and I knew not where they'd got off to, they was all ways disappearing.

"I filled and tamped my pipe with the fresh tobacco, but the hearth was cold as stone. I said to my son,

"Run over to Widow Gilbert's house and get a hot ember."

"Josiah was my first born, me being but fifteen years of age when I had him, and he now is a fully grown man of twenty-four years.

"I said to him, "When you get back here, we'll smoke the pipe, and you can tell me what you heard in town. Which tavern did you go to, boy?"

"Greenleaf's," said he.

"And I've seen the devil himself in there."

"Then he went outside, and over to the neighbors' house for some fire, leaving me to wonder about the devil, and so impatient for my smoke that I grabbed a scant handful of the brown leaf from its rolled paper packet, and ate it. Twas good, and I was wont to get another, but Josiah was soon back with the fire, and I lit the pipe with it.

"He turned round to the hearth and tried to make it blaze up with some dry pine wood and needles that sputtered and cracked so that it sounded like musket fire and took to flaming so high that it scared me, and he pissed upon it to make it die down."

The jury men found Goody Wescott's propensity for adding details of her family's uncouth living habits to her story amusing. Several of them tried to cover their inappropriate smirks by putting their hands to their mouths.

"I was feeling aright then and held out the pipe to my son, and he set down on the log stool and smoked, and told me what he'd seen in Wethersfield.

"Before going into Goodwife Greenleaf's, he'd been headed toward a different Ordinary, but when he got closer he saw, walking from the other side of the street and crossing over the road, our neighbor's manservant.

"He was all dressed in black clothes, with a black cloak upon him, and was walking close upon another fellow's arm, and this other fellow wore spectacles to conceal his strange shining eyes, and my son did look upon the manservant in full daylight without the manservant even taking the slightest notice of him there on the street. And my son did see that the manservant wore no boots upon his feet, but in the place where his feet should be there were, instead, the hooves of a goat!"

At these words, many people in the courthouse turned around to get a good look at William, who, having come there only to offer support to Lydia, was too surprised by Goodwife Wescott's unexpected accusation to be defensive. He looked about at some of the curiously frightened faces turned toward him, his lips parted slightly in disbelief.

He was wearing the same cloak, which was actually very dark green. Upon his feet he wore his usual work boots, oiled for the occasion.

"And when the manservant, with his companion, who was at least thirty years younger than he, entered into the tavern, my son did see, coming out from behind the cloak a most frightful thing. Twas a long tail covered in scales like a dragon, and ending with a hook as if made to catch its victim and reel him in, with some evil motive to be sure."

No one dared to look behind the tall manservant for a tail, for if found, it would have been too unnerving. All attention returned again to Goody Wescott.

"Not only was Josiah quite certain that Magistrate Gilbert's manservant was Satan, but his companion also did show signs of being something other than a man, for the nails on his hands were long and curved like the claws of a lynx, and his ears, below his hat, were pointed like a cat's. I do not doubt that Satan cohorts with a lynx in the woods at night, for to hear that animal's screams does set all my hairs standing up, and makes my blood turn cold.

"Seeing these two creatures enter into that Ordinary tavern in Wethersfield, my son was convinced twas a meeting place for demons and witches, and he was much afeared.

"He turned around and ran away from there, not stopping until he came to Goodwife Greenleaf's Ordinary, where, said he, many kindly gentlefolk were inside, eating and drinking and gaming before a great hearth."

"In any case, twould be useless for me to be vengeful against the Devil, for it would do me no good. I am a God fearing lady and must accept what has happened to my family and be glad for the meagerness of my life as it is, and not covet what my neighbors—the Devil and his Woman and their Child—have got, for coveting such things from inhuman creatures would bring yet more harm upon us."

"Have you any other evidence against Lydia Goodwife Gilbert?" Governor Allyn asked her.

Elizabeth Wescott shrugged her shoulders, but made no answer, as she was preparing for another show of weeping.

"You will now state your accusations."

Lifting her face to regard the audience, Goodwife Wescott spoke clear and loud,

"As a woman alone Goody Gilbert has broken the law by living in a house with no man as head of the holdings, and especially as she shared the house with an unmarried man not related to her. Most of all, though, she is possessed by Satan, and is known by all to practice witchcraft."

Magistrate Allyn placed his index finger along the side of his nose and then rapidly slipped the finger into and out again from his nostril. He saw Lydia watching him, and looked down and grinned at the Bible.

"What have you to say in response to these accusations, Goody Gilbert?" he said.

"I do not see the reason why you, "Governor" Allyn, have allowed Goody Wescott to give voice to unjust accusations against my daughter and my husband's manservant, when—"

Before she could finish her sentence, an old man she recognized as Goodman Mills, rose from the right side of the courthouse and shouted,

"Hang the witch now!"

Giving him no notice, she continued,

"When this is a trial against me. And it would cause me to laugh, were the charges not so deadly, to hear my neighbor's fantastic, and purely invented tales."

Daniel Wescott, his son Josiah, and several other men now stood, and waved their hats and hands in the air, shouting,

"Hang her!"

"Bring the Executioner!"

"The witch must die!"

Then many people started bellowing out their opinions, and there was soon too much fracas in the courtroom for Lydia Gilbert to go on in her defense, nor for any hope of order being restored. After some minutes of riotousness, Governor Allyn was forced to call out for a short pause in the proceedings.

The two large men, the jailers who had escorted Lydia Gilbert into the courthouse, now took her by the armpits and walked her, with much difficulty, through the crowd to the courtroom door. All the while, she was screaming, in an attempt to be heard,

"Goody Wescott is a liar, and I never did to her but what was neighborly and Christian! She has no right in making accusation against William, who has done naught but work hard for us all of more than thirty years! I gave her food and soap, though she broke down our fence and set fire to my garden!"

Lydia was dragged down the steps, outside into the cold. A young woman came quickly behind, carrying a knit shawl of thick white wool. Miraculously, the jailers stopped for a few moments and allowed Lydia's daughter to wrap the shawl around her mother's shoulders and tie it at her waist. Her daughter embraced her briefly. Then the jailers abruptly jerked Lydia away, and took her back to the jail, where she was again locked in, alone.

CHAPTER THREE

ONCE AGAIN IN the dark underground room, Lydia stood in her accustomed place, several steps down from the door and near the wall, where it was a little warmer, but still far enough from the piles and puddles of excrement on the lower steps and the floor.

Having heard the name of Reliance upon her neighbor's lips, and in court, as if she, her dear youngest child, were also on trial, had roused Lydia's ire, and this, combined with the rush of seeing so many people all together in the courthouse after more than a fortnight of seeing no one, and the pure joy of her daughter Elizabeth's embrace, and the soft warmth of the woolen shawl, made her feel suddenly wildly alive.

What had Reliance to do with this trial?! She thought of the girl, now seventeen years of age, as more childish than her other two daughters had been at the same age, and in need of more care and protection, perhaps because, despite her aptitude for book learning, she seemed unable to adequately perform many necessary household tasks.

The cosy shawl held the pleasant scent of home, and of her daughters. She leaned against the wall, and, closing her eyes, a picture of one day in June, about a year and a half earlier came into her mind. Thomas had been away at Saybrook at the time to see about some cargo shipped in on The Mary Glen from Barbadoes, and William, Lydia, and her daughters had finished that morning to stack the hay.

In the house there was Indian rye bread and fresh butter and pot cheese and strawberry conserve and salad, and Lydia took all of these things and wrapped them in muslin, and placed them into a rush basket with a bottle of small beer, and invited her two daughters Elizabeth and Reliance to come to the edge of the river with her for a picnic. There was a big rock in the sun, with a flat top large enough for the three of them to sit upon and eat while watching the water flowing downstream.

Her daughters were at that time getting nearly as old as her sister Rebecca and she had been when they'd married their husbands and set sail in the ship, The Mary and John, for the long voyage to New England. On that voyage Lydia was pregnant with her eldest daughter Sarah. It was an exciting time for her—she was young, starting off on a new life all of her own making, and knew not what lay ahead, but she was not afraid; she felt secure with her husband Thomas Gilbert.

She looked at her two younger daughters and thought how well they'd grown, and it seemed only a short while ago that they were little tykes with hair soft as angel's golden thread, diverting themselves and each other for hours with a corn husk doll, or, in Reliance's case, even from the age of three years, by carefully copying out all the words from the page of a book, and then coming to Lydia to know what she had written.

In this curious way Reliance had taught herself to read at a very early age, and not only in English, but in French and Latin as well. She had always been the strangest of Lydia's children, and there was even a time, when she was about eight years old, that Thomas had thought she had a mental handicap, because her thoughts were so quick that often her parents could not understand them until a long time later, when they had finally worked out what it was that had come so quickly into the child's mind.

While they sat there eating bread and butter, a young Pequot girl came down to the river's edge on the other side, and walked into the water until it reached her knees. Then she lifted her tunic up over her waist to expose her nakedness underneath. She was about seven years old, and Lydia and her daughters sat in silence, watching her as she waded deeper, very slowly, into the river, until it came up as high as her chest. Then she reached out both of her hands and grabbed, fighting under the water with a fish she had caught. After some moments, she brought out a great shining trout with her small hands, and turned and went with it back to dry land, not even bothering to put her tunic back down to cover her little brown bottom, but walking off into the woods as she was.

Elizabeth said, "If only Mariah Wescott were able to catch a fish as well as she, the family wouldn't have to eat cat!"

"Twould be a fine thing to be able to catch a fish so easily," Reliance said.

Lydia said, "I suppose we could, each of us, take a lesson from that small Pequot girl, and learn to do it so well ourselves."

With these words she decided to try her own hands at catching a trout, believing all that was needed was patience, and fast nimble hands. But it would not be that day, nor the next, for there was plenty of food in the larder to eat. It would be for another time, and Lydia hoped her girls would try, too.

Reliance had brought a book that Thomas had got from Reverend Woodbridge—they were poems written by a Massachusetts lady named Anne Bradstreet, and she wished to read these aloud once she had finished eating.

Elizabeth and Lydia put the butter crock and the rest of the conserve, the linens and ale bottle, back into the rush basket, and Elizabeth took a small handful of breadcrumbs over to a little tree covered in brambles to leave for the birds. But when Lydia expected her to be back again to hear the poems, she was not. She looked over to see her daughter standing perfectly still in her summer gown, with her Bristol red bonnet, and the long golden plait of hair hanging down her back almost to her knees. A ray of sunlight shown upon her back, and lit up her hair and bonnet so they were as bright as fire, and Lydia felt a proud happiness to see what a fine and beautiful young woman she and Thomas had added to the world. She was observing something behind the brambles, and the expression on her face was concentrated on whatever was there. Although Lydia very much desired to know what Elizabeth was looking at, she could not bring herself to speak or move. Her daughter seemed to be in another world.

Reliance then opened the leather cover of the book of poems, and, not knowing what her sister was doing, called out,

"Elizabeth! Come over here and listen to me read!"

Elizabeth stepped back suddenly, and the expression on her face changed to one of surprised disappointment, and then, after some moments, she turned to Reliance and said,

"You've frightened away a fawn!"

She came striding toward the warm rock, and there was tenderness in her eyes when she said,

"It was sleeping there, surely waiting for its mother to return. A small, spotted fawn, with a sweet little nose and big dark eyes full of fear and wildness."

Lydia thought that she would one day make a fine mother, although she did not like her beau much, and hoped Elizabeth would soon find a different one. She kept these feelings to herself.

Reliance began to read,

"To sing of wars, of captains and of kings,

Of cities funded, commonwealths begun,

For my mean pen are too superior things:

Or how they all, or each their dates have run.

Let poets and historians set these forth,

My obscure lines shall not so dim their worth."

She read beautifully, with a clear and resonant young voice. Lydia liked the content of the poem, and found much familiar in it.

She went on reading, slowing her cadence when she came to these lines:

"I am obnoxious to each carping tongue

Who says my hand a needle better fits,

A poet's pen all scorn I should thus wrong,

For such despite they cast on female wits.

If what I do prove well, it won't advance,

They'll say it's stol'n, or else it was by chance."

As she read, Reliance's eyes opened wider, and she nodded her head slightly. Lydia knew she sometimes wrote, but she did not know what, as Reliance would show no one. If she had not been her mother Lydia might have thought her daughter wrote poetry, but in truth she knew the girl's mind was not lyrical enough for that, and she seemed better suited to write essays or expository articles. Yet, if she wrote such things, and even if she were to let her parents or sisters see what she wrote, being not even a woman but only a girl, there was no chance that her writing would be considered with seriousness by anyone outside of her family, and for that matter, perhaps not even by her own father, important and educated man as he was.

Reliance had learned to keep her special gift a secret, practiced only alone and behind closed draperies, just as Lydia had done as a girl with her healing and prescient powers.

Neither Lydia nor Thomas Gilbert knew how great their daughter Reliance's intelligence was, nor in what activity she had been involved because of it. No one, save Thomas's loyal manservant William, had any notion of what this teenage girl was up to, and why she often burnt candles all night upstairs alone in the cold attic room.

It had all started about two years earlier, when Magistrate Bennet, from Boston, had requested the Greek and Latin tutor, Master Phillips, to do a five page translation from Greek into English. It was a passage from Plato's Republic that he wished to incorporate into the Commonwealth of Massachusetts' Code of Laws. The magistrate had asked Master Phillips because his own understanding of Greek was only middling, and he had only two days until he was to present the revised code to the General Court. This request was made on a Tuesday afternoon, and the translation was to be done for the morning of Thursday.

Master Phillips was a good tutor, one of the best in New England, but he was quite busy that autumn with his students. He thought of his very best ex-pupil, whose strength in Greek and Latin at the age of twelve had surpassed his own. This was Thomas Gilbert's girl, Reliance. Phillips was well acquainted with Gilbert's servant William Farnsworth, and so, secretly, the tutor passed the translation on to Reliance via William, giving his word that the girl would keep any money that Magistrate Bennet would pay him for it. He did this with the assurance that neither she nor William would tell anyone, but that the girl would work anonymously.

Since she had stopped needing a tutor three or four years earlier, Reliance had not seen Master Phillips, who boarded in town with the Quincys, but William often met with him. The two men deviated from what was then considered normal, by being in love with each other and of the same sex.

William had taken Reliance into his confidence concerning this and other matters because she was young and curious, and she had noticed something and had asked, and also because he thought her to be different from most other people, but not in the same way as himself. He felt he could not keep secrets from Reliance, but he believed his secrets were safe with her.

William was several years older than Thomas Gilbert, that is, he was in his early sixties, but still vigorous and strong from a lifetime of hard physical labor. Reliance was her parents' youngest child, and cursed to be a girl with too strong an intellect, born in the wrong time and place. Her mother recognized this to an extent, and favored the girl, sometimes allowing her to sit idly reading Socrates or Descartes when she could be mending stockings or separating seeds. Sometimes, if it was a banned book, Lydia looked the other way, and pretended not to see what Reliance was reading.

So Reliance got by and even rose above where a more ordinary girl would have been left behind, for she could not even sew a straight line on linen.

She did the translation for Magistrate Bennet, in Master Phillips' name. It was not difficult for her, as she had read and reread Plato's Republic many times in Greek and was nearly able to translate it from memory.

William gave the translation to Master Phillips on Wednesday afternoon, and on Saturday morning, secretly in the barn, he presented Reliance with a gold coin, the first coin she had ever had of her own.

It was a fine feeling to earn money for something she could do well, even though she had to do it in someone else's name.

Master Phillips didn't expect what followed, and neither did Reliance, but not only did Magistrate Bennet return to him another time not long afterwards for a further translation, he recommended Master Phillips to other highly placed men, the Governors of Connecticut and Massachusetts among them. Since she had worked so well, and because he had little time, Master Phillips continued to covertly pass the work on to Reliance. The documents were mostly translations from Latin or Greek, and simple for the girl to do. Some of the men began requesting translations from French, which she could also do, and only one Master Phillips had to turn down for it was from an old German language neither of them knew.

Each time Master Phillips returned the translations to these important men, neatly done in Reliance's own hand, he was given some coins, which he passed on to William, who then passed them to her. The gold and silver pieces grew to be a hand full, and she did not know where to keep them, for she had neither pocket nor a purse, as it was thought that a girl had no need of a purse.

One day while left alone in the house to bake a gingerbread, Reliance came across a silver glove that had been hidden away in a nutmeg tin. She took it out and looked at it carefully, and thought that it must have been sewn by her mother, for it was hand made of stuff, and well done, too. Because there was only one glove, the left one, Reliance believed that her mother must have lost the other, and the one remaining would be of little value to her. Thinking that this glove was a thing Lydia had no practical use for, and that she would not miss it, and thinking also that it was pretty and would work well as a purse for all of her gold and silver pieces, Reliance took it.

Up until then she had kept the money inside her long stocking, but it bothered her when she lay down to sleep, and when the number of coins grew they fell down into her shoe underneath her foot, and she started to limp. Her sisters noticed the limp and wondered if she had fallen. Reliance felt the money had become like an affliction that caused her pain.

And so, with much relief, she took the coins from out of her stock-ing and dropped them lightly, one by one, into the silver glove. Once she had them in there she didn't know where to put it. She had no hiding place but on her person, and such a glove would be hard to hide, except by pinning it inside her petticoat, but the coins would tinkle when she moved and give themselves away.

She thought of the barn, where only the animals would see her in the act of hiding the glove, and they would tell no one. She hid it behind a slat in the wall and covered it with a wad of straw, and told only William, who, spending much time there, would eventually have come across it anyway.

When she returned to the house the gingerbread had stayed too long in the hearth oven and had burnt black, and was smoking. She hurried to clear away the smoke and to set things right again by trying to make a second gingerbread but found there were no more eggs, so she made cookies instead. She went to give the first gingerbread to the pigs, but in the meanwhile the fire grew too hot, and when she returned from the sty the cookies had burnt as black as the bread.

Lydia was still leaning against the wall when the jailers returned for her. Comforted by the warmth and the scent of the wool shawl given to her by her daughter Elizabeth, she felt relaxed and strong, and ready to defend Reliance against her neighbor's unfair accusation.

CHAPTER FOUR

SHE ENTERED THE courthouse with her uncovered head held high, walking on her own, with a jailer on each side. The crowd had settled down, and, at Lydia's entrance, everyone stopped talking, and watched her in terrified silence. The people who seated near the aisle, and blocking it at some places with their sprawling legs, now neatly tucked themselves away to allow her a wide berth. She looked around as she made her way to the front of the courthouse, and not a single person whose eyes she tried to meet would look directly at her.

Governor Allyn was already behind the stand. When she had reached her place in front of the wooden stool, the Searcher, who, before, had been standing close behind her, now stepped back. Lydia stood facing the audience for some time looking for William, but she no longer saw him at the back of the courthouse. Reliance was sitting quietly between Judith and Mercy Stiles, as before, but now she did not try to avoid looking at her mother.

In truth, Reliance had no fear that Elizabeth Wescott's accusation would bring her to trial, for she felt herself to be protected, because of her anonymous written work. She knew more about Governor Allyn than he, or Lydia, or anyone else, knew she did.

Upon returning from one of his day trips to Hartford, William had given Reliance a letter written by Magistrate Allyn, to be transcribed with grammatical and spelling corrections in her neat handwriting on fine parchment. Very often these studied men of law, who should have known Latin and Greek and French well enough to write their own words in it, did not even know how to properly express themselves in English. This was the reason why they paid their golden and silver

coins to the Latin tutor to do the translations, and now even transcriptions, for they had neither time nor expertise enough in the written
language to do it themselves.

Occasionally Reliance had the opportunity to transcribe or translate
a letter from a Magistrate to a Governor and then to transcribe the other
one's response. In this way she got to understand much of what went
on between these governing men, and what they conversed about and
what new ideas they had in mind for the future of the New England
colonies. Sometimes their letters even revealed an inkling of what
might happen next back in the English Commonwealth.

This letter written by Magistrate Allyn was addressed to Governor
Hopkins. He wrote of instituting stricter punishments in Connecticut on
religious dissidents and heretics such as Quakers, Anabaptists, and
practitioners of witchcraft, as was already done in Massachusetts. Now,
said he, these heretics receive only a fine or a public flogging, and perhaps, if their offense be great or many, imprisonment. But Magistrate
Allyn believed that flogging and imprisonment did little to discourage
these people from preaching their dangerous ideas in public, and if it
were possible he would like to increase the punishment for the first
offense to flogging, imprisonment, and stripping the heretics, if
freemen, of all voting privileges for the remainder of their lives. If the
offender be a woman or a servant, the number of lashes of a whip to the
naked body should be increased. For the second offense, whether
freeman, servant or woman, Magistrate Allyn believed the appropriate
punishment would be cutting out the tongue if the offense be minor,
and death by hanging if the offense be great. If one of these heretics
should attempt to seek refuge in Rhode Island, he would be sentenced
to immediate death by hanging. He wrote that the current punishments
were ineffective, and not strong enough to deter sinners, adding that he
himself continually witnessed their dangerous public outbursts. He had
ended this letter urging Governor Hopkins to agree, and to support him
in obtaining approval in Connecticut, under the rules of the New
England Federation, concerning this change.

This was what Magistrate Allyn had written, with bad punctuation and many grammatical errors, to the frequently absent Governor of the Connecticut Commonwealth. Reliance did not agree with the letter's content, but, being a girl, was not entitled to an opinion in such matters.

Now, as she sat in court watching her own mother being tried for witchcraft, and knowing that the final word, whatever decision the men of the jury reached, would be Governor Allyn's, acting as Judge, she wondered if she could have done something to change what she believed would be the tragic outcome.

It had been difficult for her to rewrite Allyn's cruel letter, and even then she had wished to change the words and make them gentle and forgiving toward the Quakers and those other people whose religion was not the generally accepted one. Her own view on the matter was that if people were not free to practice their own religion in all of the colonies of New England, but must exile themselves to Rhode Island, it was too similar to the circumstances under which her own parents and so many others had left England to come to the New World. She had thought, if Puritans can not tolerate religious dissidents, although they themselves were also dissidents previously, then will the Quakers who are exiled to Rhode Island also not tolerate others who believe not in that same religion, and on and on, until each group of people believing in one religious idea or doctrine cannot live amongst others of any other group, but each must have its own place separate from the rest. And when such people meet in one another's homes or at church, or in a town green or ordinary or other meeting place, their conversations will have no grit nor spice to them, for each will know what the other's beliefs are, and what will they have to discuss or dispute?

To Reliance's way of thinking, when she rewrote the letter, such a utopian existence would be dull, but it seemed that was the very thing Magistrate Allyn and others of his kind wanted to bring to fruition. Now she saw that the results of his narrow-minded bigotry were far worse than dullness.

She remembered a time the previous summer, in this same court meeting house. It was during Sunday meeting, and Reverend Stiles was reading from Ecclesiastes. When he came to the part, "To everything there is a season, and a time to every purpose under heaven", into the meeting house walked Peter Grigson the Quaker, stark naked. He walked down the central aisle and to the pulpit, where he stopped and stood facing Reverend Stiles, who, having his eyes down to read from the book, did not notice the naked man for some moments.

Everyone, including the boys who usually caused a loud ruckus fighting and pinching one another at the back of the meetinghouse, was silent. It was suddenly so silent that if a baby's belly were to have rumbled it would have seemed a thunderous roar.

All eyes were on the back of the naked man, and on Reverend Stiles with his head down, his eye glasses upon the bridge of his nose, reading on and on. Reliance, during those moments, had thought that the Reverend must believe his delivery of this passage from Ecclesiastes, heard by all present dozens of times previously, had become of deep significance for the entire congregation, and for that reason all were quiet.

Finally, the Reverend noticed that there was someone standing before him, and, still speaking the last words that remained in his mind's eye from the page, he stared at Peter Grigson the Quaker, and let the words coming from his lips finish.

Then the naked man turned to face the congregation, and everyone looked upon his gnarly private parts. With deep passion he shouted that the people's spirits were as naked as he was, and that they should be ashamed to present themselves in a church that represented a religion as intolerant as Presbyterianism, for there was only one God, and weren't all human beings equal?

At this point, the Reverend, along with three or four other men from the congregation, grabbed the naked one on the arms and legs and carried him out of the meetinghouse. He yelled and continued shouting his sermon all the way, and could be heard even when he was outside, but no one was listening to his words for the spectacle was too impelling.

Then everyone began talking and making so much noise that the Reverend realized it would be useless for him to return and continue his Bible reading. After some time the people all left the meetinghouse, and only the next day heard what had become of Peter Grigson the Quaker.

Since he already had committed, many times, the offense of not attending Sunday meeting, and had also committed the offense of calling meetings in his own home among Quakers, and he'd previously been flogged and fined for these offenses, it was decided that he must be imprisoned, and then banished to Rhode Island. As far as anyone knew, he had gone there, taking with him his common law wife and his son, for he was never seen in Windsor or thereabouts again. Soon after he left, his little house, and the few things that remained inside it, was burnt to the ground. Now, because of Governor Allyn, had Peter Grigson committed the same crime, he would risk being hung.

Reliance wondered what sort of place Rhode Island might be. She thought she would like to travel there and live with the heretics for a while, but of course she never spoke aloud of this desire to anyone.

When she had finished copying the corrected letter neatly onto fine parchment, using the black ink and the quill William had brought, she rolled it up and hid it beneath her cloak.

She had been able to do this work after dinner so she would not need to stay up late burning candles. Her mother sometimes saw her writing, but Reliance kept the writing pages hidden inside a big book while doing it, and her mother never asked questions.

As usual, she had given the Magistrate's letter to William, who was in the barn at that time of day feeding the animals. As he took it from her hand she had already been thinking of the coins she would receive for it, and adding up how much money she would have.

Some part of her believed it must be wrong to aid an evil man like Magistrate Allyn, whose beliefs and ideas were opposed to those held by her father. To carry on doing these writings in secrecy from her own family and the rest of the community was perhaps wrong, too. But the money was a pretty reward, and even greater was the satisfaction she received in knowing what actions these great statesmen were contemplating, and being able to play a small hidden part in it.

Shortly before her father had left, suddenly and without himself even knowing about it beforehand, Reliance had copied out and transcribed another long letter from Magistrate Allyn to Governor Hopkins. From the previous transactions between these two she understood that Master Allyn wished to be elected as Governor of Connecticut when Hopkins' term was over at the end of October, and she also understood, not by Hopkins' response to Allyn, for that she never did see, as he wrote his own, but by Allyn's next communication to Hopkins, that Hopkins was in favor of this and would support him.

In one of these letters, so badly written, from Allyn to Hopkins, he urged the Governor to send Reliance's father, Magistrate Thomas Gilbert, to England. Besides being a delegate to the New England Confederation, and a fourth term magistrate, her father, like Governor Hopkins himself, was also a ship owner with a thriving trade business by sea. Cromwell had a plan up his sleeve to restore the Navigation Acts, and, at the same time put an end to the Anglo-Dutch war.

Governor Hopkins made frequent trips back to England, and had been living there for many months, in fact all of the months of the current year, 1654. Perhaps he planned not to return to Connecticut at all, but to govern from afar. But since the number of magistrates had been reduced from the necessary six as written in the Fundamental Orders, to two according to the new Code, there were only Magistrate Gilbert and Magistrate Allyn for Connecticut.

As Master Allyn wished to be chosen by the colony's deputies to Governorship in October, it would be greatly advantageous for him to have the only other voting magistrate from the Commonwealth of

Connecticut abroad during the election time, making himself the only practical choice.

These were the ideas, anyway, that Reliance formed by conjecturing on what

Allyn had written and what she had transcribed. Of course she could not be certain that what she thought was truth, and neither, whether her thoughts be true or false, could she speak about them, nor of any of the hidden knowledge she had. She was not even tempted to do so, although she saw that her mother had been very sad at first after her father had left, not understanding why he had gone so suddenly, and why he had said nothing of it to her.

It was because he had not known, but only Reliance knew this. She could do nothing to console her mother at that time, just as she could say nothing now about what she had done to help the Magistrate become Governor, and her own mother's judge. She must pretend to be ignorant of everything except what she learned from reading literature and philosophy books.

Although Lydia had not yet been given the opportunity to defend herself against Goody Wescott's accusations, that woman was seated again where she had been previously, beside her daughter Mariah.

During the pause, Lydia had prepared the questions and comments she wished to say before Goody Wescott and the jury and the rest of the people, and she stood now, ready.

But when Governor Allyn spoke, he did not call on Lydia, nor ask Goody Wescott to return to the front.

He said,

"We shall proceed to the next testimony. Daniel Goodman Wescott, will you step forward."

"I would like to comment on Goodwife Wescott's testimony," Lydia said loudly.

She did not look at the Governor.

She saw that Daniel Wescott had already stood, and she turned her face to watch as the small but stocky long-haired man seated near the front of the meeting house pushed through several standing people to make his way, limping, to the Judge's stand.

"You may be heard," the Governor said offhandedly.

"She said the cat was mine, but it wasn't. We never fed him, and no one of our household lured him to remain in our barn. He came of his own accord, and was there not long, perhaps a couple of fortnights. He made a good job of eating all the mice."

The Governor held the Bible out to Daniel Wescott and said,

"Do you give oath to the following testimony in the name of our lord God?"

Lydia continued, although she was being ignored.

"The Wescotts never wash, and so I have on occasion given them gifts of soap. They do not tend to their land nor to their holdings, nor to their own children. Their deceased daughter Mehetabel had been afflicted with epilepsies of the brain, which Goody Wescott often asked me to treat."

To her right and slightly behind her, Daniel Wescott took his oath.

"Aye," he said.

Lydia Gilbert looked directly at Elizabeth Wescott sitting in the audience. Having been caught off guard, her neighbor quickly turned her face downward, twisted her whole self sideways toward her daughter, and then spit on the palms of her hands and held them in front of her face, toward Lydia, as if she were trying to shield herself.

Lydia remained temporarily speechless.

Governor Allyn said, "Goodwife Gilbert, have you anything more to say?"

Into her mind there suddenly came a passage from Corinthians I, Old Paul's letter, and she began to recite it aloud from memory,

"There are varieties of gifts, but the same spirit; and there are varieties of services, but the same Lord; and there are varieties of activities, but it is the same God who activates all of them in everyone.

To each is given the manifestation of the spirit for the common good. To one is given the utterance of wisdom, and to another the utterance of knowledge according to the same spirit, to another faith by the same spirit, to another gifts of healing by the same spirit, to another the working of miracles, to another prophecy, and to another the discernment of spirits, to another various kinds of tongues. All these are activated by one and the same spirit who allots to each one individually just as the spirit chooses."

As she repeated the words she identified to herself where men of law had erred, for they had read only those holy words that served their own purpose, and her interpretation of this passage was that if a woman were possessed of the special gift of healing, or of prophecy, it was God, and not the devil, who had given her such gifts.

Her sudden and flawless chanting of these words had an effect opposite to what she had hoped upon the townspeople and the men of the jury, for not everyone present was familiar with this passage, and to them the words could have been put into her mind by Satan.

In a silence so complete it seemed to ring, everyone stared in terror at Lydia Gilbert standing before them, her grinning bald head shining above the immaculate white of the shawl like an otherworldly orb.

And then she spoke again, her voice oddly powerful as her words broke the hush,

"In reply to Elizabeth Goodwife Wescott's accusation, Governor Allyn, I will say that all the powers in my possession are natural and I do not practice witchcraft."

CHAPTER FIVE

FROM BEHIND, DANIEL Wescott's filthy britches were roughly patched over previous patches, and his blouse hung out, torn. He wore neither jacket nor shoes, but only a stained bodkin sewn from strips of cat pelt.

Lydia looked at the back of her neighbor, and smiled. Previously she would have judged him unfairly, criticizing his slovenly appearance, but now, aware that she was even more unclean than he, she chose to assert her spiritual superiority to the situation with insolence. She knew that it was said, among some of the townspeople, that she had the evil eye, and the power, by looking upon a person or a thing, to inflict misfortune. She herself had begun to wonder if this were true, for despite that Wescott's land was of the same quality as that of her husband's, while her husband's had flourished, the neighbor's produced nothing, and the Wescott family had suffered much adversity.

Goodman Wescott turned from the Judge but avoided looking at Goody Gilbert. He looked past her, or around her, as if she were not there, and, perhaps she was not, for the creature before him bore little resemblance to the lady he had known as his neighbor. She had been fine looking, with chestnut hair that shone when she removed her bonnet sometimes while making soap. He had watched her on occasion through the window hole when his wife was napping. The old stick of a creature before him now wore no bonnet and had only a few tufts of hair upon her head. Her arms were bound behind her back, but, even so, she seemed to have no bosom beneath that bodice.

He, too, stood with his hands behind his back, although his were not bound with a cord. By holding his hands such, he could more easily retain the truth hiding within the words his wife, Elizabeth, had instructed him to say. Elizabeth's discontent with life, and the envy she had of her neighbor, were two of the reasons he stood here now, and these were forces stronger even than hemp rope.

"Daniel Goodman Wescott, of Windsor, you may give your testimony," said the Governor.

Wescott spoke in a wavering voice, for he was nervous, having never before been in front of so many people.

He said,

"When my eldest daughter Mehetabel was nearing the end of her nine months' term, one day, while walking in the fields, she saw Goody Gilbert gathering herbs."

Lydia blinked her eyes hard several times, seeming suddenly to come to her senses, as Goodman Wescott continued,

"My daughter was seized with a pinching and a pricking upon her back, and when she turned she saw a black cat who spoke to her and told her if she did go with him he should give her fine things—golden rings and silken underclothes, and a crimson glass chalice, and such other things as harlots possess, as I recall."

For a moment Lydia did not know what this man before her in the court meetinghouse was talking about. Was he referring to Wrastle Fuller, the wheelwright? Once again she looked out into the crowded room, but could see no face that belonged to the wheelwright. She was faint with hunger. She remembered that Daniel Wescott was accusing her of witchcraft, and that it had been his wife, Elizabeth, who had made the first accusation against her, two months before.

Governor Allyn spoke:

"Could you clarify, Goodman Wescott, whether you meant to say you yourself recall the cat's words, or you recall your deceased daughter reporting to you what the cat told her?"

Lydia regarded Goodman Wescott from the side dressed in his furry bodkin. Had she heard right, had he really testified, before the eyes of God and man, of a cat speaking to his mildly retarded daughter, Mehetabel? Were the jurors to believe such a testimony? Perhaps there was some allegorical truth in what this simple man said though, for eating so frequently the unclean flesh of cats could have contributed to Mehetabel's child being stillborn. Lydia herself now was so hungry that she thought she, too, would eat cat if it were offered to her.

"Verily, I myself never heard that cat speak!" said Goodman Wescott.

He suddenly brought both of his hands out from behind his back and threw them up by his ears.

Then, checking himself, he returned his hands to their place behind him and continued,

"I repeat only what my honest daughter Mehetabel said to me before she went to heaven."

He looked at the rafters of the ceiling, for he felt Goody Gilbert's eyes upon him.

The Governor urged him to continue.

Wescott said,

"The cat spoke out loud to my daughter, and then he took her to an underground room, where she beheld a table set with dishes of divers meats, and he urged her to eat her fill, which she did. Soon afterwards the door sprung open, and Goody Gilbert flew in and perched herself upon the pommel of a chair."

Was it the image of herself perched like a bird upon the pommel of a chair or the suggestion of a banquet table covered with nourishing food that made Lydia smile, in the direction of the Searcher woman, despite herself? The Searcher glared at her for a moment, then, frightened, quickly looked away.

Wescott continued,

"My daughter did say, I am certain you are a witch, or you could not sit so—And then nine black cats ran out from under Goody

Gilbert's skirts, and she turned herself head over heels and was gone from the room.

"The very next day my daughter told me this misadventure, and suddenly afterward, she fell into a fit and a fever, and my good wife went for Goody Gilbert—"

"Why, pray, did your wife implore help from the same woman who purportedly had been the cause of your daughter's fit?" demanded the Governor.

For a moment Goodman Wescott appeared to be stumped by this question, but, after some wringing of his hands behind him, he replied,

"Goody Gilbert heals with herbery. Mehetabel was in a terrible fit, and my wife knew not what else to do."

"Had your wife employed Goodwife Gilbert as a healer on previous occasions?" Governor Allyn asked.

Goodman Wescott was quick to answer untruthfully.

"Never! For she feared her! We all feared Goody Gilbert, because of her strange ways, and the strange ways of her daughter Reliance, and their servant—"

At these words Lydia suddenly interjected loudly,

"Who is't being tried—myself or my daughter, or my husband's manservant?"

"That's enough, Goody Gilbert, keep still. You, Daniel Wescott, get on with your testimony," said Governor Allyn.

Lydia Gilbert continued, "And he tells not the truth, for his good wife called me many times to cure Mehetabel's fits. And how many times was your good wife at my door asking for Indian meal, or butter, or milk? And your son, taking grain from our barn, and asking me to sew his trousers because no one else in your holdings would do it for him!"

"Keep quiet, Lydia Gilbert. There will be a time for you to speak, when Goodman Wescott has finished his testimony. Not now, keep your mouth shut!" the Governor shouted at her.

"You may resume your testimony."

"Goody Gilbert then came into our home and poisoned my daughter," Daniel Wescott said.

"She told my wife twas medicine that would stop the fit. I can still see her inside my mind, perched there on the side of the bed, her hands pressing an iron star form upon my daughter's belly. And I can hear her, too. She was chanting some dark magical versification to bring up the powers of Satan. The sound of her voice, low at first, very nearly raised up into a terrificant scream, and, since the words were a jumble and not of the human sort, my good wife was frightened into a faint, and only woke up after the witch's curse had taken effect. For the poison she'd brought with her, under the disguise of an herbal cure, had the opposite effect from what she had said it would. Mehetabel never came out of that fit, but only fell more deeply into it, writhing and trembling far worse than ever before had I been witness to. The witch then left our house, and when my good wife came awake again from her faint, she saw that the birthing pains had come upon Mehetabel, and I was obliged to leave the house with my son Josiah.

"After my daughter had spent many hours in the female suffering, my good wife finally had to pull the dead babe out feet first with fire tongs, and, soon after, Mehetabel expired. Her final words were, "Goody Gilbert hath put a curse upon me!""

A gasp rose up from the crowd in the courthouse.

Until this moment Lydia had not known that the birth was breech, nor that Elizabeth Wescott had tried to yank the baby out of Mehetabel with iron tongs. Knowing the Wescotts' living habits, she thought that the tongs had likely not been clean ones, but were probably covered with rancid grease, or dried dung. Hearing these details of the stillbirth, Lydia felt a weight lifted from her, and she smiled, for now she could believe that Mehetabel's child had not been killed by the strong herbs she had administered to the mother, but by the unfortunate circumstances of its birth.

In the courtroom Daniel Wescott continued,

"Goody Gilbert is a witch, and she killed my daughter and my unborn grandchild."

His voice cracked as he said these words, and he wiped a tear from his eye, then dropped his head down to his breast.

Notwithstanding his falsified testimony, the truth of his emotion choked Lydia's throat with sorrow, for Mehetabel had been a baby at the same time as her own daughter Elizabeth. Lydia's sorrow for her neighbors' loss was compounded by the bitter feeling, which she did not fully understand, that she knew they had for her.

"Lydia, Goodwife Gilbert, have you any questions, comments, or words in your defense, regarding the testimony of Daniel Goodman Wescott?" said Governor Allyn.

"I well remember this episode, for I did go over it many times in my mind this past fortnight while I was kept in jail."

"Proceed," said the Governor.

"When Mehetabel was nearing the end of her nine months' term, her mother summoned me. The girl, who was seventeen years of age, was not experiencing birth pangs yet, but had fallen into a violent fit.

"Because of my knowledge of herbs and plants I had, previous to this episode administered healing medicine to Mehetabel for her affliction, epilepsy of the brain, and I knew which cures had helped her other times.

"I was washing by the brook in the morning when Goody Wescott came. She told me that Mehetabel had gone into a fit, and she feared for the unborn child, and asked me to help her with an herb concoction.

"I gathered the laundry and returned to my house for the cures.

"Other times I had given Mehetabel dried hellebore root with cinnamon for good results, but since the girl was now with child I hesitated, not knowing what effect this strong medicine might have upon the baby inside her.

"Marsh mallow would not hurt the child, though I did not think it would help the mother much. Having to make the choice, I chose the milder medicine, and, in case of dire urgency, I grabbed a piece of hellebore root and one of cinnamon bark, but hoped not to have to use them.

"As I came out of my house I called to Goody Wescott to leave the rest of the linen which she had started to hang, and to get to her hearth to make a fire and boil a pot of water as fast as she could.

"She ran ahead.

"When I entered her house, she was just getting the tinder lit. The girl Mehetabel, enormous with child, wailed, and made such a thrashing around on the bed at the front of the house that I was afraid, as I had never before seen her in so bad a state. When I moved closer, I saw that Mehetabel was bleeding from the nose, and her eyes were rolled back in her head so that they appeared white. She sat up straight and clutched at her own face and tore at her mouth, making it bleed, too. She emitted a shout so loud and frightful that it made the hairs at the back of my neck stand up. Then Mehetabel's eyeballs reappeared, colored, in their sockets, light and faded, nearly yellow.

"She looked directly at me with those pale eyes and shouted some incomprehensible words. They sounded like, "In dues meum cata strophe und gunter cats flyon!"

When Lydia spoke these strange words, all eyes in the courthouse, which had been upon her, now darted away, downward, or up to the ceiling rafters, or to the windows.

"For all the world," she continued, "although words alone cannot hurt anyone, I could see this nonsense fly at me in the form of little arrows with sharpened flint heads, and there I stood with nine arrows stuck into my face and chest. I saw them there, stuck into my own flesh, I swear to it."

Goodwife Wescott stood abruptly and shouted,

"The witch lies! She lies! Satan speaks through her! Who among us did not hear his voice just now!"

"Silence in the court!" Governor Allyn said.

Adults who held children on their laps now covered the children's ears with their hands, and the fear amongst the crowd nearly bordered on panic.

Lydia lowered her voice slightly to get everyone's full attention, and continued,

"I sat on the edge of the bed, near the foot posts, and felt a liquid heat, like blood, running down my face and all inside my bodice where it cooled and chilled my stomach.

"When I touched my face my hands came away clean; the wounds were inside my skin."

She paused for a moment, and, when she resumed speaking it was in a slightly louder voice.

"Then something else inside my skin made me change my mind about the medicine. Mehetabel would receive the hellebore root boiled with cinnamon, and, God help her, the girl was so violently stricken that I made the brew quite strong.

"It calmed her at once, and her mother was glad of it, and urged me to give her some more. The girl lay exhausted, asleep with eyes closed, spread out wide on the bed. She had no need of more medicine, but I left the rest of it with Goody Wescott, and took leave of her house.

"While I was walking out of her gate, I saw Goody Wescott's husband and her grown son coming from the direction of the swamps with buckets full of frogs. And I saw that Goodman Wescott carried over his shoulder a dead thing, a cat, a gray one.

"I went back to my own yard and finished hanging up the laundry, taking note that two lace handkerchieves and one pair of white cotton stockings were missing."

As she recounted, she remembered once again the details of that dreadful stillbirth.

"Then, after sun set, I was sitting down to supper with my

daughters when we heard the terrible sound of Mehetabel screaming and shouting so loud that, although she was in her own parents' house, it seemed as if she were in ours.

"While the girls wondered that Mehetabel was giving birth already, my heart beat so fast that I worried my breast might not be able to contain it, for I feared that Goody Wescott might have given her daughter the rest of the medicine, and where a small amount can cure, too large a dose of the same can kill.

"My daughters asked me why I looked so peaked and worried, and I said,

"Tis the screaming. I fear something has bestruck Mehetabel or the child she carries."

"Is't not normal for a woman to scream in labor?" they asked.

"Tis too much," I said. "Perhaps I should go to Wescotts and help."

"Said they, "Go, if you think best. Though they have not called you."

"More screams came from the Wescott's, but these were not Mehetabel's; they were of the mother and sister, and there were no cries of a babe.

"Perhaps you should go," they told me.

"Mehetabel was near the same age as my daughter Elizabeth and they had played together when they were young.

"I told them that when I was there that morning Mehetabel was having a fit, and I thought to give her only marshmallow to cure it, but her fit was so bad that marshmallow could not help it. And when Goody Wescott urged me to administer stronger medicine, I gave the girl some hellebore, and left the rest with her. I said I feared the mother had used the strong medicine.

"It had steeped so long with the cinnamon bark as to make it very strong indeed.

"I knew I must return to the Wescotts then and try to make things right.

"We then heard the approach of running footsteps, and a breathless voice calling out,

"Missus Gilbert! Your help is needed! Come now!"

"It was Josiah, the grown son. He had thrown an old bodkin over his shirt, and he stood in the doorway with the full moonlight from without, and the fire and candle light from within, shining down and on his dirty face, which was twisted with worry and distress.

"Mehetabel's child has come, but still born, and my sister is not well at all. She won't stop bleeding."

"I ran over there with him, and inside the house, the baby, grey in flesh, and a well-formed girl, lay dead on the table, with a half eaten skinned roast cat beside it. This sight made me wretch, for I know that eating the flesh of cat, rat, bat and dog poisons one's blood.

"The mother and father, and also the younger sister, were in such a state, they did not notice that I had entered the house. Mehetabel lay still on the bed where I had seen her last, her eyes closed, and the linens and all her petticoats and apron soaked in blood. The mattress seemed to be a marsh of blood, and Mehetabel was sinking into it, slowly, and in remarkable peace.

"In heaven's name, give her something to stop the bleeding!" Goody Wescott cried out to me.

"Although I knew it was too late, and the medicine would be of no effect, I quickly returned home for half a dram of the red powder from dried and beaten amaranthus flowers which I mixed to a paste in red wine. But before I returned to the Wescotts', and even before I had the paste blended, the girl had drawn her dying breath. When I saw her again she had already begun dreaming the transitory dreams of the dead, as she faded away from this world, her soul leaving the body that had served her so ill, it still lying in the pool of blood which kept leaking out, ever more slowly until it stopped and began to congeal.

"But to please the dead girl's mother, and also because I had already mixed the paste, I spread it upon her pale lips, and upon her thickening tongue, all the while praying to Jesus to take her soul to heaven.

"I am afeard tis too late," I told Goody Wescott then, and I placed my hand upon her arm to comfort her.

"But she flew into a sudden hysterical rage, and screamed at me, and pounded me with her fists, and scratched at my hands and face with her nails.

"Her husband was now nowhere nearby, nor was her son, and the younger daughter lay sobbing with her face down upon her sister's body.

"Even though Elizabeth Wescott was then lighter than I in body, in her state of hysteria it was if she had the strength of two men in her, and try as I did to restrain her with my arms, I could not do it. Goody Wescott continued scratching and punching at me so that I was forced to flee her house, and run back to my own house, where I shut the door tight behind me."

CHAPTER SIX

LYDIA WATCHED DANIEL Wescott limp slowly back to his place on the bench beside his grown son.

Governor Allyn then called out the name of that son, Josiah Wescott.

Although he was about twenty-three years of age, because of his lack of grace, both kinetic and sensorial, he gave the impression of being younger.

As he approached the front of the meetinghouse, he fixed his eyes on Goody Gilbert, and was not afraid nor intimidated by her, as the others were. He had known Lydia Gilbert all of his life, and he considered her as a second mother—one more capable and emotionally mature than his biological mother.

Lydia knew him to be a gentle and harmless fool.

She smiled encouragingly as he approached her, and then looked over at him as he took his oath upon the Bible.

She suspected that like his father, Josiah had been instructed by Elizabeth Wescott what words to say as evidence against her. As he began his testimony, she knew this to be true.

He testified thus:

"One morning early Missus Gilbert was afore her house, stirring lard in her cauldron, making soap. She sang a song in the devil's tongue, and on her shoulder there was a hare. The steam from that pot had an evil odor, something akin to singed horse hooves and wormwood and sheep's urine, and as it rose it formed itself into a rat, a dog, and a crooked foal, who then gathered together with her and the hare to form a Devil's Circle around the cauldron."

The image Josiah's words created made a formidable impression upon the townspeople, and there was an expectant silence in the meetinghouse.

Because of this silence, what would have otherwise been an inaudible comment from one of the jurymen was heard by all, and especially by Lydia, who stood so close.

"Rubbish," he said.

It was the long-faced one with the sallow skin. He sat stiffly, like the others, listening, stone-faced, but his single whispered word gave Lydia new confidence.

Josiah continued,

"They danced so fast around and around—the witch with her familiars—that they turned into a smudge of black smoke,"

Hearing these words someone—a man—amongst the audience of townspeople, let out one exhaled note of laughter.

Judge Allyn glared sternly in the direction of the laugh, lifting the Bible several inches off the podium with his right hand, as if threatening to throw it at the offender. Several men sitting near the laughing man turned, with tight lips, to glare at him, and he bowed his head and was silent.

Josiah continued, "And then the smoke transformed into a ring of fire, and it rose up into the air, high up above her house and ours, and then it came down again onto the thatch of our barn's roof! I wasn't there when it happened, but I know it to be true, for my mother was watching all of this through the window hole."

At these words, Governor Allyn interjected,

"Josiah, are you telling the jury that you yourself were not a witness to these events?"

Unsure of the exact meaning of the judge's words, but knowing that his mother expected him to recount the story as she had instructed him, Josiah had no reply, but stood dumbly, his hands dangling at the ends of his long arms. He looked at the judge, then he looked at his mother, and finally, he looked to his left, at Lydia Gilbert, who was much uglier than she'd been before she'd gone away, but still had the same kind look in her eyes.

He said,

"My mother told me these things later, but I never saw them myself."

"You must present only first hand evidence, young man," said Governor Allyn.

"That is, things you have seen or heard yourself. Do you understand?"

"Yes, Governor," he said.

He continued,

"I myself heard my mother tell me that she had tried to call out to me and Pa to come and help her put out the quickly growing flames. And later I heard her tell me that she was unable to move nor to utter any words as she stood there whilst our barn burnt to its fundaments. I heard her say that Missus Gilbert had put a spell upon her. I myself heard her say these things to me."

Now there was a general soft undertone of laughter rolling through the audience. Most of the townspeople knew Josiah Wescott to be a fool, and were amused by his mistake.

Even Judge Allyn could not keep a slight smile from his lips, as he said,

"Josiah, when did you hear your mother say these things to you?"

The young man stared at the holes in the toes of his hide shoes for some moments before responding,

"Sometime in the afternoon, when Pa and me came in with a cat and basket of ducks' eggs. We found my mother sitting on the floor by the window hole, covered with black ash, which had blown in from the great fire from our still burning barn.

"Pa went to her and slapped her, and she woke up, and when he asked her how our barn had caught fire, she could not at first remember. After some little while her memory did come back to her, and she told us."

"Did you yourself ever have any occasion to witness Goodwife Gilbert practicing the craft of witchery?" Governor Allyn asked.

Because of the way he had phrased his question, Josiah was not quite certain what the Judge was asking. Believing that he had been asked what crafts Missus Gilbert was skillful at, he replied,

"Last spring, my trousers, being the only ones I have, got torn so badly in front as to reveal my member." Josiah looked down at his trousers and his crotch, as he spoke.

His words, and the spectacle he presented, were too humorous to go unheeded, and many of the townspeople, trying to stifle laughs, now let go, and were joined by many more.

The Governor, also tickled almost to the point of laughter, lifted and slammed the Bible down hard onto the podium, and called for order.

In the near quietness that followed, Josiah continued his testimony, "Now being a grown man, it seemed improper that I should go about in this way, but since neither my mother nor my sisters would sew my trousers, and I knew not how, when I went over to Missus Gilbert's to get some corn husk to smoke, she got out linen, needle and thread and showed me how to mend the breech myself."

He lifted the hem of his blouse in front to exhibit the roughly sewn rectangular patch covering the center front of his trousers.

The atmosphere in the courthouse had become notably relaxed, almost friendly.

Lydia stole a quick glance at the Searcher, who was gazing at Josiah with her lips parted.

Governor Allyn smiled very slightly at Lydia, as he saw her eyes upon him, and he asked for her defense.

Josiah turned to her, and she smiled at him gently. The warmth of her shawl and of the familiar meetinghouse had given her renewed energy.

She spoke clearly and well, saying,

"The thatch on the Wescotts' barn roof was in a very dry

condition. As you surely recall, there had been no rain for all of the month of August, nor into the first week of September. When finally the rain came that day, which was a Friday, shortly after noon, it was a meager rain, preceded and accompanied by much lightning.

"About an hour past noon I believe lightning struck the thatch on the roof of the Wescotts' barn and set it afire. I had seen a great deal of it coming down in that place from my daughter Sarah's house in town, which was where I was at the time. I had gone there to have noon dinner."

Josiah had been looking out at his mother as Lydia spoke. When she had done, he asked her,

"My mother said, er, I heard my mother say that you were in your garden making a brew in your cauldron when our barn caught fire, or shortly before—"

Lydia smiled at him, and said,

"Yes. Earlier that day, in the morning, before the storm came, I had made a batch of soap in my cauldron in the customary place between our house and yours."

"And I heard her say you put in it a man's finger and poisonous parts from a gremlin—" Josiah looked at Lydia wide-eyed.

"I had lard from the pig William had butchered, and wild rose petals, and petals from marigolds, and thyme leaf in that batch, Josiah."

As she listed the ingredients, she could smell the mixture again in her memory. It had come out of the pot in great wafts, and permeated deep into her hair and the material of her clothing, and thinking on it now she felt transported. She thought how odors and smells had a secret language all their own, of which the rest of the mind seemed to be ignorant.

"And you sang a hymn to the Devil, I heard her tell me."

"Yes, I sang, but twas no hymn to Satan. It was an old song in French, taught to me by my grandmother."

There was some low chattering going on amongst the townspeople, and, perhaps to catch their attention, Judge Allyn asked Lydia to sing some of that old song in French, if she could still remember it.

Lydia was happy to comply with the Governor's request, for she no longer felt so weak, and she knew herself to have a lovely singing voice.

She cleared her throat, and, standing alone before everyone, with her hands behind her back, she sang in a clear contralto,

"Quelle est cette odeur agreeable,

Qui ravit tous nos sens?

S'exhale t'il rien de semblable

Au mileau des fleurs di printemps?

Quelle est cette odeur agreeable, qui ravit tous nos sens?

Voici beaucoup d'autres merveilles!

Qu'entends-je dans les airs?

Quelles voix! Jamais nos oreilles

N'ont entendu pareil concerts.

Voici beaucoup d'autres merveilles!

Qu'entends-je dans les airs?"

By the time she had finished singing, all of the townspeople were silently enraptured, listening to her.

While singing, Lydia had been carried back to when she was a child, and living with her mother, who died giving birth to her brother when Lydia was nine years old. Lydia's father, a generous God-fearing man, was killed the next year when his horse slipped on wet cobbles and fell on him.

Her father was the printer in Yardley, and from a young age Lydia and her five sisters and brothers lived with the written word all around them in broadsides, booklets and merchants' lists. Once their father printed a book for them made up of little stories and rhymes they had invented.

After her parents died, the seven siblings were split up to go abide with various relatives and cousins, and the happiest times were over. Lydia and her older sister Rebecca stayed at home with their grand mother, who had come from France as a young woman, and still spoke with them at home in French. She was a musical woman, often singing, or playing a mandolin, which Rebecca brought with her to Boston, and her son Elliot learned to play beautifully.

Josiah had tears in his eyes. He looked at Lydia, and said, rather sheepishly,

"And my mother said...that your familiars danced about you..."

It seemed that no one was paying any attention to Josiah, for a low chatter started up again, as Lydia spoke slowly, and told him,

"One of your cats came along, and it seemed he was listening to me singing. And there was a sparrow perched nearby, watching me, and, as I sang, he moved closer, so that when he was in reach I stretched out a finger, and he hopped on for a moment before flying away."

Josiah and Lydia stood looking at each other, while the chatter in the courthouse grew more consistent, and loud enough that the noise of it surrounded them and drew them into its busyness.

Josiah stepped closer to Lydia, and she added,

"And whilst the soap was cooling I got a hare that my son in law had brought, to skin it and prepare it for cooking for the next day's dinner."

"I do not believe you are a witch, Missus Gilbert," Josiah confided to her. "But my mother doesn't like you."

"Josiah," Lydia looked directly into his dull eyes.

"You are old enough to speak for yourself. Tell the court what you have just told me."

He hung his head and played with the hem of his blouse a moment.

"I can't say that."

He did not lift his head as he spoke.

"You can, Josiah."

"No. Ma would beat me."

There was a sudden loud thud of the Bible coming down forcefully upon the oak wood dais. Governor Allyn called out,

"Order! Silence!"

The palaver died down to a low sibillation.

"Have you anything more to say, Goodwife Gilbert?"

"After I made the soap I rode my horse into town, to my son-in-law's, and the storm came. Later, when I returned home, I saw the Wescotts' barn had burnt to the ground because it had been struck by lightning. The fire had gone out before it had spread to their house, for that still stood. I offered to help them in some neighborly way, but when I approached Daniel Wescott he held up a scaling knife and told me to move away and to never come close to him nor to his house nor his family evermore."

"That's all, Goodwife," the Governor said.

"You may be seated."

"And you may return to your seat, Josiah."

CHAPTER SEVEN

JUDGE ALLYN CALLED for the next testimony.

A tall dry-looking woman of middle age came to the front of the meetinghouse.

Lydia had seen her amongst the townspeople in the audience before, and she was worried about what she might have to say against her.

An ominous hush now settled over the meetinghouse.

"Susanna Fuller," the judge spoke her name.

It was Wrastle's sister.

"Do you swear by the great and ever living God that you will well and truly tell on oath only that which is true so help you in Lord Jesus?"

He thrust the Bible toward her with both of his hands, as if it were a weapon.

She moved forward, toward him, without looking at Goody Gilbert.

Lydia shifted her weight from one leg to the other. It was tiring for her to stay so long on her feet, and she would have liked to sit down, but, because Governor Allyn had told her to, she would not.

Outside the glass window she could see a banner of blue sky, bright and cloudless.

Susanna Fuller took her oath.

"You may give your testimony," said the Governor.

Lydia watched Susanna, remembering now the unfriendly looks she had given her each time they had met in her brother's shop. The wheelwright's spinster sister would now have the opportunity to say publicly anything she wished against Lydia. Although, by her appearance, Susanna Fuller seemed to be a person not much given to pleasure in living, Lydia believed she would glean some enjoyment by testifying against her. The silence in the meetinghouse disturbed her, for it said, more loudly than any spoken testimony, that there was general suspicion amongst the townspeople of the nature of the relationship between Lydia and Wrastle Fuller the wheelwright.

"Lydia Gilbert came to my brother Wrastle for the first time one day last spring with an old wagon wheel for repair, and that is the only work she has ever brought him. But after that she did meet many times with my brother."

If she still believed in God, Lydia would have prayed to Him that Susanna would not add an accusation of adultery to that of witchcraft, for the former would bring shame and humiliation upon her husband even after her death, if indeed she were to be sentenced to death.

Governor Allyn sat with one gloved hand supporting his sagging jowl, watching the spinster intently from behind as she spoke.

The townspeople were listening quietly. Many of them had noticed, during the past several months, Lydia's horse tied outside the wheelwright's shop, more often than seemed necessary for a woman who owned no cart.

Susanna Fuller went on with her testimony. She was dressed in dark green and grey, and her bonnet was tied so tightly at her throat that, despite her lankness, she appeared to have a double chin.

"I came into the shop the first time, when Goodwife Gilbert brought her barrow wheel. I went there to fetch Wrastle's dinner bucket, and before I entered I heard her speaking to him in sweet and kindly words. When she saw me she quit speaking, and she soon took her leave."

Lydia stood with her face to the floor, expressionless as possible, wishing she could disappear. She wondered what words Susanna had heard her speak to Wrastle, and what else had this woman seen or heard?

"No sooner had Lydia Gilbert gone out again than my brother hit upon his thumb with a hammer, and within a short time he had splintered a fine plank of pine wood and tore his britches upon a nail. Then he did a thing I had never heard him do before—he uttered blasphemy! He maledicted the Lord when I said twas Lydia Gilbert had given him a curse with her evil eye. He told me to go home and spin him a patch!"

From the women's side of the courthouse came several sounds of shock and disbelief.

In a lowered voice, Spinster Fuller continued,

"Over some weeks' time, my brother was transformed. Oft times he seemed to sleep whilst working, and when I spoke he did not hear. Twas as if he were in a trance, and he no longer had his own mind about him. One morning early, through a crack in the door, I saw him dancing!"

At these words, many of the townspeople turned around to exchange consulting glances with one another, for dancing alone was a clear sign of bedevilment.

Lydia had wondered before if Wrastle were present in the meetinghouse, and now she knew for certain that he was not. With all of her might, she hoped that, by staying still and silent, Susanna would not say that word that she dared not even think.

The spinster continued,

"And I saw the shadow of Lydia Gilbert, naked save for a long sash about her waist, leap out of the fire to dance with my brother!"

This image scared Lydia, for, although it had never happened, there was truth in it, but she made no outward sign of fear.

"I know that Lydia Gilbert is a witch because I could no longer recognize my brother, he had changed so much in so little time, twas not natural. Soon after this strange vision, my sister in law, Humility, who had been barren for many years, was suddenly with child."

Even if he should have wanted to, Wrastle could not speak in Lydia's defense, to testify that she had treated Humility over the course of several months with herbs to cure her barrenness, for he would risk drawing suspicion upon himself. To sympathize with an accused witch would be almost the same as saying one is of the same ilk, and, she thought, it would add further proof of the other crime whose name she dared not now think on.

Susanna Fuller went on,

"Since he made acquaintance with Goodwife Gilbert, my brother did take to easy laughter, and he sometimes disappeared for long hours to where I knew not. Even now when he speaks of Lydia Gilbert, which is not infrequently, a strange light comes in his eyes, and I am certain she has possessed his soul, in exchange for the child soon to be born."

Lydia was certain the spinster suspected her of having had illicit relations with her brother. But being bent on proving her a witch, perhaps the sentiments of an ordinary lonely woman would be overridden by what she knew the public wanted to hear. Or perhaps Lydia was wrong, and Susanna never had suspected anything between her and Wrastle, besides that she had enchanted him. And maybe Susanna was right, and that was all she had done, and all that she was guilty of.

"She brought bewitched herbs, and taught my brother various incantations to plant a demon child inside my sister in law's body."

These were the thornback's words, and they were unjust, and made Lydia wonder at Susanna's reasonment. Her anger rose up, for these words would only do harm to her brother and to his innocent unborn child.

The blood had drained out of her bound hands and they tingled painfully, and she continued to clench and unclench them behind her, but certainly none of the townspeople were aware of this.

Susanna proceeded,

"One morning last week she came to him flying on air and caused my brother to cry out her name in his sleep.

"Lydia! Lydia! he cried. When I came close with the candle I saw his face was contorted with lust and base instincts. She has made him no better than an animal."

The Governor leered at Lydia. She did not look at him, but could see this from the corner of her down turned eye, and she knew what he was thinking. He had also dreamt of her in this way. He had told her that she was a sinful woman.

Susanna Fuller had finished speaking.

CHAPTER EIGHT

BEFORE MEETING HIM for the first time, Lydia had dreamt about Wrastle.

It was early April, and the sun shone warm enough already so that the earth was heated and could be worked. Some weeks before, Thomas had left unexpectedly.

At the end of the previous October she had tilled, added manure, and covered her herb plants with dried leaves. Now, when she took off the layer of rotting leaves, she found new sprouts of calendula, celery, tarragon and thyme awakening.

"Tis too soon, Mistress," William's voice said from behind her.

Lydia was bent low to the ground, having dropped the hoe to get a closer look at the little green stems rising from below.

"No tisn't," she said, without turning to look at him.

"You'll see," said he.

He began to walk away toward the barn, but then he turned toward her again to say,

"We've yet to see the season's last snow."

She laughed at him, and when he had turned around again she threw a pebble at his back.

Lydia thought about what William might do when alone with his friends, and she wondered if it was he who played the part of the man, or the other one. She thought on how it would be to have a fifth member, and to plunge it into the orifice of someone else's body, and she wondered if she would worry that there might be a fiery portcullis or dragons' teeth deep within. Or would it be like stabbing the earth with a sharp spade to plant new seed there? Would it make her feel her own power? It was the springtime air that was making her think in this devilish way.

She stood and continued hoeing away the leaves, until the plot for herbs was all uncovered, and then she went to the shed for the wheelbarrow.

When she brought it out into the daylight, she saw that two of the wheel's spokes were rotted and broken. Maybe a mouse, over the winter, had eaten through some of it in hungry desperation. Without its spokes, the wheel was of little use, and without its wheel, so was the barrow of little use. She covered the hill of leaves with old sacks of hemp burlap weighted down with rocks, until she could get the wheel repaired.

Judith Stiles had told her there was now a wheelwright in town; he'd arrived late in the fall before, coming from England via Boston, and to Windsor, for it was here that he had a cousin who had told him of the town's need for a wheelwright. Until then people had been managing poorly with home done repair work, which did not often work so well.

With a mallet she removed the wheel from the barrow and brought it up close to the house, leaving it outside the door where she would remember to bring it to town the next day. Then she went to the pottage garden, where the rhubarb grew. She moved away the leaves there to see the strange curled little red fingers pointing up at her from inside the earth, like a demon. She uttered a funny shriek and then covered up the demon claws again and ran away.

As soon as the wheelbarrow was repaired she could clear away all of the leaves from the gardens, but now there was little more she could do there, so she went into the house to work on a knitted blanket.

Inside the darkened cool house were Elizabeth, who was churning butter in the kitchen, clad only in her petticoats, and singing, and Reliance sitting in the rocking chair by the window, and reading. She was reading a book in Italian, given to Thomas Gilbert by the Holland counsel man, called La Decamerone. Lydia could only begin to comprehend what the words in these stories meant, for, knowing some French, she could piece together a bit of the Italian, but not so well. What she understood about the book was that it was a collection of one hundred stories, on ten different themes, and spoke on people from all walks of life. She also knew the book to be sinful in its explicitness, for Thomas had told her this much. Reliance was sixteen years old, and could read Italian well, and was of a mind wise enough that Lydia did not doubt that she could handle reading whatever a man's hand could dare to write.

Though Reliance should have been shucking more corn for the animals, Lydia withheld herself from reprimanding her. The girl looked so involved with the book that it seemed a pity to send her away from it. Despite the strangeness of her preferences, and her high intelligence, Reliance was a sympathetic and kind girl to whom other persons were easily drawn.

"Finished with the garden already, mother?" Elizabeth called.

Lydia turned and looked in at the stillroom where Elizabeth churned. Her bare arms pumped up and down, the muscles under her white skin tensed, perspiration underneath.

"Not finished," Lydia said.

"The barrow wheel needs mending. I shall take it to town on the morrow. To the new wheelwright."

"A wheelwright? In Windsor?"

"Tis so. Here since autumn."

"Mother, shall I color the butter or leave it white?"

"As you wish."

"I shall leave it white, then. Tis coming now."

Lydia went to the other room, where Reliance sat reading. She seemed not to hear her mother enter and sit down in Thomas's high backed chair.

Next to the chair was her basket of knitting.

The blanket was made of thick new wool, uncolored, and still oily. She knit it up closely, in a heavy, twisted stitch.

As she knit, her mind wandered. The rhythm of doing the same stitch over and over, moving her fingers tediously in the same way was a meditation, and it settled her mind and brought peace.

The only noises in the room were the gentle clacking of the wooden needles, and the soft rustling of Reliance's turning pages. After some time, a surprising picture came into Lydia's mind.

She saw herself taking the barrow wheel into the wheelwright's shop. It was a hot day and she wore nothing save a red chemise, tied around the waist with a violet satin ribbon that was so long it dragged behind her upon the dirt floor of the shop. Her hair was undone and hung loosely down her back to her knees. The wheelwright, a young man quite pleasing to look at with his auburn hair and his large skillful hands, did not acknowledge any oddness in Lydia's appearance, but welcomed her pleasantly.

Without saying a word to one another, the wheelwright put his arms around Lydia, and, quite like a wheel, began to dance with her in an circle ever faster, and dangerously close to his work bench. Tools were lain there carelessly—a barely balanced hammer, saws with sharpened teeth facing outwards and near to tippling off.

She laughed and laughed so hard that her chemise slipped from my shoulders, leaving her naked to the waist.

The wheelwright then took hold of one end of the long violet ribbon and spun her so fast in a spiraling circle that her undergarment fell to the floor in a pool of red stuff, and she danced naked before the young man, who was smiling joyfully. He then did lay her over his lathe, and take down his trousers so they could fornicate there quite crudely.

Reliance slammed her book shut. Lydia stopped knitting and looked at her daughter's reddened face.

"Well!" said Reliance.

"What is it?" Lydia asked, alarmed, but trying to sound calm.

"Ah, mother! There are some things I am perhaps not yet ready to read!"

"Concerning what, dearest girl?"

Now Lydia, too, felt her face blushing.

"I shall read you a small part of it," she said.

Lydia put the needles through the wound ball of wool, and rolled the blanket and placed it in the basket beside her.

Reliance opened the book again, rifling through until she had found her place.

She began reading in Italian.

"I do not understand all of it," said Lydia. "But I can get the gist."

As her daughter read aloud, Lydia understood that her mind had been reading the book along with her daughter while her fingers knitted innocently. She did not know how this could be, but so it was.

CHAPTER NINE

SOME WEEKS LATER, after she had brought the wheel for repair to the new wheelwright, she had returned again to his shop to see whether it was done. It was on the same day that Lydia had given the strong herbs to her neighbors' daughter, and because she could not forget any detail of that horrible day, she recalled also a strange conversation she had had a during the noon meal with her girls and with William.

Reliance had been reading Descartes' book that morning when she should have been mending, and she wished to discuss it.

Soon enough her words had drawn Lydia in, for what she said made her think of Mehetabel in her fit, and frightened her.

"One part of Cartesian doubt states that we may doubt our senses," Reliance had said. "And that because one perceives oneself to be seated upon a bench eating one's dinner at home, in fact one could be but dreaming of doing this, and be, rather, naked and asleep in bed."

The words made William smile and wave his rough large hand in her direction. He was a practical man. But what she said made Lydia think on the arrows launched into her with Mehetabel's strange words. Had that really happened? If neither her own eyes nor ears could be trusted to know what was real, could what she imagined be what was real instead? She kept these thoughts to herself, but she still felt the wounds on her face and neck.

"When will you do the mending, then, Reliance?" Lydia asked.

"Tis done, mother," said she.

Lydia supposed the time she had been at the Wescott's had, like a dream, passed in a space different than that measured by the sun.

It had left her uneasy to have administered such strong medicine to Mehetabel. She had known the girl since she was little more than a baby, and now she wondered if she had done right.

She tried to forget her unease, and after dinner wrote a letter to her sister Rebecca in Boston. Then, having some free hours ahead, Lydia decided to ride her horse into town. She would post the letter, buy some laces, perhaps stop at her friend's house for tea, and also at the wheelwright's to see if he had got the barrow's wheel fixed yet.

By half past three she had finished at the post and the milliner's, and so walked her horse Aisley across the street, where she hitched her in front of Judith Stiles' house. They had met twenty years earlier upon Thomas and Lydia's arrival in Windsor. Her husband Edward was the Reverend at meeting, and he was a learned man, and just, and kind as well. Everyone attended Sunday meeting, as it was law, but even though he had a captive congregation, the Reverend was neither too long winded, nor superstitious in his preaching and so the hours passed easily enough, and often gave food for thought.

She started up the Stiles' front steps, but hadn't gotten half the way when their servant girl, a Mohegan of about fourteen years, opened the door and told her that neither the Reverend nor the missus were at home, as they had had to go to Wethersfield for some business, and only Mercy, their daughter, was at home, but she was engaged in lessons with her tutor, Master Barnes.

Lydia thanked her but could no longer remember her name. She told her to tell Judith that she had been by, and to leave her salutations with Mercy.

Her heart was sinking, because she had wanted to tell Judith what had happened at the Wescotts' that morning, but she would have to keep it inside a little longer.

She unhitched Aisley, remounted, and headed in the direction of Goodman Fuller, the Wheelwright's. And, as she went, now concentrating on her destination, the mare's steps grew quicker and lighter, and she had to check the reins to keep her at a walk. They were not headed in the direction toward home, so all Lydia could make of the horse's excitement was that it mirrored her own. Did the pressure of her thigh and knee against the mare's side, did her fingers woven in the leather of the reins, convey to the mare's bit what Lydia was feeling? The quivering in her belly, the beating of her heart, did these rhythms cause the horse to move the way Lydia would have had she been the one on the ground?

Goodman Fuller was at work, and had company in the person of old Goodman Mills, who was becoming weaker of mind with each passing year. He now went about in a matchcoat with biscuit crumbs in his beard, and pap on the lips of his toothless mouth, talking nonsense to whomever he could entrap long enough to feign listening.

His wife and grown children had tried all means to keep him at home, but to no avail.

When Lydia entered the wheelwright's shop, Goodman Fuller was good naturedly mumbling responses of this or that whenever the old man paused a moment from his spittle filled speech. Perhaps the Wheelwright did not much mind the old man's company, as his daily toil was solitary and time could weigh tediously with so much aloneness.

Both men looked at her when she entered—the old one with rheumy pale eyes, the younger man with kindness and welcome.

Lydia wished both men a Good Day, and they greeted her likewise.

"Ah, Goodwife Gilbert, you've come for the barrow wheel," Master Fuller said.

"Tis no urgency," said Lydia.

"But being in town I thought to stop here and see you."

As she realized what words she had uttered her face flushed red with embarrassment.

"I meant to say, to see about the wheel."

Goodman Fuller smiled, and in his eyes Lydia saw that he did not much mind her mistake.

"The barrow wheel—" he looked toward it, leaning against the wall where he'd placed it a fortnight earlier, still untouched.

"It shall be done day after the morrow."

"Then I shall see you in two days," she said, blushing again.

She felt hot and foolish, and she quickly bade them both Good Day again and left the wheelwright's shop.

The next time she saw him was a Thursday afternoon. It was an overcast day, but the clouds were high, and no rain would come. She was wearing her red woolen cloak, for without the sunshine the air was chilly, and by sundown, it would be cooler still.

Under the cloak she had taken care to dress in a clean waist, the green one because it set off the color of her eyes, and her brown riding skirt. She wore clean petticoats scented with lavender, too. All this, she had told herself, was because she would be having tea with her friend Judith Stiles and daughter Mercy. But Lydia would be stopping at the Wheelwright's, too.

The third Thursday of the month was market day.

Aisley pricked her ears and pranced as she neared town. She lifted her nose to take in the distant smells of other horses, and she whinnied a greeting from afar to some companion in town, whose answer both the horse and Lydia heard.

The market was bustling with ladies and women in need of new stuff for spring dresses, and one could find there besides every sort of bric-a-brac: spices, straw hats for summer, pipes, ribbons, sugar, and, if one asked, cards for playing, which were kept hidden below the table. Children were running about here and there, several quite dangerously in the path of an oncoming ox cart, which swerved away just in time not to run them aground.

On Meeting Way, where the Stiles' house was, Lydia met Judith and Mercy and their servant girl walking toward the market square. Judith asked her to join them for an hour or so at the market before tea, saying she could leave Aisley in their stable. They waited while she went to their carriage house and stable, to leave her horse.

Walking fast, Lydia soon caught up with the Stiles', and they all spent a pleasant hour at the market.

Back at Stiles' house, the servant girl brought out ginger cakes and sassafras tea. The ladies also tasted coffee. The Reverend had been given a tin full of it by his cousin. This fellow had traveled to Paris in the autumn and found the strong beverage to be newly fashionable. To Lydia's tastes it was too harsh and bitter, like smoking tobacco, and not to her liking.

At four o'clock, Mercy had a lesson with the tutor, and Judith and Lydia were left alone in the sewing room.

Lydia knew she would now have to tell her friend about Mehetabel.

"The coffee drink has made me jittery," said Judith.

Perhaps she said this as a reflection on the way she perceived Lydia to be feeling.

"It isn't a thing I could regularly partake of," said Lydia.

She looked around the drawing room at the new pictures Judith had put up on the walls.

They were small colored prints of people doing various work—a basket maker, a potter, a woman weaving a chair seat, a lawyer reading a book—each framed in polished cherry wood. Judith had shown Lydia these pictures when they'd entered the house, telling her they were a gift from Master Frantelmi, whom she'd seen last month in Boston with her husband.

As she looked at these things, Lydia was thinking of Mehetabel lying in the blood filled bed. She could see again her swollen, bloody dead lips and her thickened tongue as she wiped them with a damp rag and spread the red paste over them. She saw the girl's eyes rolled back into her head in the same was as Jesus's eyes were painted in the crucifixion pictures she had seen as a girl in England.

She began to weep.

"What is it, friend?" asked Judith.

She came close and placed her hand on Lydia's head, and then on her shoulder.

Lydia was overcome with fear and sadness and guilt and regret mingled up with something more, and over which she had no control.

While her friend rubbed her shoulders Lydia wept with closed eyes. Judith untied her bonnet and softly massaged Lydia's head.

After some moments, once she had regained herself somewhat, Judith asked Lydia if she wished to tell her what was making her weep.

"My neighbors," said Lydia.

"The unkempt family?"

"The Wescotts."

"The elder girl was delivered of a stillborn child four days ago, and she herself did bleed to death."

Lydia held her lips tight while saying these words, and did not look at Judith.

"And I did…" she began to speak, but could not continue.

Kindly and gently Judith asked her, "What did you?"

"Goody Wescott had urged my help earlier that same day, for the girl was in a violent fit."

"I knew the girl to be weak of mind," Judith said.

"Was she fitful as well?"

"Indeed yes," said Lydia.

She began to feel calmer then, as if she could tell everything to her friend, just as it had happened.

"To quell the fit I used a strong tincture, even though in so doing I knew it could harm the babe within her."

Judith said nothing, but looked on Lydia to continue.

"The girl was in an awful state and I was afeared of her."

"Now Judith looked at her hard and said,

"Afeared of her or for her? What is your meaning?"

In her mind, Lydia heard the terrible sound of those strange words Mehetabel had screamed at her, and she felt again the sting of the little arrows.

"I was afeared of her. She screamed so, in words I could not understand, and these words seemed.."

She could not tell Judith the rest of it.

"My friend, " said Judith.

"You were afeared that her affliction might take her life, I think. And as a healer, you administered the medicine you believed would help the girl. You were trying to help her, Lydia. You are guilty of no crime."

"I knew the tincture to be probably too strong for the babe within," said Lydia.

"You sought to save the girl's life, and, if need be, had to sacrifice another, not yet started."

"Tis true."

"That is true."

They sat quietly for a while, and then, not wanting to think any more upon it, Lydia changed the subject, and enquired of her friend's husband, who had been congested at the last Sunday's meeting.

She spoke for some moments of her husband's health, and then she said something that surprised Lydia.

"I wonder, Lydia," she asked, "Do you feel lonely?"

It was Judith Stiles way to not mince words, and Lydia caught her meaning.

Her question made Lydia blush, despite herself.

At first she could not answer, but then she spoke,

"You know me well enough to know I do verily miss my husband. I have had no letter from him as yet."

Judith contemplated Lydia's words some moments, and then a sparkle came into her eye and she said,

"I imagine you do miss him also verily in the way we shall not mention?"

"Well, yes," Lydia started.

She felt her face again flushing red.

"Have you made acquaintance with the wheelwright?" Judith smiled uncannily.

"The wheelwright, Wrastle Fuller," Lydia said, all at once, and in a whisper.

Judith's eyes widened and her smile broadened to show all of her teeth.

"I have seen him but once," she remarked. "He's a married man, is he not?"

"Aye," Lydia said. "But no children. He's younger, maybe fifteen years, than you or I."

"Is his wife pretty?" Judith asked.

"I have not seen her," said Lydia.

"But he certainly is."

She spoke these words, and although there was no harm in them, they made her feel excited and giddy, as if she were young again and had a suitor. But these were imaginings, and could only be blamed on her state of aloneness, and were not thoughts she thought she should allow herself to have.

"I must go by there before I return home," Lydia told Judith.

"Would you wish to come with me?"

"Now, friend?" Judith stood up. "Yes, let us go there!"

She called for the servant girl, whose name was Ponka, to bring their cloaks, and off they went to the wheelwright's shop, on foot.

Because of the market there was no one but Goodman Fuller, working and alone in his shop. When Judith and Lydia entered, his back was toward them, and he did not hear them, as he was making such a noise with his hammer. Lydia saw her barrow wheel near the door, repaired as if it were new again, but it made her heart sink, as now she wondered what other reason would she have to go there.

"Goodman Fuller!" Lydia called out from where Judith and she stood just inside the door.

He did not hear her. They stood there for some time, Lydia looking at his broad shoulders, and the muscles of his buttocks beneath the stuff of his britches as he worked. Judith stepped into the shop and fingered a set of four wheels, small enough for a mouse's carriage, that had been set upon his table. Lydia too, stepped into the shop, upon the dirt floor.

From where she stood closer to him now she could see his ankles and feet in their leather shoes.

He stopped hammering and turned for something. Suddenly seeing Judith and Lydia standing there, he started, and then lay down his hammer, brushed his hands on his leather apron, and, smiling at the ladies, he said,

"I did not hear you coming in. You frightened me!"

"I've come for my barrow wheel," Lydia said.

Judith was smiling at him.

He looked over at the repaired wheel.

"Tis ready," Lydia commented.

He walked out from behind the table, brushing again his hands upon his leather apron.

"Goodwife Gilbert," he said. "You are a healer with herbs, are you not?"

"Some say I have healed them or their loved ones," Lydia said, thinking again on Mehetabel.

"My wife has need of your skill," he said.

Lydia had heard that his wife suffered female problems with her courses and that she was unable to get with child.

She breathed deeply and told him,

"I would gladly help your wife, Goodman Fuller. Shall I go to her to speak on it?"

"I shall tell you what her ailments are and you shall teach me what needs to be done for her, so that I can help her myself."

His words surprised Lydia, and pleased her greatly. He would not ask her to be solely responsible for his wife.

CHAPTER TEN

LYDIA RETURNED THERE on Thursday.

She had no other reason to go to town, but to buy a loaf of bread for the noon meal, and, as usual, she would ask at the post if there were a letter for her.

She considered how it occasionally happens that one person has a strong affect on another, and, like animals, the two recognize an opening for deeper relating, and that this occurs not so often, but when it does, it happens on the instant and cannot be explained.

Lydia herself had experienced strong liaisons with persons of both sexes, although when the person, such as her friend Judith, was a lady, there was no desire for physical mingling, while with a man such a desire always entered into it, but sometimes in a lesser, and sometimes in a greater, way.

In all the years of her marriage only on two occasions had Lydia shared friendships with gentlemen. These were the tutor of her eldest daughter, Batholomew Culham, a man her same age, in whom she found a true companion of spirit. This gentleman had bad teeth and his breath stunk, and by thinking on those things it was not difficult for her to resist his physical embrace. After less than a year he went away to the Maine territory, where he knew some people, to build a house. Lydia never had any word from him after that and she believed him to be dead.

The other fellow, a married man named Joseph Quincy, was old enough to be her father, and by this characteristic she could exclude thoughts of physical desire, and make him, in her mind, equal to a lady friend. They were close for a number of years, and enjoyed many happy times together, visiting and talking with his wife present, or else doing small tasks together, for he was a veterinary surgeon and Lydia sometimes accompanied him on his calls, which she found to be of great interest.

Joseph Quincy had passed away two years before, when he'd slipped off the north side roof of his barn in early spring. His wife, Priscilla, who had lived many years in Boston, gave Lydia fine purple funeral gloves. She wore these sometimes while weeding the garden on dry days. For although they were made of kidskin, she did not wear them otherwise, and when she saw them on her hands pulling up weeds —a useful and meditative task—she was reminded of her late friend and considered how their lives had touched one another's.

With the wheelwright Lydia believed she could have some kind of friendship, although, because she was alone and he was handsome and young, a chaste liaison might prove difficult.

She tied Aisley at the post on the roadside outside his shop, and walked down the sloping path to the entrance.

The door was open, and no one, save Mister Fuller, was inside. He had been watching her approach, and now stood facing her, and filing a rim.

"Good morning, Goodwife Gilbert," said he.

His face lit up when he smiled.

"Good morning, Mister Fuller. I've come to instruct you how to best help your good wife with her troubles. Twould be fitting for me to speak with her first directly, if I may call on her—?"

Lydia was pleased with herself for this show of sobriety and prudence, and she looked at him, but the smile had not left his face, and his blue eyes were warm and generous.

"Certainly," said he. "You can call on her now, if you like. I will show you in."

She watched as he put down the file, and left the wheel rim against the table. Without taking off his apron, he came close to her, and, placing one large hand upon her forearm, said,

"Come."

They left the shop. Behind, and through an empty yard she followed him, noticing how straight he walked, and with sure steps.

He went up the short stair to the front door, and before he opened the door, he said, "She's been expecting you. She will be glad you've come."

He opened the door and Lydia followed him into the small house.

His wife was sitting by the far window, in a high backed chair, doing crewel work, but when Lydia entered she stood up and lay aside her sewing.

The wheelwright stood between the two women, and introduced Lydia to his wife as Goodwife Gilbert, and told Lydia her name, Humility. It suited her well, for she seemed nothing if not humble.

She stepped forward and took Lydia's gloved hand in her own bare one, and, looking her directly in the eyes she said,

"My husband tells me you are a skillful healer, and may have some cure for my barrenness."

Her brown eyes were full of sorrow and the longing to nurture a child. She was a lady of about thirty years, smaller than Lydia in stature, and very thin, and pallid.

"I'll be returning to my rim," Wrastle Fuller said.

Ever smiling, he looked at the two women standing together.

"I will leave you ladies alone, and do ask you, Goodwife Gilbert, to inform me upon your leaving."

He turned and left the house, and Lydia was alone with his wife.

"Let us sit down."

Humility instructed Lydia to take a seat on the bench at the other side of the window, while she returned to her high backed chair.

"Goodwife Fuller," Lydia said, but Humility corrected her and told her to call her by her Christian name.

"Humility. You must therefore call me Lydia."

She smiled at this and nodded.

"How long have you and your husband been living together as man and wife?"

"Six years," she said.

"Does he come to you nightly, or almost nightly?"

Lydia removed her gloves and untied her hat ribbons.

"Before he did, when I could stand it. But I suffer from wrenching pains in my belly and in my back now, almost all ways, and the pain oft times so harsh I take but two steps and I fall to the floor, and all I can do is get to my bed and try to bear it out."

"Do your courses come regularly?"

"No. Sometimes they come again after only a fortnight, and so heavy it seems a river is rushing out of me. And sometimes two or three moons pass and courses I have naught. This fills me with false hope, and makes me all the sadder when they do come, and I see I have no child in me."

Lydia's heart went to the lady, and she stood, and moved to her and embraced her while she wept.

They stayed like this for a while, then Lydia told her what treatments to take, saying she would leave the receipts with her husband, as he'd desired.

She then took her leave of the lady and of her burdensome sorrow, so that once she was again outside in the bright morning light, and could hear the wheelwright whistling from inside his shop as he worked, and saw by chance, a hummingbird sucking nectar from the blue nepeta flowers in the sun by the split rail fence, she felt as if she had swallowed the life from the wheelwright's good wife; doubly alive and glad of it.

Her violet hat ribbons still dangled down loose on her breast, and she held both her gloves in one hand when she entered again into the shop and explained to Master Fuller what herbs she would procure for him and what to do with them to aid his wife.

He was standing still before her, and empty-handed.

"Will you tell me, Goodwife Gilbert, where you go to find such herbs?" said he.

His eyes were beaming into hers and she did not draw hers away, although she knew not to was wrong, and courting Satan.

"I will show you," said Lydia, but it was the devil who spoke. "Come with me on the morrow."

Neither he nor she looked away, and the demonic spirits in their eyes spoke silently to one another.

He placed his hand again upon her forearm for a moment.

"I thank you, lady. You are a true help," said his voice.

"Until tomorrow, then," said Lydia.

She drew her arm away.

"Good day," said he.

She turned toward the shop's door.

"Good day," said Lydia.

She walked out and nearly ran against a lady—his thornback sister Susanna—coming in.

Lydia was filled with shame. For although she had done no sinful act, she had thought upon it, and so it was as if she had already done it

"Good day, Miss Fuller," she murmured, and hurried toward her waiting horse.

CHAPTER ELEVEN

THE HAY HAD not yet been cut, and the grass was so long a man could creep upon the ground and be unseen. There was a pasture she often went to on higher ground and far from the river, where she found aromatic herbs growing naturally. Artemisia and nettle by where the woods sprung up; feverfew, wild garlic, costmary, horehound and sorrel hidden among the pasture grasses.

She led Wrastle there to get comfrey for his wife. During the hours since their meeting the previous day, while she milked the cows, or did the books, read, made soup, chopped wood, swept the floor, and whatever else she did, thoughts of Wrastle had followed her although she had tried to block them from her mind.

She had considered not coming with him, and she knew that not coming would have been the right thing to do, but, after much internal debate, she did come, convinced that she was not weak.

Although she knew she should not be alone with him in such a place, as she knew she must not read the cards nor the book of Descartes, and neither must she burn dried herbs in a candle flame to obtain that which she needed or desired, it seemed she could not stop doing them, and her desire to do them anyway outweighed her wish to do what was supposed to be right.

The weather that week had been dry, so there were few flies, and with Wrastle a few steps behind her, she walked up the cow path through the pasture and to its edge. As in a dream the sunlight shone on their shoulders and upon each blade of grass, making some look white, and others shining green. There was no breeze, and the sky was blue and cloudless, and the bedstraw and grass as they walked through it let go its scent, and butterflies—orange, blue, white and yellow, fluttering from thistle to scabiosa seemed like silent music. Wrastle came close beside her.

"You know where to find everything, Goodwife Gilbert."

Lydia stopped walking. The grass was waist high, and when she looked down at her apron, it was covered with seed.

They looked directly into one another's eyes. His were blue, with some flecks of green, and, as they stood there gazing at one another, Lydia felt herself disappear and become mingled with him. This new soul hovered somewhere in the air between them. If they were to act upon this mingling feeling it would be called fornication, and such an unclean act, if known, would result in their deaths.

She said, "Who is't told you so?"

He moved closer, which she liked, but did not like, and she moved away.

Lydia had not realized, in the months she'd been alone, how much her need had been neglected.

He said, "Everyone knows it."

At first she did not know what he was talking about, so she did not answer, but looked at him.

She saw that his lips were smiling but that was only a small part of what she saw. His whole countenance smiled at her, like the sun smiled upon the pasture. His merry eyes, cheeks, lips, the slight blush on his skin; his soul shone through his face, and his face was a bright light.

It was as if she were again seventeen, or fourteen, or a hundred and twenty, she felt as if she was both outside of her body and more fully in it.

She said, "Let us find the comfrey now—over at the edge of the field, I should think."

And he, "Lead me where you will, good lady. I place my trust in you."

She turned her back to him, and began walking, rather fast, and the long grass was encumbering. Soon, her feet became tangled in her skirt and petticoats and the grass altogether, and she fell down.

Wrastle then fell upon her.

She could smell the apple and salt smell of his skin, and feel his breath on her neck.

She had washed that week and put on clean under petticoats and bodice, and the white stuff shone blinding in the sunlight.

She stayed down not even long enough to notice the beetles and ants below her, but stood again quickly and straightened her bonnet, which had got askew. He did not rise at first, but lay spread out upon the tangled bedstraw, and squinted up at her. She moved so that her shadow was no longer cast on his face, and, with the bright sun in his eyes, he could not see her, and he rose.

This was a dangerous game, and she would not go alone with the wheelwright again to such a suggestive place.

She walked on more slowly toward the edge of the field, and said to him, without turning to face him,

"I am fifteen years older than you are."

"And I am fifteen years younger than you," he said in saucy response. "Together that would make us without age."

Then Lydia heard the sound, far off, of Goodman Woodmason's sheep coming, and with them would be his boy Pip.

She and Wrastle reached the place quickly and, walking with distance between them, went to where she had known comfrey would be growing. In her apron she collected a useful quantity for his wife.

The next time she returned to the wheelwright's shop, Lydia brought a small muslin bag of dried herbs with her. These, for his wife, had a way of loosening a woman's flow and making it come more regularly. They were very mild but of good effect. Since Humility had told Lydia how many days previous she'd had her courses she knew the best time to drink the tisanes to be beginning that day, for three days.

She found Goodman Fuller alone, tooling spokes, and waited some moments before he finished, and looked up from his work to see her standing before him with the muslin sack. She was wearing her green waist and the gridolin bonnet, and she knew the colors of these garments were flattering on her, but she didn't know why she should be concerned about her appearance, unless she were not in full possession of herself, but was being driven by Satan.

When his eyes met hers she saw happiness there, and she understood that this same devil that drove her toward him also pushed the wheelwright toward her.

"Good Day, Goody Gilbert," he said, and she responded in turn.

"I've brought a sack of herbs for your wife," said Lydia.

"I have all ready instructed how she must use them, but I shall repeat these instructions to you, as you are in charge of her treatment, and must know."

As she told him instructions, she saw the way he was looking at her with admiration in his eyes, and her face burned red.

She gazed upon his hand, for it was great and strong, but gentle. And then she thought when they had gone to White's field, and the grass they had briefly lain down upon together. And she thought, I am almost old enough to be his mother, and certainly could be his old auntie. He is looking at the wrinkles upon my face, or at some gray hairs amidst the brown ones in my head. Before him he sees a hag, and, comparing me to his pretty wife he laughs inside himself at my foolishness.

Then Lydia sneaked a look into his eyes and she sensed no ill, fearful, nor worrisome ideas from him, but only a pure and fiercely shining love that frightened her.

Someone entered the shop, and the wheelwright put his hand away into his leather apron. Lydia saw his expression change and become hardened but smiling, at once. When she turned to see who was there, it was his sister, Susanna Fuller, who lived together with Wrastle and his wife, and took care of all the household tasks that Humility could not manage.

Her thin lips and stern glance gave the impression she was made of hard dry wood that could not be bent. Lydia believed it was in great part his sister's presence in the wheelwright's house that prevented Humility from conceiving a child, and Wrastle himself was none too pleased by her rule in his home, as she, being the elder sibling, had dominion over him.

"Good Day, Goodwife Gilbert," said she.

She did not hold out her hand.

"Good Day," Lydia said.

She went on glaring at her brother, and then set the tin dinner pail she'd held in her hand onto a corner of the workbench, and said to him,

"Brother, I am going to Goodwife Woodmason's for some cheese, and shall leave Humility alone now."

"Tis no matter sister, and you needn't have brought my dinner in a pail, as I shall take these herbs to Humility, and we'll eat our dinner together."

"She won't be eating. She's not well."

"I'll make her a tisane, which she may sip abed."

Lydia knew that Susanna would not leave the shop until she'd watched her leave first, for there was something in her looks and tone of voice that said she considered her untrustworthy in the company of her brother.

She bid brother and sister good day, and took her leave of the wheelwright's shop, disappointed for the short time it had taken to complete this simple effort.

The following Thursday morning the weather was lovely, and Lydia rode into town, bringing with her two baskets full of strewing herbs and sachets for Eldridge's store in exchange for sugar, flour, salt and spices. The baskets were in the form of panniers attached with leather straps to each side of the saddle. She had woven them herself from willow branches. They were greatly convenient for occasions when she was selling or buying or trading goods, but her mare did not love them, for they bumped against her flanks, and she could travel only at a walk.

When she had almost reached Eldridge's, on the main street, Lydia saw, by chance, Wrastle Fuller walking along the road in the direction of his shop, whistling. She came up from behind him, and when they were level—himself and the horse—she greeted him, and he, with his blue merry eyes, wished Lydia a good morning as well.

As they walked a few paces together, he looked at her mischievously and said that he would be taking his noon meal out of doors and alone, and asked her tentatively if she would care to eat with him.

"Then you must bring a loaf of bread," said he.

"As I have naught."

"That I shall," said Lydia.

"Meet me at noon, in the grove of trees behind White's field."

She loosened her hold on Aisley's reins and let her walk on at a faster pace, taking the muttered invitation to this secret meeting, which thrilled her with its devilishness, along with her. The thought of it thrilled her the rest of the morning as she did business with Mister and Missus Eldridge, bought manchet loaves at the bakery, posted a letter to her sister Rebecca, and had one from her besides, and stopped in to see her daughters Elizabeth and Sarah and her grand-daughter, Sarah's child.

It was nearing noon and Sarah urged her mother to stay and to have dinner at her house, but Lydia excused herself, telling her she had to go back for there was much to do while the weather held fine.

White's field was below Wrastle's shop, sloping toward the river, and on one side of it—the far side—was a grove of chestnut and hickory trees. Since the grove was in the same direction as home, Lydia rode Aisley right down into White's field. The herbage and wild flowers in the middle of the field were already up again, and Daniel White would not take kindly to her walking her horse through it.

She kept to the southern edge of the field, moving slowly. Because there had been no rain for a week, the ground was hard and their combined weight over the horse's four hooves did little damage.

When she reached the far edge of the field there was finally the cool relief of the shade trees to enjoy, and the blinding darkness allowed Lydia to relax her eyes from squinting.

Wrastle had said to meet him in the grove at noon, which it was now, but the grove was not so small, and Lydia wondered under which tree she might find him.

There was a rough path, overgrown with prickly blackberry vines. She led her horse along this for a few minutes, but she was sorry because the animal's legs and chest were getting scratched by thorns.

After some minutes the path widened, and the ground grew soft and quiet, and the air fragrant with the scent of turpentine, for in the center of the chestnut and hickory grove, there was a pinewoods.

It was then that she heard Wrastle's voice singing, and ahead, she saw him, standing under a pine tree and plucking music from a mandolin.

She drew up Aisley's reins and stopped and sat upon her horse and listened to Wrastle from a distance.

She thought he did not see her, for in the shade of the trees, a brown horse and a lady dressed in green could easily become invisible. But when he had finished his song, he looked directly at her and called out,

"What are you doing? Come over here!"

She dismounted then, and led Aisley over to where Wrastle was, and on the ground under the tree by him there were two burlap sacks— one, empty and the other one partly full.

"I shall tie my mare," said Lydia.

She led Aisley to a stout low branch, slipped off her bridle and bit and tied her halter rope to the tree easily, so the horse could root among the undergrowth for forage. Then Lydia loosened the girth and brought out the manchet loaves from her basket, and went back to Wrastle.

He invited her to sit upon the empty burlap bag. He sat beside her, but not so close that they were touching. From the other bag he took a piece of cured ham, some butter in a small crockery dish, a bottle of Madeira wine, and a small covered leathern jack full of honey. From his pocket he got his knife to cut a loaf in half. Then he spread butter thickly on one side of the loaf and sliced thin leaves of ham onto it, and closed the top and gave it to Lydia, not looking at her but saying,

"I hope you like this."

She was very hungry, but she watched while he cut open the second loaf and prepared it in the same way for himself, and then he opened the wine and said,

"We have no cup. We will have to drink from the bottle."

He set the bottle between them, and they sat on the burlap, both facing the same direction, watching Lydia's horse, which stood several yards away munching peacefully.

They ate, not speaking, and there were no sounds save the birds and cracking branches, and their mastication and swallowing. Lydia knew that what they were doing was wrong and that she should not have gone there. If someone should see them it could mean terrible gossip and even an accusation of adultery.

But the food was good and salty. She helped herself to the wine, and he, too, drank a lot of it. Between them they quickly drank one half of the bottle. Then he got the jack full of honey and set it between them and said,

"I am not accustomed to drinking wine, and now I'm drunk. I found a hive in my cherry tree last week, so we have some good honey."

He opened the jack.

"But no spoon," he said.

He plunged his finger in up to his knuckle and brought it out dripping amber gold. Then he quickly brought his fingertip to her lips and she could do nothing but open them or the honey would drip down upon her bodice and be wasted. So she opened her lips and he slid his finger into her mouth and she closed her lips around it and sucked the perfumed honey off it, blushing red to the roots of her hair.

"How is it, lady?"

Lydia could hardly speak.

"Very fine," she whispered.

He put his finger down into the jack again, and though she did not wish him to, he repeated the same action again, so that her mouth was full of sweet honey and her lips sticky and wet with it, and it was indeed very fine honey.

Perhaps as a cause of the wine, Lydia moved more closely to him so that her body touched against his. Sitting thus, their shoulders and hips lightly against one another, she could hardly breathe, for she was frightened what might come next—it was what she wanted but did not want.

After some minutes he moved away, and put his finger one more time into the honey jack before closing it. Taking this dripping golden finger he made as if to place it in her mouth, but, at the last, spread it upon her lips, and then, before she could move apart from him, he licked and kissed her, lingering, there.

Lydia's eyes were open just a slit and she saw his eyes were open wide, and watching her, and when she opened hers entirely, he kissed ever more passionately, so that she began to lose her senses, and felt as if she might faint, and she had to stop, and gently pushed him away.

After some moments he gazed at her and spoke clearly,

"Please forgive me, Lydia. I have the greatest respect for you, but the beast inside of me is called forth in your presence. I know not how to explain this."

She made no answer, but softly touched his hand that lay between them.

As they sat thus in silence, Lydia saw that her horse had stopped eating the vines, and had lifted her head in alarm, high and with her ears pointed. Lydia's heart beat fast, for she feared it was a man or a woman, but when she heard the soft cracking of the dry branches nearby, she turned her head to see a young stag. It paused for an instant in the shade, his majestic head still and tensed, and, sensing a human presence, leapt quickly away. Lydia felt the vibrations from his footfalls in the earth beneath her. Wrastle had not seen, and she did not tell him.

"Wrastle's drunk," said he. "What shall I do now?"

She looked at his face; his merry eyes and the pretty smile were of a boy.

"You'll carry on as usual," she said.

She then rose up from the burlap and he did likewise. While they shook and folded the burlap, and put away the butter and ham and honey and wine, and he cleaned his knife, there was a sadness between them that she wished she could not feel.

He then played a pretty, cheerful tune on his mandolin, and afterward he put it in its case, and Lydia told him to go on ahead of her, that he should go first for he was on foot, and she would soon follow on horseback.

But he waited and watched her as she tied her hat ribbons neatly beneath her chin.

He came close and kissed her on her gloved left hand, and said,

"Will I see you again?" but in half jest.

She answered him,

"In the presence of your good wife."

He did not smile, but turned to depart, and she went to her horse.

As she tightened the girth, she thought that the ride home would set her back into herself.

It was about two hours past noon, and she hoped that, upon her return, there would be no one about to ask where she had eaten her dinner.

CHAPTER TWELVE

FOR SEVERAL MONTHS she avoided him. And then the next time they had seen each other was in September, after Lydia had first been accused of witchcraft by Elizabeth Wescott.

She had gone, as usual, on a Thursday morning for market, and to leave herb sachets at the apothecary's. All of the week before she had seen no one, save William, and on Sunday her daughters and son in law.

On the way by the wheelwright's shop she turned her head to see if Wrastle were inside, and saw him looking out at her, but though she wished to stop, she was unsure whether to do it, for, because of the accusation, she was being carefully scrutinized by the townspeople, and must be accountable for all of her actions.

Notwithstanding this, she suddenly turned Aisley to the right, toward the wheelwright's, but as she did so she saw with dismay that in the doorway Wrastle was not standing alone, but there were his sister and his wife with him.

She turned her horse again back on course to the road, but not before both women had seen her. She should stop and inquire about Humility, for if all had gone well she should be with child, but now Lydia in the proper state of mind for pleasantries.

The air had taken on a briskness and for some days there had been ground frost in the early hours. Winter would be with upon them soon, and the Gilberts were well supplied and ready for it, but the thought of its coming filled Lydia's soul with emptiness.

The past months without Thomas, and with Elizabeth away most of the time as well, had made her lonely for company. The winter was the worst time to be alone, for adverse weather made the walls of her house grow thick and impenetrable.

When she reached the main street, where market was, it was, as usual, filled up and noisily resonant with the moving, speaking bodies of women, men, children, horses, oxen, dogs and the smells of all these warm bodies and their variety of excrements, essences and pomades.

Despite her dark mood, Lydia's spirits were lifted and she dismounted from her horse and led her by the reins through the crowded market.

That day there was a woman from Mystic who came only now and again to sell her fisherman husband's catch, and she displayed a great codfish cut in two—each half at least a yard long, and many oysters and clams, and striped sea bass. There were so many women gathered round her table to look and to buy that one would think none of them had ever seen a fish before.

There was Mercy Goodwell selling her honey and wax candles, and the family from Hartford with their large display of dry goods, ribbons, brass and bone and jet buttons, and woolen caps. There was Woodmason's boy selling cheeses, and the strange old woman with her willow baskets. There was also a little girl Lydia had never seen before, about nine years old. She was dirty and ragged, and stood behind a covered box upon which were eight or ten eggs so large they could not have come from a hen, nor even from a goose. Their shells were thick and shiny. Alongside these giant eggs were soft plumes dyed bright red with cochineal. The wood box was covered with a crimson cloth, the display should have attracted much attention, but no one was stopping there to talk to the little girl nor to buy from her.

Lydia stood some feet away and saw the look in the girl's eyes—as if she were in a far off place, and not at the Windsor market at all—and for a moment she feared that the child and her fanciful eggs did not really exist. For she did not look at Lydia, and seemed to see no one, and no one else but she seemed to see the girl. Lydia grew dizzy and cold. She looked away and thought to lead her horse out of the market place, but some thing forced her to stay there, and to move closer.

Aisley took no notice of the little girl and the enormous eggs and the feathers, although she was standing directly in front of the box.

Lydia moved so close that her hips were pressed against the edge of the box, she could feel the gravity of the wood on her bones, it was as real as the road that her two feet stood upon.

She saw herself as a skeleton, like the pictures Nicholas, her son in law, kept inside a drawer for reference, and which she and the girls had looked upon and studied many times while he was out of the house. Her hip bones, like stumps of lost wings forming the edges of a rounded cradle, and the slender bones of her legs, so fine she wondered why they did not snap into pieces, and her feet, bonier than a flounder fish. She had transformed into a skeletal woman thing, and one bony hand held the frayed and disintegrating rope that tied around the muzzle of a skeletal horse. She looked again at the little girl, and she, too, was only a frame of bones standing there, her deformed teeth clenched in a fearsome smile, the hollows where her eyes should be empty of eyes.

Lydia spoke to her saying, "What ever fowl do such large eggs come out of, child?"

The girl stood unmoving and did not answer, and when Lydia turned her eyes again upon the eggs, the shells had broken apart, and from them hatched crimson and black birds, fully plumaged, with black feet and black sharp beaks, and eyes as round and as yellow as reales. The cloth covering the box had disappeared, and so had the fancy plumes, and so had the girl. And then the little birds flew together high up into the sky and far away so they were no longer visible.

All that, a moment previous, had been before her, and that she had touched with her bones, now was gone, leaving nothing.

The horse grew restless and stamped her hoof, and when Lydia looked at her she was full fleshed and furred as she should be, and when she looked at her own hands, they too, were corporal and moving.

As Lydia turned to her left, intending to walk in that direction toward Judith Stiles' house, someone caught her on the left shoulder. She turned to see who it was.

Feeling still light headed and confused, she was not all together certain, when her eyes met with the personage of Wrastle Fuller, that it was really him, and for some moments she stared at him without speaking.

"Lydia," he said. "You wear a look of bafflement. Are you unwell? Why did you not stop in at my shop before? What is the matter?"

After some moments all she could say was,

"Wrastle. Goodman Fuller."

She paused for a time to breathe, and to look, without touching him, to discern if he were indeed real.

"You did not hear of my summons to court," said Lydia.

"Indeed."

"You know what the accusation was then?"

He uttered no word, but nodded his head, and by the upturned corners of his lips he said he did not believe it.

The two of them could not stand together without conversing too long in a public place, for people would take notice.

"How is your good wife?" Lydia inquired.

"With child," said he.

He could not keep the pride and joy out of his eyes. His countenance had lit up like a bonfire.

"I'm glad for both of you."

She meant it truly.

Then he spoke some strange words she could not understand the meaning of.

He said,

"Goodwife Gilbert, you can still make things right, if you will it."

She looked again at his face and what she saw made her tremble.

For the man standing before her was not the young one she had loved as a friend, but was an older man familiar to her, it was Allyn.

She could make no answer come forth from her lips, but turned her gaze to the ground, turned her body around, and led her horse away from this cruel game that her senses were intent on playing. She went away from the townspeople, away from the market place.

As soon as she was distant enough from the crowds, Lydia mounted her horse, and, rather than going in the direction of her friend's house, she went to the apothecary, where she silently left her herb packs, and did not look into the eyes of the young man who would soon become her son in law. Quickly she left town, and rode home at a trot, following the way most likely to bring her into contact with no one.

She did not wish to see people she believed she could trust and yet be unsure if they were indeed who she thought they were.

Suddenly nothing was as it seemed and everything had changed.

Lydia rode her horse down the back way. She entered into the woods and took the Pequot path.

The horse trotted fast and agile over roots and stones and fallen branches, her black-tipped ears always pricked and moving from side to side and forward, listening to every bird or squirrel that moved in the underbrush and distinguishing these sounds from the lighter ones of a leaf or an acorn falling, or those of other sounds for which her senses were always awake—the ones that threatened.

She stopped short just as she was rounding a bend in the path, where the oak and the chestnut trees grew thick. Beneath her Lydia felt all of the muscles in her horse's body tense, her head and neck lifted and arched, her tail formed a stiff spout, and she blew fearfully through her nostrils. Her muscles were so full of tension it seemed she was ready to burst and escape. Rarely did Aisley show such fear.

Carefully Lydia looked up, and, moving hardly at all, she looked around her, and as deeply into the trees as she was able. She saw nothing out of the ordinary.

She tried to nudge the horse with her leg to move forward, but Aisley stayed at that place, snorting and trembling.

Then Lydia saw, coming toward them from around the bend, a

pack of brush wolves. There were two adults and three or four young ones. Their wild eyes stared, and the horse spun around, and, despite Lydia's best efforts to maintain control of her with reins and bit, she was not under control. She galloped back again along the same path they'd come on, and took no heed of the low branches that Lydia had moved away with her hand, or ducked her head under previously, so that now her face became scratched by thorny locust branches many times, and once so badly that she felt a piece of her cheek flesh tear away to stay behind with the branch. Her eyes teared, for they were moving very fast, and it was difficult to see ahead of her. In her excitement Aisley kept tossing her head up and down.

When Lydia ducked under a low branch, the horse tossed her own head upwards at the same moment, and at the meeting of their skulls Lydia felt the crack of bone in her face just below her eye, and then immediately a great swelling. Within moments the eye was swollen shut, but no matter that she pulled as hard as she could on the reins to slow her down, It was as if Lydia were a feather attached to Aisley's mane, and the horse took no notice of her.

On the other side of the river, she went in the direction of town, intending, Lydia was certain, to take the usual pathway home.

It was not until they were nearly on the road outside the wheelwright's that, foaming with white sweat, her horse finally slowed to a walk.

Lydia's bonnet had fallen behind her shoulders, and she pulled it back up onto her head, as far forward as she could, to hide her damaged face.

Her skirt was badly torn, and she held it together with one hand, and hoped only to get through this part as quickly as possible without being seen.

By the time she reached home, Aisley was dry, and Lydia was relieved not to find William in the barn, for she wished that no one, not even William, would see her until she could first see herself in the silver serving spoon that she kept shined and polished for that purpose.

When she got inside and found the spoon, she saw that her right eye red and the entire socket were two or three times normal size, and blood was streaking down both cheeks. She knew she could not hide these injuries away from everyone indefinitely, for it would take some weeks at least for her face to return to normal.

Later that evening she had a laugh when William saw her and she let him believe for a few moments that Magistrate Allyn had done it.

And when Reliance returned from town the next day and saw it, and it looked even more swollen and worse, Lydia told her that she had had a fight with the devil.

Reliance's eyes grew wide with wonderment, like a little child, and then Lydia saw her daughter's reason take control, and she said,

"Who was victorious, mother?"

Lydia answered her, "Indeed, twas I."

Over the following fortnight, each day when she checked her eye in the spoon's back there were new colors in it like a rainbow. First it was deep violet, then with streaks of rose and crimson, then gradually it took on green markings within the violet, and finally, yellow. After another week the swelling had gone down enough for Lydia to make a trip again into town.

For those three weeks she had avoided being seen, not even going to Sunday meeting, feigning unwellness, which was not exactly false. But Lydia missed being in company, and greatly longed to speak to her friend, and to look in on Humility Fuller.

She made a paste of finely ground sage and rose petals mixed with milk, and put this on her face and all around her eye to cover up the remainders of the injury, and she wore her black hat, for it had the widest brim.

CHAPTER THIRTEEN

THE LAST TIME she had seen him alone was in October. She had gone to his shop, and he was alone, and happy to see her.

She removed her gloves and said to him, "Goodman Fuller, how is your goodwife, and how are you?"

"Both very well, Goody Gilbert. Perhaps I should turn the question back to you."

He lay down the spoke he was tooling and took in a long look of Lydia, and by the changes in his eyes she could see that he noticed the still unhealed injury to her face, but he said nothing about it.

"Well myself, thank you," she answered him.

She would let him think as he wished.

"Humility is joyous," said he.

"I have never known her to be happier."

"I'm glad of it, Goodman Fuller."

Wrastle caught the sincerity in Lydia's voice and on her face.

"As I am glad for the friendship you and I did share."

"Are we not still friends?" he said.

There was some alarm in his voice, but she understood he no longer needed her except as a familiar acquaintance.

"I think not," said Lydia.

He knew she spoke the truth, and he said,

"You have given me great happiness, Lydia. I shall not forget it, and neither shall Humility. You have brought blessings upon us and I am grateful for it."

"Tis God's will," she said.

He was looking at the skin on the backs of her ungloved hands, spotted and papery from working among the herbs under the sun and in the wind and cold and the heat. The contrast between her hands and his, which were fifteen years less used, and both bigger and stronger and some way smoother than hers, was notable, and not pleasing to either of them. She drew her hands away from the bench. The coldness returned to them—it started along the sides and tips of her fingers and slowly filled up both hands with an excruciating chill like death must be.

She hid the old things in her skirt folds, but he left his upon the bench in soft fists.

"If you should need my help for anything, Lydia, I am all ways at your service."

Step by step, and very slowly, Lydia found herself backing away from him.

When she had gotten to the doorway and saw that he was still smiling at her in the same way he had been smiling when he'd finished speaking, she did not know how to answer him for he seemed to be very far away and small.

She took two more steps backward and was out the door, and, once she had turned her back on him, Wrastle Fuller had disappeared.

As Lydia returned to her horse, she asked herself, Which one of us has disappeared? He or I? For in his life she no longer held a post, and perhaps his life, being at the start of something, was of more importance, and therefore larger, than her own. If indeed this be true then she thought it was she herself who had disappeared, not he.

She already felt the life ebbing away from her.

She put on one glove, and realized that she had dropped the other.

"Goody Gilbert!" Wrastle's voice called from behind her.

But she did not turn, for she wished that he would not remember her as an old woman, but as that other person he had loved only months before.

Again he called, but by then she had reached the horse, and

occupied herself untying the knot she had made in the reins, and she did this with her back turned toward him.

She felt him looking at her back, and seeing its smallness, and the drooping of her shoulders as her spine began to fold down into itself, and she did not want his pity, nor did she want to meet his eyes.

In the courthouse, before all of the townspeople and the jury, and Judge Governor Allyn, Lydia stood, and slowly looked up without lifting her head too high.

Susanna Fuller, the spinster, was gazing out at the audience.

"What say you in your defense, Goodwife Gilbert?" the Governor asked.

"My dealings with Goodman Fuller," Lydia said meekly, "have been nothing if not natural and Godly."

CHAPTER FOURTEEN

SUSANNA FULLER RETREATED back into the cloud of townspeople.

The judge called another name, but Lydia did not hear it clearly.

Someone, a man, rose from near the back of the courthouse.

Lydia watched as he made his way with careful and deliberate steps, through the swamp of people, and when, finally, he reached the front, he took oath.

It was Surgeon Carver, her son in law.

Why was he being called forth so soon, for the defense? Would not James Stiles be testifying against her? She was surprised that her son in law would defend her, for doing so could dishonor him as a surgeon. Also, she knew that he had kept company with Governor Allyn in the previous months, and she had thought they shared sympathies.

For some moments Lydia was filled with gladness, believing that Surgeon Carver was going to help her, and perhaps her punishment would be minimal.

But the hope in her heart became a bitter nothing when she heard him say he stood to accuse, and not to defend.

He was her eldest daughter's husband, and the father of her grand child. What could he have to say against her?

Nicholas Carver stood for a moment facing her, and gazed at her shrunkenness and her bald head.

She closed her lips tightly, in disapproval at what he was doing, but did not look down or away from him.

He began his testimony,

"I would that I had not been witness to the evidence that Lydia

Gilbert, my own wife's mother, did present to me these past several months, which proves her, beyond any doubt, to be in regular affiliation with Satan, and a practitioner of witch craft. If I had known previously these things of which I shall soon speak, I never would have allowed her presence in my house."

Nicholas was well spoken, and, because he was respected as the town's only medical doctor, his words captured the alert attention of all persons present. For certainly a medical doctor would tell only the unembellished bare truth.

"With my own eyes I saw Lydia Gilbert practice sorcery with the aid of the Devil, using a bewitched glove," he said.

Lydia looked to Governor Allyn, who seemed to be smiling contently at her son-in-law's words, for the damage they would do to her. She was outraged. How could this man she considered to be a member of her own family speak in public against her?

"One afternoon toward evening in early spring, there came to the Gilberts' holdings unexpected visitors: a man and his wife and baby traveling through from New York, on their way to the Maine territory. They had come from Boston, carrying all of their belongings on the back of a pony, along the post road.

"I was behind the barn with my father in law, Thomas Gilbert, and his manservant; we were trying to repair an old sleigh. I had ridden out to the holdings after noon dinner, but would have to return early, for my wife was with child, and she had remained with her sister at my house in town.

"I saw the travelers arrive, and go inside with Lydia Gilbert.

"When Thomas and I came in for a drink of ale before I went back to town, I met them.

"The man's clothes and the skin of his face were filthy with dust, and his shoes had come unsewn at the toes, and showed his bare feet. He carried an old sack over his shoulder, full of household bric-a-brac. He was about twenty-five years of age, and his wife was very thin and had no coat. She was much younger than he, no more than seventeen. In the cradle of her arms she held the crying baby.

"The baby was unwell. The girl said that it had had a fever for two days.

"My mother in law gave them a basin of warmed water to wash their hands and faces, and then went to her still room where she keeps herbs and potions. The baby was crying constantly. I watched this, knowing that she, my mother-in-law, had practiced herbery for many years, and believed in its efficacy. As a studied doctor of human physic, I knew then, as I know now, that herbs and plants and potions alone can do nothing to heal. These remedies can only work if the herbalist is also in connection with the powers of evil."

The audience remained silent, concentrating, taking in Nicholas's every word as if it were a prescription for guaranteed happy immortality.

Lydia's legs were tired, and, uttering a loud sigh of disgust, she sat down heavily upon the wooden chair behind her.

Nicholas glanced at her in peeved annoyance and continued,

"When Lydia returned to the room she had some things with her which she placed upon the board, all the while muttering strange incantations under her breath. I noticed that, along with the dried flowers and herbs, and tree bark, she had left a single fancy decorated glove.

"I also noticed that when my sister in law, Reliance, saw the glove upon the table, her face took on a strange expression of confused anger for a fleet moment. She set her eyes upon it before taking the bucket of dirty water outside.

"The travelers sat down by the hearth, and Lydia told the young mother that she would give the baby a concoction to make its fever subside.

"Then she went to the still room for the ale, and brought it back in an earthen pitcher. I had taken the glove up from the board and was turning it round and round in my hand to look at it. It was decorated

with the signs and symbols used by practitioners of the dark arts—
symbols to conjure the power of Satan."

As Nicholas said these last few words his brown eyes, with their
black eyebrows, intensified, and he slowed the rhythm of his speech
and raised the timbre of his voice to great effect. The audience seemed
to be sitting on nails, for no one moved nor made any sound.

He exhaled, and continued speaking, slightly faster.

"She poured ale into four tankards and left these on the board table
against the wall. She carried a tankard to the traveler's wife, and gave it
to her and told her to give her the baby."

Slowing his pace once again, to emphasize the importance of the
following words, he spoke,

"I said to her, "What a fine glove, Lydia. But where's its partner?"

"Lydia snatched it away from me and said,

"Lost, many years ago!"

"I watched, as she slipped her left hand into the glove, while
holding the baby on her right elbow. She pressed the gloved hand
against his head, and uttered strange words in a low voice, so that no
one would hear them, for certainly these were to beckon the powers of
the devil close to her. The baby took a deep and sudden breath like a
hiccough, and then all together stopped his crying and was silent.

"Very soon, he fell into a deep sleep."

Nicholas stopped speaking and, with his eyebrows raised, he
looked around at all of the people before him, and at the men in the jury
behind him.

Certain that all attention present was upon him, he continued.

"She kept her gloved hand on his head, and held the baby close to
her body. After some few minutes, she noticed that I was watching her,
and she turned away, but so as to seem she had not noticed what I'd
been looking at.

"For a long time Lydia wore the glove on her hand, pressed against
the child's head, and every time I looked at her she turned her back and

moved further into the shadows, as if to hide herself and the glove she wore.

"Finally, because I had finished my ale, and it would soon be dark, I said I must be leaving.

When I stepped near the board to put my empty tankard upon it, I asked Lydia,

"Why do you now wear that unmatched glove?"

She made no answer immediately, and, looking closely at the baby's sleeping face, I said,

"Yours is a calming touch, Lydia. I think his fever has broken. But what is the meaning of the glove?"

"Now, the attention of Thomas and the traveler were upon the glove, too, but still Lydia did not respond.

"Finally, she smiled strangely, and said,

"Tis so pretty I put it once again upon my hand. Tis a pity the other's lost."

"Then she handed the slumbering baby back to its mother, and removed the glove from her hand, and put it upon the table.

"I knew there was something evil that remained in that glove, and that it should not stay in the house, and so I snatched it from the table and quickly threw it into the fire.

"Lydia looked shocked, and I said to her,

"Tis no use holding onto an unmated glove!"

"Thomas agreed to this. Lydia went, angrily, close to the hearth, clearly upset to see the glove burning. It released an unnatural stink of sulfur, and made shrieking sounds, and then the flames turned blue, before they died away completely, leaving only a thick black smoke."

CHAPTER FIFTEEN

WHEN SHE WAS 15 years old, Lydia had sewn a left hand glove. It was not an everyday glove to be worn against cold, or while riding, or working in the garden. No, this particular glove was intended to intensify and convey the power she felt she already possessed in her left hand.

Even at that young age, Lydia had asked herself why it was believed that humans were higher beings than other animals. She thought it was because of their hands, and their minds. For of all God's creatures human beings alone had the power to create anything they could imagine with their hands. This power was no small thing. It was what made civilization. Lydia believed it to be of magnificent value.

Realizing this, she decided to sew, according to the size and model of her own left hand, one glove of fine kidskin dyed a nearly silver hue. She had got this from her aunt, the milliner, in exchange for her help in sewing decorations on to ladies' hats.

Once she had sewn the glove's body she decorated it with lace and ribbons, small azure glass beads, the dyed lilac plume of an ostrich, and the symbol for the star sign of Taurus, and a spiral, carefully embroidered in lilac and silver threads. She did not dare to show it to anyone for she believed the glove revealed too much of her own spirit and beliefs.

She kept the glove hidden, and no one, save herself, knew of it, from the time of its making until many years later when, after having carefully brought it with her when she came to the New World, rolled up and packed inside a spice tin, she again found it in an unlikely place.

One morning when she went to the barn her eye caught upon something glinting and silvery stuck in the wood slats of the barn wall. When she stepped closer and put her hand to it, she saw it was the glove. She pulled it out of the slat and questioned aloud how and why the glove had got there.

She asked, "Why ever was my old glove behind the barn slat? Do any of you animals know? Can someone answer me? Minnie, do you know?"

Minnie did not utter a word, and neither did Mercury, nor the heifer, nor the cat, nor the chickens, nor the oxen. Lydia's mare, Aisley, pricked her ears to listen to her mistress's words, and although she probably would have liked to, she could not answer.

When Lydia reached her left hand into the glove to put it on, she found several silver and golden coins inside each finger. She emptied these into her palm, and saw that they were Spanish coins. Six or seven of them were small gold escudos with a Maltese cross encircled by a flower, and the rest were of silver—two or four, and even a couple of pieces of eight reales, with their shields and crosses that reminded her too much of the old world she had left behind, but which still held sway over the new.

Who had moved the glove from its hiding place in the spice tin to behind a slat in the barn to store money in? It would have had to be someone who lived in her house, and she would most likely suspect Reliance, but she could not imagine where her daughter could have got the coins. If William had stashed the coins there—perhaps they had been a gift from a wealthy fellow—why would he have put them inside her glove? She did not know the why nor the how, but, after so much time had passed by she had unexpectedly found the wherefore of her old forgotten glove.

Holding the coins in her right hand, she put the glove on her left, and found it still fit. She moved her hand around in the air lyrically, like she had done as a girl, drawing power toward her.

The house door closed and she heard William coming toward the barn to feed the animals. Suddenly she realized that she had stood there for a long time doing nothing when there were a dozen things she should be doing.

She removed the glove from her hand, dropped some coins into each finger, worried momentarily whether she had put the proper coin into each proper finger, and placed the folded glove back behind the same slat where it had been. Whoever had put the coins in the fingers would be coming back for them at some time, so perhaps she would discover who had put it there.

William entered the barn, tall and bald and looking outwardly somber as usual. Lydia turned to him, pretending to be startled, from where she stood by Minnie and the heifer's stall.

"How be the little one, lady?" he said.

"Seems to be very well, William," said Lydia.

She searched his face for any sign of suspicion or guilt, but saw none. He looked tired, and as if he had slept poorly the night before.

"How be you?" she asked.

"Middling, lady. A bit tired, but all right."

He turned his back to her, and started going about his chore, then, having noticed that the glove had been disturbed, faced her again and, rubbing his bald head, said,

"Forgive my impropriety, lady, but I should tell you that I found your glove here yesterday morn whilst feeding the horses. At least I think tis your glove though I had not seen it previously. It looks to be your handiwork."

He glanced toward the slat.

"However would it be here?" said Lydia.

She walked closer to it but not right away. She acted as if she did not know where it was.

"I know not," said he.

By his words she believed he was telling the truth.

Then she reached for the glove and snatched it from behind the slat, and examined it.

"Yes, tis my glove. One that I sewed many years ago."

She held it up into a ray of sunlight coming in from the west side door, and the glass beads glittered.

"But what's inside?" she said.

She shook the coins out into the palm of her hand.

Lydia looked into William's kind blue eyes, and saw by a glimmer there that he knew the answer to this mystery but was trying to handle it tactfully, by telling her about it as he had. If the coins were his, she wanted him to keep them.

"These coins are not mine," she said.

"Whosoever they belong to shall surely come back here looking for them, so I shall leave them here on this ledge, inside my old pocket, and let us all be content with the outcome this time."

William agreed, but turned toward the hay just as his face reddened all the way to cover his entire head. Lydia was not surprised if he had come across the old glove accidentally, as he sometimes cooked for the family, and may have sooner or later opened the spice tin where she had hidden it so many years ago.

Having seen the glove again brought many pleasant thoughts and scenes of when she was young to Lydia's mind, for even after her parents were dead and she and her siblings scattered throughout England, because she was young she was carefree.

Her aunt, to whom she went to work at the millinery shop, was the spinster sister of Lydia's mother, and did in many ways remind her of her mother, for although she was not as pretty, her eyes were similar, and she had a playfulness about her like her mother. The aunt coddled Lydia, even as a young woman, sometimes letting her keep cuttings of this or that ribbon or lace or dried flower or plume, or any other pretty thing that caught her fancy, and if there was a lull in the handiwork of ladies' things, Lydia was allowed to spend that time making whatever she wanted from these pieces.

At the age of fourteen years Lydia had begun to be so deluged with prophetic dreams that, rather than fear them, she decided to put to good use. She kept a journal—a small black leather bound book, one of many salvaged from her father's shop. Into this journal she wrote her dreams each morning when she awoke, and when the event she had dreamt about happened in reality, she wrote that, too, with its date, on the paper alongside the one with the dream on it.

Within some six months' time she found that, by thinking on what she wished to happen, or what she wanted the dream to foresee would happen, Lydia could make it real. She could say to herself upon retiring, "This night I shall dream on Missus Binghampton coming into the shop tomorrow and buying five pairs yellow gloves", and so she would dream it, and the next day the mentioned lady would appear at the shop and buy the gloves just as she had in the dream.

At first she believed that she was controlling what was to come. But if she thought up a purely fantastical scene, such as, "tomorrow the earth shall open up in front of the church and swallow the minister, and the sun shall shine all night long," she would not dream it, and it would not come to pass. And even while thinking on it she knew it would never occur in life. Perhaps not believing in it made it false, but she believed that, rather than controlling with her thoughts what had not yet happened, she was thinking on what was yet to happen. In a word, Lydia was able to see the future.

She kept the journal private and neither spoke of it nor showed it to anyone. She never told anyone about her strange gift, until many years later when she confessed it to her sister Rebecca.

Although Lydia did not flaunt this ability, she was pleased with it.

Once she had met a lady, a friend of her grandmother's, who could read the cards. This strange old woman lived alone in a tiny hut by the brook behind the mill with twenty cats. People said she was a witch. She could see the future in the cards.

One day Lydia went with her grandmother to visit the withered old hag, who wore a heavy winter cloak over her clothes, and she smelled so foul that it brought stinging tears to the girl's eyes.

Inside, the hut was dark and filthy, as if never swept nor cleaned at all, and Lydia soon saw that the old woman was blind, for her eyes shown all white, with no color to them.

While she struggled to breathe, leaning next to her grand mother, and standing before the rickety table, the old witch took from her apron pocket a deck of cards and laid them out on the table without a word, letting her gnarled and yellow fingers linger some moments over each card as she unturned it, reading them in this way, as if her eyes were inside the points of her digits. The cards, though very worn, were decorated with gold leaf, and beautifully drawn, especially the animal figures.

Lydia watched carefully.

Her grand mother had been to the old witch's hut once previous, some years before Lydia's mother had died, and all that the witch had seen in the cards had come to be.

Now her grand mother was returning once again because she had been having the same disturbing dream night after night, and knowing not what it meant she thought that by having her future looked at by the witch something might be illuminated that otherwise she could make no sense of.

Her grand mother would not tell Lydia the content of her dream, although she begged her many times. Likewise she did not think it was proper for an impressionable young lady to accompany her to such a place. She had not wanted Lydia to come along, but the girl pleaded with her, the greatest reason for which was that she was afraid her grandmother might fall, as she sometimes grew dizzy while walking, and needed someone to lean against. Also, Lydia was curious about the old witch.

When she had finished turning over the cards, which numbered ten, she held both her hands over them, about half an arms' length up, and spread her fingers wide, with the palms of her hands downward, and then, for some very long moments which seemed never to end, her hands moved up and down over the cards, very slowly, as if by gentle undulating waves of water. From the woman's chest and throat came a low hum like an animal's growl, and this sound, and the vision of the withered old woman with her staring white eyes, and her bent fingers lit up by a single candle, was eerie, and Lydia wished for it to end. No sooner had she wished it than it did end, and the old woman placed her hands on the edge of the table and spoke, saying,

"Thy children shall be scattered to the oceans like a handful of sand, and time will take thee away from this earth quickly and in the dark of the moon. In this child now present there is a great power. This could be an affliction if not used with care, for she is comely and will marry an important man, and herself shall be sought after and looked up to amongst women.

"The shadow of death lurks nigh and will soon take away thine youngest boy."

With a great flourish of both of her hands that seemed, to Lydia's eyes, to raise a cloud of brilliantly lighted dust, the old witch fell silent and was finished.

Lydia looked at her grandmother, whose face appeared pale, even in that dimly lit room.

Was it her youngest brother, Blaze, who was to die? She had not seen him for several years, for he had gone to live with her father's cousins.

And what could the old hag know of her powers, of which she had never spoken to any soul, and what could she have meant by saying these powers might be an affliction?

The grand mother dropped a coin into the old woman's wrinkled palm and thanked her.

Then off they went, out of that terrible hut with its smells of cat urine and rotting fish.

She wanted to ask her grand mother what those words, "could be an affliction" might mean, but she knew that to bring up the subject would be the same as admitting that she herself knew that she had great power, and of this she would not speak. To ask whether her grand mother's dreams had been of Blaze dying Lydia dared not either, for if this had been the subject of her unspoken worries, now she would be even more worried. So the girl kept silent as they walked, until, once again in town, Lydia took hold of her grandmother's hand in her own, and asked her,

"Was your question answered, grand mother?"

The older woman looked into the girl's eyes for a long while without speaking, but only nodding her head very slowly. Lydia grew uncomfortable, but by her grandmother's look understood that she had known of her prophetic power and was now certain of it.

Then she said, "Yes, my dear," and turned to continue walking, leaning against Lydia.

Lydia was aware then that those things of which no one speaks are often the things most clearly understood between people.

Later, some days or even a fortnight or so later, or perhaps it was still longer than that, she decided to make the glove. She had come to believe that, by placing her left hand over an affliction, such as a strained tendon, or a wound, she could help heal it.

One day on the way home from buying a cheese from the shepherd's wife she had tripped on some rocks while going down hill, and twisted her ankle. It hurt terribly to walk on that foot, but once she got near home she put forth her best effort to walk without limping so that no one would know she was hurt. And that night when she was in bed the pain and swelling of the ankle was such that, thinking again on the blind old hag and her words, Lydia tried repeating some words in Latin, imagining inside her mind that her ankle was healed and well. She called for good air to surround the injury, all the while holding and stroking the ankle with her left hand.

In the morning the leg was almost as if it had never been hurt at all.

It was for the increase of this healing power that she had decided to sew the left hand glove.

She had used it rarely, for she did not have many occasions for healing her own body, being well and sound. She used it on her aunt's horse, which had suffered girth galls, and her grandmother's dog, who'd had warts. The glove worked very well when it was upon her hand, but it frightened her a little bit, because she worried that she might not be able to keep such power hidden for long, and if it were discovered she would be condemned to live a life like the one the haggard witch lived—isolated, loved by no one, an outcast. No man would marry a soothsayer or a witch, unless he did not know what she was.

When, at the age of twenty-two, she met Thomas Gilbert, and fell in love with him, Lydia put away the glove and forgot it.

CHAPTER SIXTEEN

SOME DAYS AFTER Lydia had unexpectedly found her old glove again in the barn slat, Reliance, coming to the barn early to milk the cows, discovered it was missing. She had slept only a few hours that night, for she had been working on a translation for Governor Allyn, and had left the barn door wide opened to get some light in there. When she went for the milking stool and pail from the hay room, she thought to check behind the few remaining bales, for the money glove.

It was not there!

In its place was something else—her mother's old worn brown velvet pocket. Her face prickled with an unfamiliar feeling, and, as the cows lowed impatiently behind her thoughts of all sorts rushed into her mind—

Her mother had discovered her secret!

William had betrayed her and told her mother she was earning money by doing translations for Magistrates and for the Governors!

Her mother had seen how much money was there!

Someone else had found the glove, or taken it—one of the Wescotts—Josiah, when he came to steal corn!

She opened the pocket clasp and put her hand inside, and took out the coins to count. They were all there.

She was humiliated.

Since when had her mother known?

Why had William not told her that she knew?

It had been her secret and now it was no secret at all. She was like a little child who discovers that the adults have been lying to him about

God and the angels, although they never admit that this is nothing but an invention.

She thought she would have to hide her money in a different place.

The cows were lowing with more insistence, and she heard the back door of the house shut as her mother left it.

Quickly Reliance shoved the pocket back into the slat and grabbed the stool and the milk pail.

Lydia entered the barn as Reliance crossed over to the cows' stable. Lydia's silhouette in front of the barn door was black, with the grey morning light behind her.

"Good morning, child," she said.

"Good morning, mother," Reliance replied.

She quickly moved into the stable, and set the stool down in the straw next to Minnie.

While she milked, the sounds of the animals rustling about, and of her mother feeding them, and then cleaning out their stables, and the rhythmic sound of the milk spurting into the tin pail mingled with Reliance's angry feelings and, in her tiredness, she faded in and out of waking and sleeping, and slowly the anger dissolved.

She, too, could play the game of silence and secrets. She decided to leave the pocket where it was, and continue adding new coins to it there. She would never tell her mother that she knew she had seen it, nor ask William anything, nor say a word about her discovery to anyone.

CHAPTER SEVENTEEN

IN THE COURTHOUSE, Nicholas Carver continued his testimony.

"Lydia Gilbert is able to change shape and form, and did it one day in my barn, coming in as a snake which crawled upon the floor, which then transformed itself into an old beggar woman. I recognized her not, and would not have thought it was my own mother-in-law, except that she then transmuted a third time, to her usual aspect, which is not the same aspect she presents to us now."

Suddenly Lydia rose from the wooden stool she had been seated on and said,

"I remember the episode you speak of very well, Nicholas. But it had naught to do with magical transmutation, for you know as well as I do that you had your mind on other things that day and simply did not at first recognize me because I was wearing a large brimmed hat to conceal my swollen eye!"

Judge Allyn lifted the Bible threateningly to stop Lydia speaking out, but Nicholas Carver said to him,

"Let her speak, Judge. She only damages herself by doing so."

His words incensed her, and she continued,

"I came to your barn at midday, with my horse, as I had done many times before, Surgeon Carver. You were in there, and when you saw me against the light you were blinded and did not know who I was!

"You shouted at me rudely.

"Who's that?" you said.

"Old woman, this is not a public stable! Are you deaf?"

"You were very rough, which surprised me, and I knew not how to answer you.

"Finally, I said, "Nicholas, do you not recognize me?"

"I came closer to you with my horse, and you looked straight at me without any recognition, so that I began to believe you had lost your senses.

"I stood before you, not three yards away, and I waited for your answer, or some sign of recognition, but it did not come.

"Finally you spoke, saying,

"Have you not a home to go to, good woman, that you seek refuge for yourself and your horse in someone else's barn? Where do you come from? Are you traveling alone?"

"Then I did not know what to make of you, Nicholas, for surely you had either lost your mind or were gaming strangely with me, and I was frightened. Tis true that the swollen and blackened eye changed the appearance of my face somewhat, but surely not beyond recognition. Then I thought, if you should suddenly realize twas I, your own mother-in-law, 'twould be greatly embarrassing to both of us, so I pulled my hat lower upon my forehead and kept my eyes down turned.

"I answered you in a very low voice, hardly discernable as my own.

"I said, "I am traveling alone, sir, but seek not lodging. By entering your barn I have made an honest mistake, for I thought I was in a different place. Please forgive me. I shall leave now."

"As I was turning to leave, you said,

"Is that not Goodwife Gilbert's horse?"

"Aye, tis," said I.

"You then asked me who I was.

"I removed the hat from my head, and looked you full in the face.

"Can you not see, Nicholas, that I am your wife Sarah's mother Lydia?"

As Lydia spoke these words before the townspeople and the jury, she looked deeply into Nicholas Carver's eyes.

His face reddened deeply, but listening to her story, he said not a word.

Lydia continued,

"And then you said, "Certainly I knew twas you, Lydia, as soon as you removed your hat and moved out of the doorway. The light from outside was shining in my eyes and made you appear as a phantom without clear features."

"Do you remember saying those words to me, Surgeon Carver?"

"Have you finished telling your tale?" he said.

For some moments she stood and regarded him. Then she said,

"No. For you repeated it a second time. I handed my horse to you, and, whilst you removed the tack, I asked you again, for you had given me a fright. I said, "Nicholas, what is it you see when you look upon me? Is my eye still so very swollen that I seem not to be myself?"

As Lydia spoke to him this time he avoided looking at her, but smirked cleverly, first toward the audience, and then toward Governor Allyn.

Some of the townspeople laughed lowly, as if they were in on a private joke between themselves and the doctor, and a general low mumbling broke out as Lydia said,

"You said again, "Twas the bright western light in my eyes."

He made no acknowledgement of having heard her, but encouraged mocking laughter from the townspeople with his facial expressions.

Lydia did not repeat herself, but sat down again in resignation.

When Nicholas resumed speaking, the audience hushed.

"Furthermore, aside from breaking the law by keeping playing cards, Lydia Gilbert uses these same charmed cards for telling fortunes."

He took a few steps forward and raised the volume of his voice slightly, saying,

"She kept these cards hidden away in my own house, while she was staying under my roof, only taking them out when I was not present. I would not have known about them except that my sister in law, Reliance, informed me. Lydia Gilbert tried to lead my wife and my two sisters in law astray with the regular use of these unlawful cards. She played at them, telling fortunes, even in the presence of my infant daughter.

"Now we are all aware what the Bible states, "There shall not be found among you anyone that maketh his son or daughter to pass through the fire, or that uses divination—"

As Nicholas Carver spoke these words, many of the townspeople joined in, reciting from memory,

"Or an observer of times, or an enchanter, or a witch. Or a charmer, or a consulter with familiar spirits, or a wizard, or a necromancer."

More and more voices joined in, until the words, themselves spoken in unison like a magic chant, echoed loudly off the walls and the rafters inside the meetinghouse building.

"For all of these things are an ABOMINATION unto the LORD: and because of these ABOMINATIONS the LORD thy God doth drive them out from before thee!"

Several voices went on reciting, but, because Surgeon Carver had finished, they soon died away.

He stood before the townspeople and the jury, smiling triumphantly.

Judge Allyn allowed him to gloat for a few moments and then addressed Lydia,

"Do you deny that you used cards for divination, Goodwife Gilbert?"

Lydia remained seated, and, looking the Governor straight in the eyes, spoke not a word.

She was remembering the time Surgeon Carver found out about the cards. It was at his house, indeed, and happened the same day the first accusation summons came. After the noon meal, according to their usual habit, Lydia and her daughters gathered in the small sitting room. Sarah's husband, being the only man present, did not usually tarry, but took his leave to go outdoors and walk and converse with some acquaintance or neighbor. Only then would Sarah bring out her own pack of cards, which she kept unknown from her husband. But that one day, before Nicholas had gone out, there was a knocking upon the door.

He went to open it, and from the chair where Lydia sat she could see it was the messenger from the courthouse. He handed Nicholas a piece of paper, for Missus Lydia Gilbert.

Nicholas accepted the paper and closed the door again.

With trembling hands she broke the seal, and unfolded the paper to read that Magistrate Allyn was summoning her to appear at his house next Thursday, September twenty third, at two hours past noon to answer to an accusation made against her for witch craft.

At first the surprise of this last word came as a great relief, when she saw the accusation was not for adultery, and Lydia almost laughed, but she took pause and thought about the words for some moments— witchcraft! It was not a minor accusation.

She put the paper on her lap and said,

"Tis a summons."

Reliance stared hard at her mother, her eyes demanding more information.

Sarah leaned forward in her chair, causing the ball of yarn upon her lap to fall to the floor and begin to roll and unravel.

"I've been summoned by Magistrate Allyn, for next Thursday. To answer to an accusation."

Lydia refolded the summons and tucked it into the pocket of her skirt, then searched inside the small sack on the floor beside her, for her handwork.

Everyone in the room remained idle and tense, unable to utter a single word, but waiting to hear the details of the summons.

For some moments Lydia did not speak, but continued on her work with the needle and thread.

At last she said, "Are you all perhaps waiting for me to divulge of what crime I have been accused?"

Reliance was nodding her head vigorously up and down.

"Witch craft," said Lydia.

She knew that if there were such a thing as witches she would probably qualify as one, and she also knew who her accusers likely were. The Wescotts had long feared her for possessing what they believed to be the unnatural power of attracting good fortune, which consisted of nothing more than hard work and intelligence.

"You? A witch?" Sarah said.

"You have done naught but goodness and kind deeds for this community, I say, being a person willing to go out of your way to help another, with no desire for personal gain. How could you ever be considered all the evil things implied by the name of witch? There must surely be a mistake. The summons was brought to the wrong house."

Nicholas shook his head; he had accepted the summons, and heard the messenger speak Lydia's name.

Sarah got up from her chair, picking up her ball of wool on the way. She took the summons from her mother's pocket, unfolded it and read it aloud, and then said,

"Who would think to accuse you in this way?"

"Our good neighbors, the Wescotts, I do think."

She clicked her tongue and dropped the summons in Lydia's lap.

"They are wasting time and no more. No Magistrate would find the wife of another Magistrate guilty of such a crime. And what proof have they against you?"

"What proof need they have?" said Lydia.

"Tis true I can heal with herbs and with my hands. And tis true I use the cards for divining."

As soon as she had uttered these last words, she realized she should not have spoken so freely in front of her son-in-law, and she wished she could take them back.

Nicholas commented,

"I know naught about cards for divining, Lydia. Certainly none shall be found under my roof. And I think there is only innocuous quackery in practicing herbery, for any apothecary can tell you that few plants have real physical effect on a man but that what effect he might believe he undergoes is mere fancy."

And then, inexplicably, Reliance said,

"There are cards here, Nicholas."

He looked at her and then at Sarah and at Elizabeth, and then he looked to Lydia, unhappily confused.

No one spoke. Reliance stood up and went to the drawer in the dresser where the cards were kept.

Lydia could not understand why Reliance wished to incite Sarah's husband this way, for she thought it would have been easier to say nothing and keep the cards unseen, as she had done for years with Thomas.

Reliance took the deck and turned, leaving the drawer open, and unwrapped the cards from their covering of printed paper, and brought the deck close for Nicholas to see.

He took it from her and riffled through the cards, then said,

"These we'd best burn straight away. I shall not ask questions, nor utter another word about them, and neither should you.

"Is there anything else I should know?"

Sarah was trembling visibly and looked pale, but she kept her face down toward the floorboards. In her hands she twisted a strand of the wool she'd been knitting on round and round and into a tight knot. She twisted the stuff so tightly that her knuckles grew white.

Once again Reliance spoke, saying,

"To my knowledge there is nothing else here that could be considered a tool of witchery, nor as evidence against my mother in the charge of witch craft."

"I know of nothing," said Elizabeth.

"Nor I," Sarah said, with sudden great release of nervousness.

"Then so be it," said Lydia.

"I shall appear before Magistrate Allyn on Thursday, and face the accusation."

After some moments of uncomfortable silence, and believing that all was settled and calm, Nicholas, who had remained on his feet, strode to the door with the announcement that he was going out for his customary stroll.

He flung the door wide open to the street, bright golden and hazy with dust and sunshine. There was a great burst of light. When he closed it again behind him, the room returned to being darkened and cool as a crypt.

CHAPTER EIGHTEEN

LYDIA HAD ONCE told Reliance that because she was born beneath the star sign of Acquarius people trusted her with their secrets. They told her things she did not ask to hear, believing their confidences safe with her.

About a month before her marriage to Dr. Carver, Sarah told Reliance that she loved him, but considered him as a brother to her, and so her love lacked passion, and she fretted about consummating the marriage, because there was someone else she loved with passion but could not marry. This information coming from her sister's lips shocked and startled Reliance. Sarah had drunk a pint of mother's ale, and Reliance knew she spoke her heart's truth.

She asked her,

"Who raises your passion?"

Sarah blushed and perhaps she then wished she had told her sister none of it, but she answered,

"Tis Elliot, our cousin."

He was handsome, and well spoken, and of the same age as Sarah. He lived in Boston, and came to Windsor only a few times a year.

"You're sweet on him," Reliance said.

It seemed natural. She thought she could be as well. He was a person one couldn't help but love.

Reliance stared at her sister a moment; her face turned from pink to rose to nearly scarlet, and then suddenly almost white.

Then she changed the subject to embroidery stitches.

In truth, Sarah knew that her only child was not Nicholas Carver's, but Elliot's. It was not difficult for her to pretend the child was her husband's, because no one, except perhaps Reliance, doubted otherwise.

Her cousin Elliot had stopped in Windsor, in July, on his way to New Haven. Weary from travel, he had stopped at the Carvers' house for the night, to rest, and to feed his horse, and to sup with Sarah and her husband, and to sleep.

The previous time Sarah had seen Elliot was shortly before she married Surgeon Carver. That time she and her cousin had confessed their love to one another, and even kissed and held each other, in the barn by the cows, and when she had emerged with pieces of straw on her clothes and bonnet, Sarah had been afraid that her mother or father would see her, and she hurried inside the house and made herself busy with the housework.

That night she had lain in bed next to her sisters and was unable to sleep, but lay awake turning to and fro for many hours thinking on what she had done. He was the one her soul desired, but he was her first cousin and she was already betrothed to surgeon Carver, so it was impossible for them to marry.

The next morning Elliot had left the house before dawn, and Sarah knew that it was no use to write letters to each other, nor to spend time thinking on things that could never be, so when Nicholas Carver had asked her hand in marriage she had agreed to it. They were married in May. She did not feel for the surgeon what she felt for her cousin, but she considered him her friend and believed he would make a good husband.

Their first months of life together as husband and wife Sarah was content, and had nothing to complain about, for although he was cold by nature, Nicholas was not unkind, and he provided well. He had tried in earnest to get her with child from the start, but something would not take.

When Elliot arrived at their house in July to eat with them and to sleep beneath their roof, Sarah lay awake again all the night, as she had done two years earlier, thinking about him. She thought about herself as well, and she wept silently for reasons she did not know.

Morning came and Sarah discovered that her husband had already gone out, having been called very early by Goody Blossom for her child. She found herself alone with cousin Elliot for a time lasting the better part of an hour before he had to leave again on his journey.

She offered him tea, and bread, and he took the tea, and then offered the bread to her lips.

They had known one another since they were toddlers, and had no pretenses. Being alone with him she felt again as she had as a young girl when they used to play together sometimes during visits in the summer. She was forward, and pushed the bread away from her lips and kissed his mouth, and he did not turn away, but brought her close to him, and encircled her body with his embrace.

Before they knew what was happening, they lay upon the floor together, their bodies joined as one in coupling. It was at that moment that her daughter, Elinor, was conceived. Sarah never told Elliot that she was his child, but if he had thought to work out the passing months between one event and the other, he would know. Whether he knew or not was of little concern to Sarah, though, for either way it would change nothing.

CHAPTER NINETEEN

NOW NICHOLAS CARVER stood before hundreds of people, many of whom had been his patients, to accuse his wife's mother of witchcraft.

After Thomas Gilbert had gone away suddenly to England at the end of the previous March, Nicholas had begun spending more time in companionship with Governor Allyn, who, at the time, had been only a Magistrate. Although Nicholas's political stance had always been more conservative than that of Thomas Gilbert, spending time with Allyn seemed to have pushed him still further in that direction.

Having gotten no response from Lydia, Governor Allyn turned his attention back to Nicholas Carver, and said,

"Have you any more evidence to add to your testimony, Surgeon Carver?"

Nicholas took a step forward, to block Lydia's image from his peripheral vision.

"Yes, Judge Allyn. One morning early I myself witnessed Lydia Gilbert conversing with the devil. She knew not that I saw her."

He spoke these terrifying words slowly, and they had a great emotional effect on the audience. There was the sound of in taken breaths, and a pregnant woman seated near the front fainted.

"She had gone into my study, although I forbade it, and was reading from one of my anatomy books. I saw the light from under the door and watched through the keyhole. The devil was standing very close to her. He appeared as a small man, about the size of a slender boy of ten or eleven years. His head seemed too large for his agile body, and he wore no clothing. His body was covered with thick fur like an animal.

"My mother-in-law sat there, at my writing bureau, regarding him as he did her. Then she stood up to make herself taller than he was, and she placed her hands upon his shoulders. I listened very carefully for either of them to utter some word. For, although this spectacle terrified me, it is in my nature, as a doctor of surgery, to fully understand everything I observe.

"Many moments passed, it seemed days or weeks passed by, while they stood confronting each other in silence. The devil prepared himself a pipe to smoke, and lit it with some fire from Lydia's lamp, and he smoked, blowing out rings from his lips and nostrils, but always keeping his yellow eyes pinned upon hers.

"When he had finished smoking, he put the pipe down onto the table, over the book, and held out his hand to her, in invitation, it seemed, to dance.

"Then he lent her his other hand as well, and he took her whole body into his spindly arms, and, in a wavering eerie voice, he uttered these words, over and over,

"Jacra Mastiga!"

"I could barely stand to watch as my own mother-in-law moved closer to the devil, almost as if she wished to merge with him physically.

"The two of them had their bodies entwined so that, with the hairiness of the one's and the whiteness of the other's, they resembled, in the low light from her betty lamp, the mildewing roots of some evil tree. They stood there like that, rocking slowly to and fro, for quite a while.

"The devil then suddenly pushed himself away from her and tore open her chemise, sending buttons flying and scattering in the room. With one of his hands holding her head back by the hair, he used his other to take her clothes off so that her nakedness was exposed. Then he placed his foul mouth upon her, and suckled fiercely. He bit at her, and she screamed out, and pounded upon his hairy back with her fists. He continued his violent sucking and biting, and then his long forked tongue came out. It roiled and coiled about her bosoms like a snake, and it went beneath her skirt and underneath her petticoats. Lydia Gilbert then fainted, on the way knocking against the lamp, which went rolling across the floor and caused a disturbing clatter.

"The devil vanished from the room as strangely as he had appeared.

"In truth, I knew not what to do, for my mother-in-law seemed to be lying in a faint upon the floor, but I questioned whether this was a part of her witch craft, and whether it would be wise to disturb her.

"For some moments I waited in anguish for her to rise. Since the lamp had gone out I could see only the faintest of shadows through the keyhole, and depended on my auditory sense.

"Finally I heard her getting to her feet again, and groping around for the door handle.

"And then she shouted out these words, "What do you want? Why do you come here?"

"This startled me very much, for my first thought was that she was speaking to me. I then realized that the devil must still be in the room with her, as she said,

"Get gone! You have finished your business here! Away with you!"

"When she opened the door, there I was, with my cloak on, bag in hand.

"Good morning," I said to her.

"But she was as if in a trance, and walked out of my study without seeing me, a strange glazed look on her face, and her clothing and hair disheveled. A peculiar odor of sulfur and rotting flesh came from within the room.

"'Tis early to be about. Are you unwell?" I said.

"She answered me not, but moved toward the room where she slept, before the hearth.

"I had to leave then, for my patient was waiting. I advised her to take a rest after dinner, and then I bid her good bye, and I left the house. When I saw her again at noon she seemed to be her usual self, but appearances can be deceiving. After paying witness to that episode I knew without a doubt that my mother-in-law, Lydia Gilbert, is a witch, and in regular contact with Satan."

Nicholas's convincing story had worked like a charm upon the audience. When he had finished speaking all eyes remained upon him and no one dared break the silence with so much as even a cough or sniffle.

Lydia sat crumpled in the chair, her head tilted up at a cynically questioning angle toward her son-in-law, who could not see her.

After some moments, Judge Allyn spoke.

"Goodwife Gilbert, you realize that this is a gravely serious accusation, and will likely require that your body be searched for the marks left upon it by the enemy of mankind, the chief of all evil, Satan."

He glanced toward the Searcher, who lifted her chin righteously.

"Have you any words in your defense? Do you deny Surgeon Carver's accusation?"

Lydia got to her feet, and, taking advantage of the profound silence, spoke in a clear strong voice.

"I know not of what my son-in-law speaks. But I count myself fortunate to have never met the devil, for I believe he does dwell in Surgeon Carver's house."

At these words, Nicholas turned around and stared at Lydia with an open mouthed look of shock.

She continued,

"Surgeon Carver has a blue chair in his study, at the table with his books and papers, and there is where he sits while studying and reading about the various maladies that infect the bodies of men.

"He said of that chair that he'd brought it over with him from Wales, where his grand father had it before him, and he'd got it from a woodcutter. Though the chair is old and worn, it was well constructed, and sturdy to sit upon, but there is something not right about it.

"One night, when I could not sleep, I lit a lamp and, although he forbade it, I went to sit on the blue chair in the study, and I secretly looked through my son in law's illustrated books.

"Twas while sitting on the chair, and looking at a drawing of a man's heart, with its system of arteries and veins, so similar to the heart of a pig, that I felt an odd draft against my face and uncovered head. It came suddenly, and was ice cold and made my hair rise up at the roots.

"For some minutes I sat there, but the draft, which came from nowhere, as the study has no window, chilled me to the bones, and covered me in gooseflesh, so that I was afraid, and hurried to get up. In my rush I knocked over the lamp, and then I hit my leg upon the chair's leg and fell upon the floor. When, finally I found the door and was able to leave the study I was in a panic. I never did see the devil, but I believe that something evil dwells in Surgeon Carver's study, and after that time I would not go in there."

The audience had remained raptly silent during Lydia's speech.

Governor Allyn, who had been listening attentively,now with a loud humph, said,

"This is nonsense, Lydia Gilbert! You are on trial! You are not permitted to make accusations against your accusers, but only question or comment on their accusations against you!"

She turned to face her judge.

"When I came to your house after the first accusation made by Goody Wescott, you did offer me immunity from further accusations in exchange for—"

He lifted the Bible and threw it down hard upon the pulpit, shouting,

"You will silence yourself, woman! These outbursts will not be tolerated! Bind her at the mouth!"

His face had reddened deeply and, to stir up a ruckus from the audience, he encouraged Nicholas Carver to join him in taunting her.

"Satan has got into her, and makes her speak nonsense! Ha!"

"The woman is possessed!"

Lydia shouted to be heard,

"You propositioned me for sexual relations! If there is a devil, tis you! Tis you! What right have you to try me for crimes I have not committed, when you yourself are so darkly stained with evil that it does turn my stomach to look upon you now!"

Realizing that the audience was now joining the Judge and Surgeon in mocking laughter, and that no one was listening to her words, she spat upon the floor in contempt.

The Searcher came from behind her with a piece of thick hemp rope and tied it tightly around her jaw, to bind her mouth. Lydia slumped down onto the wooden stool, defeated.

Before returning to his seat, Nicholas Carver spoke his final accusation,

"I accuse my wife's mother, Lydia Gilbert, of practicing the black arts, and of being a person unfit to live freely among others, for she is a menace in the community of Windsor."

CHAPTER TWENTY

THE GOVERNOR CALLED for James Stiles.

Lydia had been sitting with her chin upon her chest, her eyes closed. The rope binding her mouth was too tight, and if she lifted her head it became even tighter and cut into the skin of her face. When she heard the name of James Stiles, she looked up for an instant, to see him there, near the central aisle dividing men from women, and not far from the front. She dropped her head back down, and then he was suddenly near her at the front.

James Stiles was the Reverend's cousin, and her best friend Judith's cousin-in-law. The last time she had seen him was at Judith's house, the day of Sarah's wedding to Nicholas Carver.

Before Governor Allyn, James Stiles took his oath, then turned to stand facing the people, and began speaking.

"In September of 1651, during the temporary absence of Reverend Stiles' family from Windsor, my brother, Henry Stiles, a bachelor, went to reside with the Gilberts.

"My cousin, Reverend Stiles, is a trustworthy man, and, because he and his wife recommended the Gilberts to him, my brother was not hesitant, but transferred his belongings to their house with no consternation whatsoever.

"He had not been there but a month before I had hearsay that the relation between him and Lydia Gilbert had gone askew.

"Although he lamented not to me directly, neighbors of the Gilberts reported that they often heard Lydia screaming curses at my brother. For most of his life Henry had suffered various maladies due to his naturally weak constitution, and, apparently he had put his trust in the dubious healing capacity of Goody Gilbert. I say dubious, for, in truth, I believe that in the name of healing, she was attempting to murder my brother."

James Stiles' carefully measured words were shocking. There was a general uncomfortable shifting around of body weight in the audience and among the men of the jury, for it seemed that James Stiles was accusing Lydia Gilbert not only of practicing general witch craft, but of planning and executing the death of a late member of the community.

James Stiles continued his testimony. He was a handsome man, and he spoke convincingly.

"It is well known in Windsor that Lydia Gilbert practices healing with herbs and other suspicious materials, and I know by word of my late brother that she did use certain of her poultices and such upon him, allegedly as cures for his pains. In truth, these cures were poisonous philters intended to intensify his suffering.

"She administered these "cures" in order to put his already weak physical being into a more perilous state, which eventually would lead to his complete demise. During the months he lodged at the Gilberts I received word that Henry suffered a series of unexplained ailments. These included excruciating pains in the shoulder, arm and mouth, and their pain far outweighed any other pain he had suffered previous."

Though he gave no reason as to why Goodwife Gilbert would have desired his brother's suffering, his speech was persuasive.

Lydia sat with her bald head down. She could see no one, but sensing the tense interest from the men sitting behind her, she feared the jury would be prevailed upon by James Stiles' words.

He continued,

"On November third, a musket day, my brother Henry was inexplicably killed when the armament of Tommy Allyn suddenly fired of its own accord and without warning. The bullet split Henry's heart in two.

"I testify that Lydia Gilbert is a practicing witch under the dominion of Satan, and did use her dark powers to cause the musket to kill my brother after all of her previous attempts to kill him with poisons and potions failed."

At his last words gasps and little cries were uttered by some of the townspeople, for Tommy Allyn, the Governor's nephew, had been charged with Henry Stiles' death, three years earlier.

They, as well as Lydia, had thought that was a closed case.

Governor Allyn addressed the Searcher.

"Remove the binding rope from her mouth."

The rope was untied, and Lydia lifted her head and looked at James Stiles' profile.

"Have you words in your defense?" Governor Allyn said.

James Stiles turned to look at her arrogantly, and she stared back at him, and spoke carefully, saying,

"I was sad for the accidental death of Henry Stiles three years ago."

She looked now at the townspeople and mustered her strength, hoping that the truth in her words would strike a positive chord with the men of the jury, and act persuasively upon them.

"Some years previous to 1651 Henry Stiles had come to abide with Reverend Stiles, and it was there that my husband and I first made his acquaintance. We found him to be pleasant company, and when the Reverend, in 1651, found that he and his family would have to be away for the better part of a year, Henry, who needed a woman's help for managing a household, came to live with us. In truth I did not at all mind repaying the hospitality that my friends, the Stiles, had so often shown to us, through caring for their cousin.

"The Reverend Stiles and Judith and Mercy departed in June.

"The day previous to their departure, Henry Stiles walked to my husband's holdings, carrying with him a few possessions, and took up residence with us. He slept upstairs in the garret on a mattress I had made for him of new clean straw.

"I had known Henry Stiles only a year or two, but knew, from hearsay, something about him. Apparently, some fifteen years previous,

he had courted a lady, and was quite filled with anticipation for his
wedding to her when, on the Friday before they were to take their vows
to one another this lady was swept away by a current and drowned in
the Great River where she had gone to bathe in preparation for her
marriage. Henry was distraught, sad and silent for many months
afterward, and since that time never courted any other lady but
remained as a bachelor. Then he became aged and took to drinking
much rum in the evenings, which made his speech incomprehensible,
and while he was at my house he often fell asleep on the high backed
chair by the hearth and spent the entire night there, snoring with his
chin upon his chest.

"As I had promised my friends that I would care well for their
cousin in their absence, I was true to my word, although there were
times, during those months whilst he was living with us, that I did think
to myself, How can it be that a man of fifty two years is unable to cook
a boiled egg, nor to mend a hole in his stocking, nor to brush up the
crumbs he leaves upon the floor? The only excuses for this gross
lacking in his knowledge could be laziness, for it takes no brute force to
do these things, and even a child is capable. But I spoke naught of these
things to Henry Stiles, and did not mind serving him, but took pleasure
in it.

"Henry Stiles had a weak constitution, and was soft in his muscles
and belly, and he had a stenchful breath, for his teeth were rotting
away, and his jaws were swollen, and when he ate he had difficulty to
chew. He often asked me for compresses. He never helped with any
work in the house, except one time when he agreed to hold up his two
hands for Elizabeth to wind a skein of wool into balls for knitting a new
blanket for him, and one other time he churned the butter five minutes
while Sarah went to bring more split logs for the fire to keep him warm.

"I prepared his tea and his breakfast each morning, his dinner each
noon and his supper each evening, I washed and mended his clothes
and his bed linens, prepared him compresses, and decoctions when he
felt unwell. I made him a new pillow for his head when I'd saved

enough down from the wild geese Surgeon Carver brought. I cleaned and swept the garret where he slept, and when the nights became cooler, I had ready for him two new knit blankets, and gave him a quilt from my own bed as well. I knit him three new pairs of stockings, for his were too full of holes for further mending. Every Saturday evening I polished his shoes with beeswax.

"On November third, a Saturday, and dry and sunny, I decided to spend a good part of the day cutting the remaining dried stalks from the herb garden, and laying mulch, for the week before there had been the first hard frost. Since it was lovely weather that day, I informed Henry Stiles in the morning when I served him his breakfast that I would not be preparing dinner at midday, but would be taking some bread and cheese and ham for a picnic out of doors and that he could do the same if he pleased.

"I did not ask him to help with any work out of doors, nor, since he was home and idle, to prepare dinner for those of us who had outdoor work to do. But when I told him that I would not be serving a noon meal, he looked displeased and did not answer, but only remarked that his right arm was numb.

"I told him that perhaps a long walk in the sunshine would help his arm, and then I took his empty cup to wash and brushed up the breadcrumbs he had left upon the floor and the board.

"Later, while I was in my garden I saw Henry Stiles leave the house. He was wearing his brown great coat, the heavy woolen one into which I had recently sewn new pockets. He had both his hands deep in those pockets, and the coat buttoned all the way, and the collar turned up to cover his jaws. At the time I thought he had spent too long indoors sitting motionless, or he would have been apprehended that the day was too warm for wearing such a coat in such a way. He seemed not to see me, and I watched him walk over the hill and disappear, and then, after a little while, he reappeared in the distance, entering the woods, probably heading for the ordinary tavern in town.

"That was the last time I saw him living. It was the first Saturday of the month, muster day, and militia practice was underway in White's field, on the other side of the woods. With his brown great coat covering him up, Henry was not very visible among the brown trunks and turning leaves of the woods, and, as everyone here knows, Tommy Allyn mistakenly shot Henry in the back, causing him soon to die. Twas generally agreed, at the time, that Tommy Allyn's musket was cocked and he accidentally hit it upon a tree which caused it to fire. Perhaps the boy had had a little too much cider to drink, as they are all apt to on muster days. Any way, Tommy Allyn was found guilty in this case three years ago. I never desired Henry Stiles' premature death, and I did not ever try to poison nor to curse his health in the slightest way.

"If there is anyone present who does not recall it, three years ago the Governor's nephew was sentenced by the court to pay twenty pounds, and he lost his right for bearing arms for the period of one year. His father, Matthew, brother to Governor Allyn, paid the fine for his son, and certainly the boy has long since repented his accidental wrongdoing. The case was closed three years ago, and I see no reason for bringing it up again now."

Governor Allyn said,

"You digress, Goodwife Gilbert! You are stepping out of your place in mentioning judgments that were made in the past! Furthermore, I take your insinuation, that the unexplained firing of a rifle was due to faulty behavior on the part of my nephew, as a personal insult!"

"And well you should!" Lydia moved closer to the Governor and nearly shouted.

"If you think to put the blame on me for this crime so as to clear the name of your nephew, you are not fit to be a judge!"

Governor Allyn's face reddened with anger.

James Stiles did not look at Lydia Gilbert behind him, but his lips tightened, and anyone taking notice could see that he had clenched both his hands into tight fists.

"Must I remind you, Lydia Gilbert, that The Code of Laws clearly states that defamation of a judge is a criminal offense?"

Lydia stepped back again, but did not take her eyes off Judge Allyn. For some moments she was silent.

A woman's voice, it sounded like Elizabeth Wescott's, called out,

"Hang her now!"

And then other voices from the audience joined in, some of them in agreement that Lydia Gilbert was a witch and should be put to death, and others, in discord, taking the position that James Stiles' testimony was invalid. Arguments broke out, and very soon there was no order in the courtroom at all, but an uproar of confusion.

"I repeat," Lydia tried, in vain, to make her voice heard above the others.

"I mourned the death of Henry Stiles, and offered my sincere condolences to his brother and the rest of his family!"

During the hubbub, James Stiles turned to face Lydia Gilbert, and after she had spoken these last words, which, apparently no one but he had heard, he went up close to her and slapped her face.

"You, Lydia Gilbert, shall pay for my brother's death! You are a worshipper of Satan and not fit to live amongst the citizens of Windsor!"

Judge Allyn repeatedly slammed his Bible upon the pulpit, but the racket in the courtroom had grown so intense that no one paid him any mind. After several more attempts at gaining order, the Judge finally turned to the guards and told them to take Lydia back to the jail for another interval in the proceedings.

No one seemed to notice as she was escorted away.

CHAPTER TWENTY-ONE

OUTSIDE THE SUN shone high and bright on the snow. Lydia's daughter Sarah came running from the courthouse behind the threesome, carrying a dinner basket.

The guards were walking fast, for they were in a rush to find seating at the Ordinary before it filled for the noon meal. When Sarah caught up with them, she curtsied slightly, and, with her eyes lowered, spoke to them.

"Good men, please let me leave this basket of food for my mother. She will need strength for further questioning."

For a moment the two men stared at the young woman, whom they recognized as Surgeon Carver's wife, and then the bearded one said,

"You may."

Sarah thanked him and handed the basket to him. She looked at her mother, shrunken and ugly, and then put her arms out and drew her body close in embrace. Lydia could not hug her daughter in return, for her hands were still bound behind her. She stood with her face buried in her daughter's shoulder, taking in her scent and enjoying her touch and her warmth.

"That's all. Get ye gone now!" the guard said.

Sarah held her mother's shoulders and her gaze. Her eyes were filled with tears.

"Thank you," Lydia said.

Sarah released her, and moved away, and the guards dragged Lydia onward to the jail.

The heavy door had been left open, and, seeing this, Lydia was glad, for the jail sorely needed airing out. The sight of the place, and the smell as she was drawn near it, filled her with a heavy feeling of doom and hopelessness.

At the entrance, her hands were unbound and she was thrust forcefully down the steps. The jailer set the basket of food at the top of the steps and slammed the door shut, and hurriedly locked it.

Still surprised at being pushed down the stairs, Lydia had fallen about half the way, bruising her knee and dislocating her shoulder. Her white shawl had become soiled with excrement, but at least her hands were free and she had a basket of food.

It had been weeks since she had eaten a noon meal, weeks since she had eaten anything at all but hard bread. As she climbed up the smelly stairs, she allowed herself to feel the hunger pains in her stomach, knowing that she could finally satisfy them.

She opened the linen cloth inside the basket and found a jack with something to drink, a fresh manchet loaf, some slices of ham, a wedge of cheese, two apples, a small pumpkin tart, and a little bunch of dried sage and thyme tied together with a thread. The perfumes of these things covered, for a little while, the terrible smell in the jail. She was so excited she forgot herself and her plight and knew not what to eat first.

She bit into one of the apples using her remaining molar teeth. It was a rennet, crisp and juicy. The juice dripped down the side of her face and all over her jaw, and it was not easy eating an apple with her back teeth, but she ate it all, chewing slowly, thoroughly, savoring its flavor, and feeling its goodness travel through her body and bring it strength. She even ate the core.

Now her stomach was gurgling, as if laughing, accepting the food with joy, but she knew she must not eat too quickly or all at once. She broke off a small piece of cheese from the wedge and placed it upon her tongue, and, feeling almost as if she were a queen, she sat near the sun-warmed wood of the door, and stretched her legs out before her. She closed her eyes, taking immense pleasure in the slowly melting cheese in her mouth.

She believed that all of the accusations against her had been spoken, and there was nothing left to the trial but her own defense, and, if there be such persons, those who would speak to defend her. She knew very well that Judge Allyn wished that the jury should find her guilty. Some time ago, Thomas had told her that the judge had power over the jurors and could keep them in deliberation until they delivered the verdict he desired.

A picture of Governor Allyn came into her mind.

His face was puffed and reddened with anger. He was saying, "Must I remind you that defamation of a judge is a criminal offense?"

Perhaps the physical ecstasy of having good food to eat had made her giddy, but, rather than feeling fearful of his judgment, the thought of Allyn made her laugh. How could it be that he was in the position of judging her? Lydia could only imagine what abuses of the law Will Allyn had committed in order to rise to the position of Governor of the Commonwealth and Judge. She herself had been a first hand witness to several instances of his attempted abuse of authoritative power.

She put another piece of cheese into her mouth, and remembered the time he had come to her house at night when Thomas was away.

It was around the middle of September, a year or so ago, and she had never spoken of it to anyone.

Reliance and Elizabeth had gone to stay with Sarah, in town for a fortnight, and she was home alone, except for William, the servant.

After supper she had cleared away the trenchers, and decided she would sew linen drawstring bags for herb storage by lantern light. She was wiping the trenchers with a rag when she heard the approach of a horse outside the door.

This frightened her somewhat because it could be bad news. The Colonists were fortunate because in that part of the land the native Indian people were their allies, and so they had no enemies to fear.

She stood by the table, still and listening, as the horse came to a stop and its rider dismounted. It was a man of some weight; although he did not speak she could tell by the sound of his body hitting earth, and he seemed not young, for he groaned slightly with the drop.

Then she heard him speak a few words to the horse. Was that the voice of her husband's associate, Magistrate Allyn? He had supped at their house several times and she thought she recognized his voice. It was distinctive: not low in pitch, but of a full timbre, and loud.

What would he be doing at her house so late in the evening? It could only be bad tidings of Thomas, and this was something she did not care to hear.

She wanted to take off her leather shoes and walk quietly up the stairs, to creep under the blankets of her bed and go to sleep peacefully, dreaming soft dreams after a good day's work. She wanted to walk away from whatever bad news Master Allyn carried with him on the other side of the door. She wanted that news to wait for tomorrow, or some other time, or never at all.

But she was not one to hide, nor one who avoided responsibility when it was due.

He tapped three times upon the door, and she opened it immediately, her heart beating so hard and fast she thought she might faint.

When she saw Master Allyn's face, she did not know what to think, for it was not a face containing ill news. It seemed he had been well fed and drunk, for when he entered the light of the house she saw that his cheeks and nose were red, and the night air was not yet cold.

"Good even to ye, Lydia," he spoke her name. It wasn't proper form, an unrelated man and woman being alone together.

The words came to her then,

"Good evening, Master Allyn. What news do you bring me at this hour?"

Her heart had quieted, but in her mind she became suspicious of something, for his comportment was strange.

"To pay ye a visit, lady," he spoke.

He took her hand in his own and brought it close to his lips, but she pulled it away. This made him laugh.

Suddenly, she was afraid of the man.

"Would you take a tankard of cider, or some other refreshment, Master Allyn?"

She said these words, hoping he would not, and all the while moving further from him, and toward the hearth.

"With thanks, yes," he said, moving along with her.

The embers of the fire still shone red, but there was little light in the room save for the lantern she carried in her hand, and she thought she would rather waste a few pieces of wood than to be together with Master Allyn in the darkened small room with no one else nearby at that moment.

"I will boil water for a tisane," she said.

She took up two logs from the pile and placed them on the embers in the hearth, and with the bellows, began forcing the flames.

As her back was turned to him, she was afraid of what he might do behind her.

When she felt him place his two hands on her hips, she stood and turned, and pushed him forcefully away.

"You'd best be on your way, Magistrate!" she shouted at him, hoping also that William, who was in the barn, might hear.

Before she knew what he was up to, the lewd man had grabbed both of her wrists, and now held them in one gross hand behind her back, just as if she were bound. He placed his other hand upon her breast, and roughly squeezed and pushed her bosom about, trying to loose it from the bodice, and hurting her. He pressed his body into hers, and, having the open hearth behind her, its flames licking noisily upward to consume the dry wood, she could not step backward.

His face came near hers, and she smelled the foul odor of his old and unwashed skin, pipe smoke, and decaying teeth. She moved her head first to one side and then to the other, and he took her jaw into his hand and held it so tightly that it hurt. Then he forced his lips upon hers and thrust his foul tongue into her mouth.

She gagged, ready to vomit.

William appeared then on the threshold of the kitchen door, still holding in his hand the pitchfork he had been using in the barn.

When Master Allyn saw William he let Lydia Gilbert free and drew both of his hands into the pockets of his jacket.

"Good evening, Goodwife Gilbert," he said.

He bowed slightly.

"I thank you for the refreshment and bid you farewell, and a safe return for your husband."

She spat at him.

"You are a sinful woman," he then said.

He turned his back and left her house.

These, his leaving words, were meant for William, the only witness, to hear.

But William had understood the Magistrate's foul intent, she was certain.

Just as her husband's manservant never spoke of where he went and what company he kept on Sunday, so he said never a word to her, nor to her husband when he returned, nor to her daughters, of Magistrate Allyn's unwanted visit. For though it was not she who had been at fault, to tell of this attempted rape would have brought shame upon her, and so, neither did she speak one word of this bad evening to anyone, not even to her friend Judith, and certainly not to her husband Thomas who had to keep business dealings with the man.

She had taken early to her bed, without completing the tasks she had planned, after rinsing her mouth with mint water a dozen times, and applying cold compress of chamomile to her bosom, and to her jaw, where he had hurt her.

Thinking on him now, as she had thought in the first days of her imprisonment, filled her once again with a feeling of angry injustice. She knew that, of the two of them, he was the more dangerous to the well being of the community, but, by the workings of dirty and, she thought, evil, hidden human forces, he had gained a certain power over her. He had the power to put her to death, and she believed he would probably use it. But he had not, nor would he ever have, overwhelming power over her living body.

She finished the cheese, took a long and refreshing drink of cider from the jack, and made a sandwich of the ham and manchet loaf.

A memory of the time he had informed her that her husband would be absent for many months came into her mind. She had been in the barn milking the cow at the time. Thomas had departed earlier in the week for Boston. They had quarreled just before he'd left, and he had not even bid her goodbye. She heard the rider approaching from the north. Her first thought was that it was Thomas returning from Boston.

The single horse was moving at a trot, which then slowed to a walk as it neared the house. Whomever it was he meant to stop, and was not one of the occasional travelers who passed by.

She moved the stool and pail and went out of the barn to see who it was. The manservant William had just come up from the river with fresh water and still carried the yoke on his shoulders.

They stood together and saw that the approaching rider looked to be Magistrate Allyn. He was wearing a long black riding cloak, and a black hat pulled down low on his forehead, and on his bright sorrel horse, lit up red in the low beams of the rising sun, and emerging from the fog, he made an impressive sight, but not a welcome one.

William set down the water buckets and the wooden yoke, and said not a word, but stood a bit closer to Lydia than was usual for him. She understood his meaning—whatever the reason for Magistrate Allyn's unexpected visit, William would not leave her alone with him.

The sunbeam faded away and the Magistrate on his horse now passed through a patch of thick fog. William and Lydia could see only a dark shadow, and the horse, with Allyn on it, in his hat and long cloak, seemed a strange beast.

When they were out of the fog, Allyn said,

"Morning, Missus Gilbert."

He touched his hat brim and then leant forward to dismount.

Lydia nodded to him in reply, but spoke not.

He alighted from his horse, onto the ground. On his boots he wore silver Spanish spurs.

He handed his horse, by the reins, to William, and William did not lead the horse away, but stood nearby and loosened the girth.

"What brings you, Magistrate?" said Lydia.

The smallness of her voice revealed her discomfort about his presence.

She could smell his horse, steaming in the fog, which had enveloped them, and the odor of it, strong and earthy, and the odor of the damp saddle leather, slightly mildewed and tonic, and the warm odor of the soggy woolen blanket seemed, like the fog, to be engulfing her.

She had wondered, was her husband dead? This bad news coming from the hated lips of Magistrate Allyn would have been a double offense, for she imagined he would receive some pleasure in telling her.

She could smell his cloak—the moist fine wool, tobacco smoke, rum soaked tavern floors—and his foul breath, and the dirty, old man smell of his person. Her eyes fell to his thick yellowed fingers spread upon his hat brim, then back to his face.

She gave him a questioning look.

He spoke,

"Good wife Gilbert, I must inform you that your husband has been called away suddenly on business to England. "

He paused and looked down at her.

She steeled her countenance at him, expressionless. With a slight nod of her head she urged him to continue.

Now he looked at her whilst he spoke.

"We were dining together last night when the news was brought to us from one of Cromwell's men. Regretfully there was not time for him

to return home before his departure, for his ship was leaving, and he
had only time enough to board."

"How long will he be away?" she asked. "Were it only yourself
and my husband at table?"

"There were two others present, Missus. There were Frothingham
and Bloodworth, too. I do not know how long he will be abroad,
perhaps as long as the better part of a year."

"And he sent no letter for me?" said she.

"He hadn't time, unfortunately, Missus. Certainly he will write
from England once he arrives there."

Magistrate Allyn put the hat back onto his head, and said,

"His horse is to be sent back here later today with the post rider. I
came ahead to inform you. Naturally I will be at your disposal during
this time."

"You may be on your way now, Magistrate. Good day," said
Lydia.

She turned and went back into the barn, leaving William standing
alone with the man and the man's horse.

She got her stool, and the partly filled pail, and took them into the
cow's stable, and sat down to finish milking. She listened as Allyn's
horse walked away toward town, and only when the sound of its hoof
steps were out of hearing, did she allow herself to shed a few tears, as
she milked with her cheek pressed hard against the cow's warm flank.

After some time she was aware of William being in the barn, and
although she had finished milking the cows and had put the stool away,
and had the pail full of milk in her hand, it seemed as if someone else
had done these things. William placed his hand upon her shoulder and
spoke some words but she did not hear them, for she could not stop
thinking of Thomas's brusque departure, and wondering why he had
not sent a letter, and when would she see him again?

Outside the barn the fog had settled in the yard. Lydia walked
through it toward the house, but was only part way when she felt to her
left the dark image of someone watching her. She thought of Allyn, but

only for a moment. For when she looked into the fog she saw the dark wild eyes of a half grown fawn staring back at her. Swiftly it turned and leapt away into the whiteness.

She swallowed the last of the ham sandwich and took another long draught from the jack of cider. The good food and drink in her belly made her feel relaxed and sleepy despite these unpleasant thoughts, and she leaned her head back against the dirty wall and closed her eyes a moment.

She remembered when she had received the first notice of her accusation for witchcraft, the one made by Goody Wescott a couple of months before she'd been jailed. The summons had called for her to appear at Allyn's house and answer to the accusation in private. At the time he was acting Judge in Windsor, although he had not yet been elected as Governor, because, with the absence of her husband, Allyn was the only magistrate.

More than answering to the accusation, she had dreaded having to go alone to his house. It was on a Tuesday, after noon. She had walked the short distance, from Surgeon Carver's house. Allyn's house was painted red clapboard. She went slowly up the three brick steps to the front door and knocked.

When his wife opened it, Lydia had breathed a sigh of relief.

"My husband is expecting you," she said.

She was a plump lady in her late fifties, or as old as sixty, with fine white hair falling out at the part. Her round face was not pretty, but neither was it unpleasant. Her blue eyes gave Lydia the impression that she was ignorant, or lazy.

Lydia followed her into the house, and to a closed door on the right. The lady opened the door and there was Allyn sitting at a writing desk. He looked up, but did not smile at his wife. Then he looked at Lydia.

"She's here," the wife said.

"Come in," Allyn said to Lydia.

"I'll be going out now," the wife said to her husband.

"To Mercy Gladwell's. I'll be back before sunset, husband."

She closed the door behind her, leaving Lydia alone with Allyn in his study.

"Come in and sit down," he said.

He did not stand, but gestured toward a high backed chair against the wall.

"I'd rather stand, thank you," Lydia said.

"I've come to answer to an accusation against me."

"Yes, I know."

He pushed his spectacles further up the bridge of his nose, against his eyes, and lifted a piece of paper that lay on his writing desk closer to him to read.

"Goodwife Elizabeth Wescott has accused you of witch craft, Lydia," he said.

She was appalled that he was using her first name, as if they were relations.

"Magistrate Allyn," she said.

"My neighbors the Wescotts have suffered much misfortune of late, but tis all of their own doing, and has naught to do with witch craft. That is a slothful family, indeed. If they would but be a bit more industrious they would have no reason to believe themselves cursed by an inexistent witch!"

"I fail to understand your words, Lydia," Allyn persisted.

He lay his index finger alongside his nose.

Lydia heard the front door close as his wife left the house.

"In short, Magistrate Allyn, I deny Elizabeth Wescott's accusation of witchcraft."

Lydia wanted to finish as quickly as possible and leave Allyn's house.

"Have you any affiliation with the devil, as Goodwife Wescott accuses?"

Magistrate Allyn dropped the piece of paper onto his desk and stood up, scraping the legs of his chair against the wood floorboards.

Standing, he was quite imposing, for he was tall, and largely built, and rather fat as well.

Lydia moved backwards toward the closed door.

"I deny the accusation. I have no affiliation with the devil."

"Lydia, do you know how serious an accusation of witchcraft is?"

Magistrate Allyn moved out from behind his writing desk and closer to Lydia. He came closer than she liked. She had her back against the door, and he came still closer.

He reached out his hand, the same one he'd had at his nose, to touch her chin.

She moved his hand away from her face with her own, but he persisted, and his strength was far greater than hers. He held her chin tightly in his hand, as an angry mother would her naughty child's.

"One accusation can easily enough be absolved, Lydia. But if there be more you would have to be tried before a jury. Do you know what the punishment for practicing witchcraft is?"

She did not answer him. Her fingernails were digging into his wrist, trying to get his hand off of her face.

"Do you know, Lydia?"

The stench of his foul breath made it hard for her to breath.

"It is death."

"But there is something you can do to make certain that no more accusations are brought upon you."

She wanted to spit into his face, but was frightened of what he might do in reaction. Her legs were close to his and she could have kicked him, but she stay still, frozen by good sense.

"Do you wish to know what that is?"

She did not need to hear what foul proposal he was intending to make to her, for she could read it in his little lecherous eyes and in the evil smell that emanated from his skin.

"No!" she said.

And then she could control herself no longer and she spat at him, and the spit hit against his reddened nose.

The shock of it made him step back, and she quickly opened the door and ran out of his house.

In truth, there was much that she could be accused of concerning wrong behavior. It was certainly true that she had broken the law countless times by playing at cards. And she had read banned books, and allowed her daughters to read freely of them, too. But these were minor infractions to the Code of Laws, and, compared to the wrong behavior of her judge, seemed negligible. And yet, Will Allyn would judge her.

She took the pumpkin tart from the basket and bit into its soft spicy filling. It had been sweetened with honey, and contained cinnamon and nutmeg. She ate small morsels of it, very slowly, savoring its flavor.

She remembered a letter she had gotten from her sister Rebecca, shortly before she'd been taken to jail. She had reported that two Connecticut women had been hung, their only crime being, "telling fortunes, which gave proof of having a covenant with familiar spirits associated with the devil", and, "knowing things past, present and to come which could not be known by strength of reason nor information from man nor divine revelation but must needs have come directly from Satan, shewing the women in question to be in communication with the devil."

At the time these words had stayed in Lydia's mind and worried her heart, for she often times had had the experience of seeing what was to come, and she did not think herself in compact with the devil.

She thought of the words written in the Old Testament warning that having familiar spirits and practicing the magic arts such as wizards do is what makes a witch, and these persons shall not be tolerated. She could not make sense of these words in relation to herself. She did not practice the magic arts, but sometimes made good use of her God-given gifts of prophecy and of healing when called upon, and that was quite different.

Certain men in power, like Governor Allyn, could choose to interpret the words of the Old Testament in the way most convenient to them, at times without regarding what the New Testament had to say on the same subject. For the true goal of these men, she thought, was not to protect the community, but to control that which they could not control; the peoples' very thoughts, beliefs and spirits.

If there was such a thing as the devil it was Magistrate Allyn imposing himself upon her body, and of such a devil she had much fear.

For of this she was sure: The devil is but the evil side of a man.

She took another drink of the cider, and, feeling more satisfied and comfortable than she had in weeks, she began to drift into sleep.

She saw Governor Allyn, reclining in an iron tub full of steaming water. Though all of his body save his head and neck, and also one hand which held a red blown glass goblet full of madiera upon which he sipped, were covered, he was naked.

It was not his first glass full of wine, as his nose and cheeks were nearly as red as the goblet and the wine it contained.

The room in which the tub sat was empty except for that object, and it was large, with a row of long red curtained windows along one wall, and the floor was scuffled wood. It was a house of ill repute, perhaps the one he frequented in Mystic.

Behind him stood an iron candelabra, which held eleven wax candles, all of them lit, making a great warm glow all around him.

And though she could not see his naked body submerged beneath the water, somehow, in her dream state she could see it. His large fat belly, and his teats, almost like those of a woman, folded down against it. His little shrunken cock and balls were nearly lost under the weight of that enormous protuberance. His thighs were thick and short and pink, and no matter how much soap he might use to wash himself, the foul rotting odor of his flesh would never depart from him. His back, too, was covered in a layer of soft and tender fat that melted down into two large hip folds to his pimpled buttocks.

The oddest thing of all was the tail that curled out like a great scaly reptilian thing from the base of his spine. It lay heavy and turgid at the bottom of the iron tub, its end, pointed like the head of a viper moved up and down of its own accord, causing rings to form on the surface of the water.

The Governor sipped his wine and smiled pleasurably.

The vision made her skin prick into shivering bumps, and she woke up with a start.

The guard had opened the door, flooding the stairwell with bright sunlight.

She was dragged to her feet by the two large men, and taken back to the courthouse.

CHAPTER TWENTY-TWO

SARAH HAD INFORMED Reliance in the afternoon of the day it happened that Lydia had been taken away to await her trial in the jail below the meetinghouse. Sarah did not know when her mother's trial would be nor how long she would have to spend in jail.

The next morning, as soon as she had finished with her chores, Reliance had ridden her father's horse into town. She wished to see her mother, and to know when her trial would be, but when she went to where the jail was, there was no one about, and the iron door was locked tight. She did not know where to find the jail guards, for she did not even know who they were. She would have liked to go to Governor Allyn's house, but that would do no good anyway because she knew he was in Boston, along with Magistrate White. And even if Allyn's wife had been at home, she would have been of no help, for she was an ignorant person with no power of jurisdiction.

Since Reverend Stiles used the meeting house on Sundays, Reliance thought there was a chance he might also have a key to the jail below, and so she went to the Stiles' house.

She tied the horse outside, and the Indian girl let her in.

Missus Stiles was at home, and she rushed to embrace Reliance, overcome with sentiment. She and Lydia had shared a close friendship for many years, and they were like sisters to one another.

"Sarah told me that your mother has been taken to jail, and that she is awaiting trial for witchcraft!" Missus Stiles said.

She was holding both of Reliance's hands, and looking at her with eyes that had recently shed tears.

"Yes, they took her yesterday," Reliance said.

"From my brother in law's house. I wanted to see her. I wish to bring her food, and her cloak, and perhaps a quilt, and a cushion for her head. I went to the jail, but I know not how to reach her, nor where I must go to ask to be let in. Governor Allyn is abroad, and also Magistrate White. I thought perhaps the Reverend might have the key?"

The Reverend's wife continued holding Reliance's gloved hands. Hers were small and warm. She was a kind and comely lady, somewhat smaller than Lydia.

"No, unfortunately the Reverend has not the keys to the jail," she said.

"I wish he had! I, too, thought he might, and so I inquired of him last night, for I would like to go to your mother and keep her company, and comfort her if she needs it. And I have a letter for her, too."

She let go of the girl's hands, and turned to get the letter, but then she turned back again and she said,

"Take off your cloak, Reliance. Sit by the fire and warm yourself."

Reliance did as she was told, leaving her cloak on the floor before the hearth where soon a little black and white spotted dog appeared, curled itself up into a ball, and lay upon it.

Missus Stiles came back with a letter in her hand. Even before she said so, Reliance knew by the seal that it was from her father.

"It's from your father," she said.

"I went to the post yesterday afternoon, and Goodman Warren gave it to me, thinking I might find a way for Lydia to have it. If only it had been a day earlier! I know that your mother had been waiting for some word or news from him for many months."

"And now she is locked up in there," said Reliance.

"Could the jailers be trusted to give it to her? If I can find them?"

"I know not," said Missus Stiles.

"Those two men are lawless ne'er do wells from that settlement on the other side of the river, and they are the crudest and the stupidest ones of them all. I would not trust them, personally."

"Then she'll have it after the trial," Reliance said.

She hoped that would be soon, and that the outcome would be good.

"You keep it for her, Reliance. It will be a glad surprise for her when she returns home again."

The girl took the letter. It was enclosed in an envelope of heavy rag paper folded into a square, and sealed with her father's signature green wax, and his initials, TG.

"I'll have Ponka bring you hot tea. Or would you prefer a nog?"

"Tea, if you please."

She called for the Mohegan girl, who was a year or two younger than Reliance. The Stiles kept her as an unpaid servant. Not like William, who had chosen to remain with the Gilberts. Ponka was a slave.

Many days passed and the magistrates did not return from Boston, and so Lydia continued to await her trial in the underground jail. Reliance knew that Governor Allyn would eventually have to return to Windsor, and that when he did her mother would be tried, but she did not know when this would be, for she had had no news of him through translations for several weeks.

She kept her father's letter on a shelf of the Welsh cabinet, weighted down with her mother's silver serving spoon. Every time she went to the cabinet for a trencher or a spoon, or for a pot to cook in, or for a pinch of spice, she saw the letter there, with her mother's name written upon it in black ink in her father's elegant hand, and she badly wished to know what was written inside of it.

So many days passed that, one day after the noon meal, when she looked upon her father's letter, she suddenly thought that it somehow might contain news useful for her mother's release from jail, and so she justified it to herself when she peeled off the wax seal intact and opened the envelope.

It gave her pleasure to see his familiar script, and to know that he had touched the paper she now held in her hands.

23 July, 1654

My Dear Lydia,

Several months have passed since my arrival in London, and still I
have had no letter from you. Is it possible that the hurried letter I wrote
to you from Boston when I learned of my imminent departure was lost
or forgotten by Magistrate Allyn, to whom I entrusted it? I believe it
must be so, for I have no other way to explain to myself the reason for
your silence, unless it be your pride. I was nervous in the days before
my departure, and so unfairly brusque with you. For my ungentle
comportment I beg you to forgive me.

There is nothing as true as the assurance I give you of my loving
memory of you. You are my preservation: I think of you incessantly to
console myself and to guide me while I am here alone.

Although my departure was abrupt, you must understand how
much I love you. I cannot imagine that someone could love you more
than I do, Lydia.

I have been well, except for my recurring problem of passing
stones in my water, for which I have been seeing a physician in
London. I am suffering a bout of low fever now, and in this state am
prevented from writing you a long letter.

I hope this one finds you, and finds you well and content, and
whether you write to me or don't write to me at all, I hope that you
believe, as I do, that you and I remain as one.

In Body and Soule,

Thomas"

Reliance noticed the date, and that it had taken over three months
for his letter to arrive in Windsor, which was longer than usual, but not
excessive.

His written words to her mother humbled the girl. She carefully
folded the heavy paper back into its envelopment, and stuck the seal
back on with a finger spot of paste made of flour, water and honey, and
she replaced the letter upon the Welsh cabinet.

She knew she should not have read it, and she would pretend she
had not, even to herself. She would try to forget those words meant for

her mother, which would surely have brought her great comfort had she been able to read them.

Reliance wondered why her father's absence was going on so long, for she knew that his meeting with Cromwell had been in May, and then there had been other issues having to do with the Navigation Acts, and discussions with Holland, but it was November now, and she thought it was time he should have returned. She hoped he was well, and had recovered from his stones. She thought perhaps she would write to him. But she hoped he would return too soon for that.

Reliance had foreseen, through reading private exchanges between Governor Hopkins and Magistrate Allyn, that all of these changes were taking place, but, having sworn to work anonymously and in secrecy, she had said nothing to anyone. A person more influenced by sentiment than she was might have broken secrecy and given warning to those unknowingly involved. She could have said something to her mother. She could have said something to her father, or written to him of these things while he was abroad. But she believed it was not her place to change history, only to record it. When she translated or rewrote the letters and other writings of important men it was as if they and those they wrote of were not real living persons that she knew, but were only people who existed in ink on paper, and she, too, when she worked for them. For, in her work she did not even have a name nor a face, but was invisible.

She knew of many secrets and goings on, but revealed nothing to anyone, and she was unknown except as a bookish unpractical girl.

One of the days before her trial, when her mother was in jail, and her father had still not returned, and after she had read her father's letter, William came to Reliance with the news that her old tutor, Master Phillips, had been offered a position in New Haven, at the college that Reverend Davenport, and Master Milford were founding, to teach languages. Governor Hopkins had been so pleased with Master Phillips' work that he was giving money to the college for his salary as a professor of Greek and Latin. Rather than being honored by this offer of a professorship, Master Phillips was worried he could not live up either to Reverend Davenport's nor the ex—Governor's expectations. He told William to ask Reliance if she would take the position in his place.

"In his place or in his name?" Reliance asked William.

She had just finished milking one of the cows, and got up to move the stool and pail to the other one. She thought that if a college did not allow young ladies to study there it could not have a lady professor teaching the young men.

William was holding a pitchfork, and did not answer. He only looked at her. Since he did not speak, Reliance turned her back to him and set down the half filled pail and the stool, and sat upon it to milk the other cow.

"Have you given thought to stop doing this literary work?" he said from behind her.

"What? Why would I? Do you wish me to stop, William?"

She turned around and looked at him as she said these words.

"I have not dominion over you, and so can wish nothing from you," he said.

Having been Thomas Gilbert's servant for so long, William never expressed his opinions directly, but his veiling of them was so thin he may as well have done so.

Reliance ignored his words.

She asked him,

"When you said that Master Phillips would give me the professorship offered to him, what was your meaning? Or rather, what was his meaning? Would I be expected to hide myself beneath his gowns and speak for him whilst he mimes?"

"I know not, Reliance. I think you could stand as yourself at New Haven."

"Disguised as a man?"

"Not as a man. As you are. I think," said he.

"Verily, your hiding and secrecy about this work you do, if I were to have an opinion on it, might be damaging, and not worth pursuing any longer. Go to New Haven, or else give it up entirely, is what I would say were I to advise you."

"When you next see Master Phillips, tell him I will speak to him on it then."

"As you see fit," he said.

Then he turned and began pitching out hay for the animals.

Reliance hurried to finish the milking for she had promised Sarah she would make an Indian pudding for that day.

CHAPTER TWENTY-THREE

LYDIA WAS LED, walking between the two jailers, the short distance back to the courthouse, and, although she had been abruptly awakened, because of the food she had eaten she felt renewed, and more vigorous than she had in weeks. She would, however, have liked to use a chamber pot before going back on trial.

At the steps to the court house a group of men lingered and joked, and as she and the guards drew near they did not stop, but, staring at her rudely, called out,

"You'll soon be back in hell where you came from!"

"I can see ye strung up already! The noose rope's already been put up, waiting for ye!"

"Hehehe! A hanging! Now that's a worthwhile spectacle!"

"Stinking heathen!"

These men had surely had too much too drink at the Ordinary, and one of them moved so close to Lydia that she was nearly dragged into him by the guards. At the last instant he spit at her and moved out of the way.

All of them guffawed and laughed horribly as she was taken up the steps and into the courthouse.

Inside there was such a loud ruckus that it seemed as if market day had moved indoors, for everyone—men, women, and children—were gathered about in clumps and groups, talking, laughing and gesticulating with much animation. As Lydia approached the front of the courthouse, she saw that even the men of the jury were merry, slapping one another on the back and blithely discussing whatever light matters they had carried over from their noon dinner. The atmosphere was one of excitement for something wonderful that was soon to happen. And Lydia knew that the wonderful thing everyone was anticipating was her death by hanging.

Despite her disgust at her fellow citizens' behavior, she held her head high and, when the guards left her at the front, she sat down upon her wooden stool and looked about at the happy faces of the people around her, and, although she was alone and had no one to talk to, she smiled.

Much time passed, and Judge Allyn continued talking and laughing with several men, including Surgeon Carver, at the back of the courthouse. No one paid any attention to Lydia, and she began to feel as if she had walked into someone else's trial. The drummer beat three o'clock, and still Judge Allyn made no move to call order to the court.

Lydia watched various men and women leave the courthouse, and then, fifteen or twenty minutes, or half an hour, later, return again, and commence new conversations with other friends and acquaintances they found inside. She needed very badly to use a chamber pot.

At least another half of an hour passed, and finally Judge Allyn made his way to the front of the courthouse, stepped up to the pulpit, and, after spending some time joking quietly with the men of the jury behind him, lifted the heavy Bible and brought it down on the oaken surface with an unconvincing thud.

No one seemed to pay him any mind.

Lydia grew unquiet. Now was the time to give hearing to anyone who might speak in her defense, and this, she believed, might be the only way to sway some of the men of the jury to vote her innocent.

Hoping to have some effect upon the townspeople, if not Judge Allyn, Lydia stood up suddenly and shouted, as loudly as she could,

"Silence!"

Many people turned and looked at her, their mouths agape, and, indeed, they became temporarily silent.

She looked over at Judge Allyn. He was lazily turning his face from the jurymen to her, and it wore an ungenuine smile. He looked at her for some moments without changing his expression. And then he turned to the townspeople and said,

"Let us please have order in the court!"

He slammed the Bible onto the pulpit with more force, and most of the people began returning to their seats. Still, another ten minutes passed before the noise in the courtroom had died down enough for Governor Allyn to be heard when he finally said,

"We will now hear from the defense, if there shall be anyone present who wishes to speak."

He looked around, his finger playing at the edge of his nostril.

"Governor Allyn—" a woman's voice from the back of the meetinghouse spoke.

Wrastle's wife, Humility, visibly with child, stood and came forward.

There was much mumbling and low gossip amongst the townspeople as she passed.

"I would like to give my good word in defense of Lydia Gilbert," she said.

"You must take your oath," the Governor said.

He stepped forward and held the Bible out to her, and, in her soft and gentle voice, Humility took oath.

Speaking in her defense was too great a risk, Lydia thought, but she made no sign of thinking so. She continued standing, smiling slightly, hoping she would not piss herself.

"For more than a year I had the good fortune to receive regular visits from Goodwife Gilbert in her capacity as a healer, for I had suffered from barrenness since the start of my marriage, for eight years. With her advice and the help of her herbal cures I was finally able to conceive a child, now six months in my womb. Goodwife Gilbert has done my good husband and myself a great service, and I now speak in her defense, for she would accept no other payment.

Lydia sensed that Humility knew she had been with Wrastle. She was certain of it. She again looked out into the audience for him, and saw him now, standing alone in the aisle near the women's side.

Wrastle was not looking at Lydia, and, although she was staring at him, he did not shift his gaze to her, but continued looking earnestly at his wife, who, in turn, kept her eyes locked into his.

By giving testimony in defense of an accused witch, Humility risked being accused herself of witchcraft, and Lydia knew that what she was doing now was a great act of courage on her part. Thinking on how she had caused Wrastle to be unfaithful to Humility at the same time that she was healing her, made Lydia feel so ashamed that she stopped looking at either of them, and sank back down onto her stool, her head lowered.

Humility continued,

"I would like to say that I have always observed Lydia Gilbert, in her dealings with us as well as with others, to be a lady for peace, and to counsel for peace. She never, to my observation, used threatening words with anyone, nor did I look on her as one given to malice. Her business dealings with my husband have always been good."

All during her testimony Goodwife Fuller had not looked at Lydia, nor at anyone but her husband Wrastle, who seemed to be willing her strength to speak from where he stood.

Now she quickly returned to her place in the audience, and Lydia could not help but watch as Wrastle took one of her gloved hands in both of his own and helped her to be seated.

CHAPTER TWENTY-FOUR

WHILE HUMILITY FULLER had been speaking, in part perhaps because of her soft voice, a general undertone of conversation had gone on amongst the townspeople.

From where she sat, Lydia could not help but hear several women, including Goodwife Gladwell and her spinster sister, in the first row discussing the best ingredients for a mince pie. From the men's side she overheard bits and pieces of lewd jokes, and then the loud guffaws of Goodman Woodmason and Goodman Elderidge.

Judge Allyn, too, was talking privately with one of the jurymen. His head was turned to one side and he did not notice when Mercy Stiles, the Reverend's daughter, quietly stepped forward. She was sixteen years of age, and Lydia thought she should not defend her, for it was probably useless. But she knew that the girl was acting according to her principles, and for that, in a small way, Lydia felt glad.

Mercy waited some moments in front of Governor Allyn at the pulpit.

Certainly he was aware of her presence there, but he rudely continued his conversation with the juryman.

Lydia heard some of what he was saying.

"She's a saucy trull, but with her coats up over her head one takes no notice…"

The juryman chuckled, and added some lewd words of his own.

Mercy's face had turned blushing red, but she continued standing patiently before the judge.

Finally, Allyn shifted his attention to the girl, and, with an unpleasant grin upon his face, said nothing to her, but gazed at her for a long time, taking her in from toes to bonnet.

She spoke with a wavering timid voice,

"I would like to testify in defense of Missus Gilbert."

The judge stared at her, and his expression slowly changed from lewdness to mock outrage.

"In defense of whom?" he said.

Mercy gestured nervously toward Lydia.

"She who stands to be accused," she stammered.

"Do you mean Goodwife Gilbert?"

"Yes."

It seemed that hardly any of the people in the audience, nor even of the jury, had witnessed this exchange of few, but significant, words. A lady could only be addressed as "Missus" if she were married to a man of great importance.

Judge Allyn then said,

"What is your age in years?"

"Sixteen."

"I would have thought younger," he said, eyeing her breasts.

"But, being of consenting age, you may take your oath."

He held the Bible toward her without himself moving, so that Mercy was forced to move closer to him.

She placed her right hand on the Bible and took oath, and then, although it seemed that no one was listening to her or even noticing that she was standing there before them, she spoke in a clear but shaky voice, saying,

"Missus, er, Goodwife Gilbert is a proper woman who has oft times spoken to me openly when my own mother was unwilling, of subjects a girl is wont to speak of with a woman. I never heard an unkind word against her until now, and I testify she has no acquaintance with the devil."

The girl's face was red with embarrassment, and she stood before the inattentive audience and then looked around nervously at the Judge, who had resumed his conversation with the juryman.

She curtseyed slightly and, even before she had returned to her seat, another young woman, Martha Bellringer, had quickly made her way to the front.

She stopped in front of Judge Allyn, and, interrupting his private conversation, asked him if she might take her oath and testify in Goodwife Gilbert's defense.

With some irritation, the judge held the Bible out for the skinny young lady, and gave her his half-hearted attention for the few seconds it took her to take oath. Then he recommenced his conversation with the jurymen.

Martha Bellringer's voice suited her, for although her body was as thin and dry-looking as a piece of iron, her voice was clear and sonorous.

She spoke, saying,

"I have known Goodwife Gilbert for over five years. When I first came with my parents to this new land I suffered many allergies, some of them so bad in summer that I could not go out of doors, and, at times I nearly suffocated for lack of breath. My parents took me to two different doctors—one of them in Hartford, and the other one was Surgeon Carver here in Windsor. And, when these good doctors could do nothing to help me, my parents had me consult with the pharmacist. Twas all to no avail, for my allergies not only persisted, they became progressively worse each year.

"It happened one Sunday after meeting that I was speaking with Elizabeth Gilbert, who is Goodwife Gilbert's daughter, and of my same age. She told me that her mother was very handy with herbal cures and might do something to help rid me of my problem.

"My parents conferred with me that I should seek Goodwife Gilbert's help, since nothing had worked so far. When I went to her house outside Windsor, accompanied by my mother, Goodwife Gilbert welcomed us warmly, asked me many questions concerning my health and habits, and then she went about preparing a cure for me in a very competent way, using only herbs she herself had grown or gathered from the fields. I followed her instructions just as she told me to, taking a variety of teas and tisanes, and using a special pomade on my skin which contained honey. Within a week I noticed a great improvement in the clearness of my head and nose, and, within a month my allergies were gone entirely.

"I testify that Goodwife Gilbert has nothing evil about her, but, in fact, is a person for good, and a valuable healer in the community of Windsor. I defend Goodwife Gilbert in her innocence."

Very few people had paid any attention to Martha, which, Lydia thought, was a pity, for her speech had been beautifully made.

As the young woman passed her to return to her seat, Lydia caught her eye and said,

"Thank you, Martha."

"I thank you, Goody. And I wish you well," Martha said.

There was a pause of some minutes in which no one stood to defend her, and Lydia thought there would be no more.

Then, from amongst the general restlessness and movement of bodies in the audience, a burly-set man was approaching the Judge's podium. It was Benjamin Sudbury. He was a kind-hearted man, and had fathered eight strapping sons on his good wife Esther. Theirs was a simple, honest, hardworking family. They lived on the east side of Windsor.

"Judge Allyn, I would like to speak in defense of Goodwife Gilbert."

He pronounced these words in a confident voice, a round, warm voice that made Lydia recall all the times he had ridden to her holdings on his plough horse to call her out to their farm for help in delivering the babies.

Judge Allyn held the Bible out to him casually, not even bothering to look at him as he took his oath, but continuing his private conversation with the juryman.

Benjamin Sudbury spoke. His voice was powerful, and pleasant to hear, but very few people were listening.

Lydia sat with her legs crossed tightly.

"I testify that my good wife Esther and I have known Goodwife Gilbert for many years—since the birth of our first son, who is now nineteen years of age. This humble lady, notwithstanding that she was the wife of a magistrate, aided my wife in the safe deliverance of all eight of our sons. Each of our sons was born without undue difficulty, and all have lived healthily and well, God willing, up to the current moment. I testify on behalf of Goodwife Gilbert, for no words against this lady could convince me—"

Benjamin turned and spoke these words to the jury. Lydia could not see if any of them were paying attention to him.

"No words could convince me that Goodwife Gilbert has any relationship with Satan, the devil, or any other word for evil. She is a good and honest lady, and there is nothing about her that might suggest a smudge on her spirit. I testify that Goodwife Lydia Gilbert is innocent of all the charges made against her."

At these words, Judge Allyn turned toward Benjamin Sudbury and said,

"I remind you, Goodman—?"

"Sudbury," he said.

"I remind you that it is not in your power to clear the accused of charges made against her."

"I meant that, in my mind, she is cleared."

"What authority does your mind carry? Are you aware of what you speak? This is a court of law, and the official procedures shall be followed. Have you anything else to say?"

"I say that Goodwife Lydia Gilbert has no affiliation with Satan."

"You may be seated."

Before returning to the audience, Goodman Sudbury stepped toward Lydia, and facing her full on, said,

"God knows you do not deserve this."

His eyes were full of kindness and love, and his words and presence gave Lydia a new feeling of strength.

Benjamin Sudbury disappeared, and, out of the crowd hobbled a tiny old lady dressed all in black.

It was Priscilla Quincy. Lydia had thought that she had returned to live in Boston after the death of her husband. If so, she was astounded that this lady would have come so far to defend her, for she had upwards of 80 years.

She was so small that it seemed Judge Allyn did not see her. She stood before him for quite some time while he looked around lazily at the state of disorder in the courtroom, picking at his nostrils.

She was wearing a black bonnet, and carried a walking stick with a brass tip, and she took this stick and used it to rap lightly upon the Bible, which lay closed on the podium in front of the judge.

"Judge!" she called up to him.

Judge Allyn leaned forward and peered over the edge of the podium, his face contorted into an expression of irritation.

"I would like to speak for the defense!"

"Come around here, then, old woman, where I can see you."

She came around to the side of the podium and Judge Allyn, holding the Bible by one corner, bent over to the side and said,

"You may take your oath."

"Yes, I shall," she said. "Please, could you tell me what words I must say?"

"Nothing," said he. "Just give your oath."

"Do you not have to ask me for it, Judge Allyn?"

He rolled his eyes and said,

"Do you give oath to the truth of the following testimony in the name of our lord God?"

Widow Quincy placed her miniature and very wrinkled right hand upon the cover of the Bible and said,

"In the name of our lord God I give my oath to the truth of the following testimony."

She then slowly turned around toward Lydia, and smiled at her warmly.

She was already hunched, and now she hunched further forward and, since no one was listening, she spoke familiarly to Lydia in a quiet voice,

"My late husband was so fond of you!"

"He was one of the dearest friends I have ever had," Lydia said.

"Why are they putting you through this?" Priscilla asked her.

"It is unreasonable and unjust!"

"I know not," Lydia said.

Lydia stood up and moved closer to Widow Quincy.

"I have urgently to pass water!"

"Oh, dear," Priscilla said.

She then moved over close to Judge Allyn who had turned around again toward the jurymen, and, using her cane to get his attention, she said,

"Judge! Governor! This lady needs to use the privy house!"

"What's that?"

"She needs to use the privy! "

"Good God, old woman, is that your testimony?"

"Of course not!"

"Well, get on with your testimony, and then we'll see about the "privy house"."

Priscilla turned to face the audience, which hardly seemed to be an audience, but had deteriorated into what appeared to be a disorganized marketplace selling nothing.

"I speak in defense of Lydia Gilbert, for she is not a witch, but a talented healer. My late husband, the veterinarian Joseph Quincy, held Lydia Gilbert in highest esteem and often times followed her advice in his treatment of your animals. As many of you remember, my husband was frequently accompanied by Lydia on his calls, for she was a great help and inspiration to him.

"She was a frequent visitor in our home, and I always found her company to be delightful and interesting. Lydia Gilbert is a person with great powers; intellectual and of love. These powers are natural and God given, and have naught, I repeat, NAUGHT, to do with the Devil. Therefore, I hereby testify that Lydia Gilbert has no association with the devil, and is not a practitioner of witchcraft."

Widow Quincy turned toward Lydia, who had remained standing, and looking up at her, said,

"This is ridiculous! No one is listening to the defense!"

She then turned to Judge Allyn and, lifting her cane in the air, said,

"I have spoken! Now give this good lady an intermission for heaven's sake!"

The Governor summoned the guards, and ordered them to take Lydia outside to "piss in the snow".

The courtroom was in such a state of mayhem that no one even noticed that the prisoner was being escorted out, except for the group of teenage boys loitering around outside the door.

The guards told Lydia to piss at the bottom of the steps. Being in such a state of urgent need, she did not protest, but squatted down like a madwoman, unable to move her skirt and petticoats out of the way, for her hands were still bound. The boys watched, jeering and taunting her, some of them bending down, vainly trying to view her private parts underneath her skirts.

Just as no one had noticed when she had been taken out, likewise no one even batted an eyelid in her direction when the guards escorted her back up to the front of the courtroom.

Feeling greatly relieved, Lydia remained standing in front of her chair.

Judge Allyn was turned all the way around, talking with the jury. His back faced the courtroom.

Lydia waited quite some time for the Judge to do something to bring order back to the courtroom.

The Searcher, who had been sitting with the jury, suddenly and inexplicably moved to stand behind her.

Lydia turned around and said to the Searcher,

"There may be others who wish to speak in my defense."

The Searcher regarded Lydia suspiciously, and acted as if she had not heard the words she'd spoken, but only an animal-like noise issuing from her lips. She made neither reply nor comment, but stepped slightly back, and turned her eyes away.

A few more minutes passed with no change in the general situation, and then, Governor Allyn finally stood up and slammed the Bible down with tremendous force, calling out,

"Order! Order! Order in the court!"

CHAPTER TWENTY-FIVE

GRADUALLY, EVERYONE RETURNED to their seats, or their standing positions in the aisle and against the walls, and, with further calls for order, the last remaining mumbles trailed off into a suspenseful silence. Now, perhaps a search would be ordered, or at least the jury would be asked to make their decision, and surely, Goody Gilbert would be found guilty.

When the judge had the audience's full attention, he stood up and began speaking.

"As is written in the Connecticut Code of Laws, in all cases that are tried by juries, if four of the six agree the verdict shall be deemed to all intents and purposes sufficient—"

As he spoke, Lydia, who was also standing, saw her husband's manservant William come back into the courthouse. Several other people noticed his entrance as well, and turned their attention toward him. He was making his way toward the front of the courthouse, pushing through the people who were standing in the central aisle.

The Governor continued speaking, seemingly unaware of William's approach.

"Upon which judgment may be entered and execution granted, as if they had all concurred."

William stood before the judge's platform, hat in hand, and cleared his throat loudly.

Judge Allyn stopped speaking and looked at the large bald man before him.

"I would like to speak in defense of Lydia Gilbert," William said.

Judge Allyn studied the manservant's rugged old face.

"We have already heard the defense."

He laid his yellowed index finger alongside his nose, and, turning his head slightly to one side, said,

"But if you've something to add, I suppose it is just that you, too, may take oath and give testimony."

Lydia was afraid of what William might say. Already, Goody Wescott had accused him of being Satan. In truth, he had been a witness to Allyn's first attempt at forcing himself upon her body. But she was afraid that, no matter what he said it would do nothing more than to create trouble for him.

All eyes in the audience and the jury were upon William, as he placed his hand, which covered the entire front of the Bible, upon the book and took oath. He was a man of few words, but the words he used were carefully chosen and blunt.

Seeing him again up close after so many weeks, Lydia remembered the time, shortly before she'd gone to live at Surgeon Carver's house in town, when William had stood to take away the trenchers, after taking dinner together with her at noon.

And she had stood, too, and turned around and put her arms about his shoulders. She had sensed at that time that he was mightily discomposed.

His arms had hung limp at his sides. No words came to his tongue, and then he had placed his hands upon her back.

She did not let go her grasp on him, and he did not push her away.

Then she had lifted her face to his. For some moments she looked into his eyes, and she had seen that he was terrified—of her—because of what he feared she desired from him.

Finally she had spoken, saying,

"William, do not think wrongly of my action. I am not holding you in my arms for any other reason than that you are, above all, the one person I can trust. I am certain you will do your best while I am away to look after Reliance, who shall need looking after, until my husband returns. This is your home as much as it is mine. The time and sweat you have put in here has made it what it is."

"You can depend upon me," he had said.

She'd held him ever tighter, and gingerly he had returned her embrace.

Then he had taken his leave of her, and went outside to begin baling the hay.

That had been the only time, in the twenty-two years she had known William, that they had ever had any physical contact, or come close to being emotive with each other.

He began his testimony. His voice was deep and clear.

"I have worked for the Gilberts, on their holdings here, for twenty-two years."

"In what capacity?" Judge Allyn asked.

"Tenured servant to Thomas Gilbert. I chose to stay on with them afterward."

"My question is different," Judge Allyn said.

"Could you tell the court and the jury what work you did for the Gilberts?"

"Do," William said.

"What work you do, then. Tell us." said the Judge.

"A variety."

"He's the black man!" screamed Elizabeth Wescott from the left side of the audience.

"Josiah saw him in Wethersfield!"

Governor Allyn glared at Goody Wescott, who had stood up to make this accusation.

"There will be silence in the court!" he said.

"Let us hear the servant's defense."

He turned his attention back to William, who was looking at him with a nettled expression of disgust.

"Specifically what are your duties?"

"Whatever needs doing," William said. "Tilling, sowing, reaping, feeding the beasts, currying or butchering them, building fences—"

"Or that monument to hell!" screamed Elizabeth Wescott.

"Goodwife Wescott," Judge Allyn said.

"If you do not keep silent, I shall ask you to leave."

She sat down, muttering to herself.

"Is it true that you built a monument of stones to the devil, as Goodwife Wescott stated previously?"

"Am I being accused?" William said.

Judge Allyn sucked at his wooden teeth.

"You will provide an answer to the question put forth."

"I am here to testify in defense of Lydia Gilbert."

"Did you construct a monument of stones in the field previously owned by Goodman Woodmason?"

"The field was full of stones. I piled them up so I could till it."

"I myself have seen the construction in Woodmason's field, and it could not be considered a pile of stones," Judge Allyn said.

"Twas a folly," William said. "No more."

"Are you telling the court and the jury that you spend your days in folly?"

"I am telling you nothing. It's you who're asking,"

"Your impertinence will help neither Goodwife Gilbert nor yourself," said the Judge.

"Could you explain the purpose of the stone construction in Woodmason's field?"

"Tis a fort for hunting song birds, and there is a well below it."

This answer stunned Judge Allyn and left him temporarily speechless.

No doubt Allyn, and many of the older people present could remember such constructions from the old country, where men had to kill song birds for meat, for large game was not so plentiful and easily caught as it was here in this new land.

In truth, the stone construction in question had never been used for hunting birds.

Thomas Gilbert had purchased the parcel of land from Woodmason as a place to sow rye. When William turned the soil, it was full of stones. He dug the whole field in one afternoon, and made a pile of the stones in a corner of the field. This soon increased to a hillock, and by sunset, it was a small mountain.

With so many stones William thought he could make a wall to separate the Gilbert property from the Wescott's, but winter was coming on, so the stones remained there for many weeks, until shortly before Yule.

One Thursday Lydia asked William to go for hemp rope in Wethersfield, insisting that she could not wait until Monday, when he normally made the trip.

In Wethersfield, while waiting inside the doorway of the rope maker's shop, William unexpectedly saw his friend, Deggory Phillips, entering White's Ordinary with Magistrate Allyn. Because Phillips received some of the transcription work to be passed on to Reliance from Magistrate Allyn, William would have thought their being together was for a business transaction, but he could see, even from across the road, that his friend was flirting with Allyn. Seeing this made William wild with anger, but he had maintained composure until the transaction was finished, and he left the shop.

Then he wanted to rush inside the Ordinary and smite a great blow unto both of their faces, and break earthenware jugs upon their heads until they were bloody and squealing in pain. His heart thundered like a militia full of drums, and even remembering it now, a year later in front of the court, he was filled with rage and jealousy.

Certainly Phillips had wooed that pig, the Magistrate, with his false translations. It was said that Magistrate Allyn would bugger man, woman, boy, girl, and certain beasts. William had thought Phillips to be made of finer stuff, but he found out he was wrong. He would have rushed in to White's Ordinary and murdered both of them had he not been intercepted that day by Reverend Winthrop.

Among his strengths and capacities, one William was most pleased with was the ability to conceal his emotions at will.

When the Reverend, an old and weather worn man of around ninety years, met up with him, they clasped gloved hands, and spoke about how the Gilberts and their daughters were faring. They discussed the tobacco crop, the Reverend's health, and the lack of rain, for a good half of an hour.

The old minister's back was to the Ordinary, making William's vision of its entry quite clear, and he never saw neither Phillips nor Allyn come out.

Once Reverend Winthrop began hobbling along in the direction of his abode, William turned away from the Ordinary, and crossed back to the rope maker, where he'd hitched Gilbert's gelding. He rode home, vowing to himself not to speak on what he'd seen, but to act accordingly.

And so, the next morning when he went outside and looked at the mountain of stones in Woodmason's field, he was moved by feelings of angry frustration to begin constructing a strange thing like nothing he had ever seen before. It began as a circle of stones an arms' span wide, and increased in height but not in width.

Between the stones he packed argil mud from the riverbank, and he mixed this with sand to make mortar. Every day he put on one or two more rows of stones, and he planned an opening, large enough for a man to enter bending down, by leaving some stones dry, and removing them and at the end.

Each day William found some little time for building up and mortaring stones. The round and narrow house increased in height, higher than he could lift a rock. After that he brought a ladder and leant it against the set stones.

The construction went up another two arms' length.

By the end of the month of May the tower was as tall as he could make it. It was the height of thrice a man. Because of its narrow dimension, it seemed to poke into heaven.

William thought about building a roof with a frame of sticks, covered with thatch. But after he had removed the stones for the doorway, he went in and looked at the sky above, and the moon moved over the sun, and a pair of bluebirds landed and perched on the edge of the wall, and sang.

"I shall put no roof upon this tower, then," he said to the birds. As he spoke, the moon moved away from the sun.

He stayed a few minutes inside the tower. Then he looked at it from the outside. Rain and the snow would fall inside were there no roof. He would have to dig a good drain. The water should fall into a deep hole, equally deep as the tower was high. He dug a drain inside the tower, and a hole that led to a spring, and made a well, and all the summer months passed.

Judge Allyn had remained silent for some moments, cogitating, and now he spoke, saying,

"Do you deny, as Goodwife Wescott testified previously, that you frequented White's Ordinary in Wethersfield in the company of an unidentified creature with yellow eyes?"

"What do you think, Judge Allyn? You've been there many times yourself. Have you seen Satan in there?"

Lydia's heart was beating very hard, for she was afraid for William, and yet, sensing his justified anger, she, too grew angry.

"You will refrain from contempt against civil authority!" Judge Allyn said.

His face had become red with outrage.

Everyone in the courtroom was silent and tense. Many believed that William truly was the devil, and they were afraid.

"As witness to the event, I make accusation against you, Governor Allyn, for looking on Thomas Gilbert's wife with lust, and attempting violation upon her body!"

"This is outright defamation of a Judge!" shouted Allyn.

"It shall not be tolerated, as stated in the Code of Laws of the State of Connecticut! This impertinent servant will be imprisoned now, to await trial and further punishment!"

"Allyn, you are a base and cheating knave! To the devil with you!"

Governor Allyn called the jailers to take William away.

Lydia saw them hesitate, frightened of him.

"You shamefully abuse your authority, Governor!"

William spat at the Judge.

Several men and grown boys from the audience crowded upon the big servant, surrounding him. They bound his hands behind him, and pushed and shoved him away to the jail.

CHAPTER TWENTY-SIX

THERE WERE WHISPERINGS of nervous excitement in the courtroom as soon as William had gone.

Governor Allyn, with a serious expression, quieted the audience, and, with great pomp, turned the page of a book he had before him upon the podium and read aloud.

"If the party suspected have the devil's mark—for when the devil makes his covent he always leaves his mark behind to know one for his own, yet it is, if no evident reason can be given for such a mark."

He looked up, and into Lydia's eyes in such a rude manner that she had to turn away. She knew what was coming.

He then turned his gaze to the Searcher, who was standing several paces behind Lydia's chair, and eagerly ordered her to inspect Lydia's body for the mark of the devil.

The Searcher spat on the floor behind her, and whispered,

"You stink of old piss!"

Then she stepped around, circling Lydia as if she were captured prey, so that she was in front of her.

When the Searcher looked at her Lydia saw a cold thing in her eye. It was a hateful look, so filled with enjoyment of her own evil that it gave Lydia goose bumps. It was the look of someone who delighted in inflicting pain and humiliation upon another.

The Searcher stepped closer to Lydia, and with rough hands pulled her mouth open to look inside it. Lydia did not struggle against her. She felt sapped of energy and of hope. The younger woman's hands were strong.

The townspeople watched. No one spoke. Not even a baby's cry broke the silence.

Governor Allyn stared insultingly.

The Searcher poked and pricked inside her mouth with a darning needle. Lydia tasted blood where the needle entered into the places left empty from some fallen teeth. But a devil's teat does not bleed.

She untied Lydia's bodice, and then her blouse beneath it, and then her underdress. Lydia stood still, like a child being undressed by its mother. Because of her bound hands, the clothes did not fall to the floor, but tangled and bunched around her arms.

With a knife the Searcher tore the band that bound Lydia's breasts. Her mind became numb. She had lost her voice. She could not even cry out in protest.

Goodwife Gilbert stood half naked before the town, humiliated, but not ashamed, for she could no longer feel shame.

The Searcher pinched at Lydia's breasts and stuck her flesh again and again with the needle until she was spotted with small droplets of blood. Upon a dark mole on her side she pricked repeatedly and always deeper, until finally it bled.

She then lifted Lydia's skirt, and her petticoats, one by one, and pushed her down roughly to sit upon the stool at the front of the courthouse, in the eyes of all. She threw the coats up over Lydia's head, so that she could see nothing. She sat with her eyes closed tightly while the Searcher forced her naked thighs open wide, so horrified by this woman's actions upon her body that she could hardly believe they were happening.

It was true, though it seemed impossible, that this could happen among God-fearing people.

Before Lydia Gilbert were friends, strangers, neighbors, people she had lived among peacefully for more than twenty years, and her secret parts were exposed to them all, as if she were an animal, or a corpse, or no one.

The Searcher roughly opened and pulled at her down there. Lydia was too numb and exhausted with disbelief to move. She poked the needle into her labia and Lydia cried out from beneath her skirts.

And then she began to tremble, and she grew cold when she heard the Searcher say,

"I have found the devil's teat, Governor."

But she was not done yet. She continued to prick at Lydia's nether parts.

"See for yourselves she is no normal woman," she said in a loud voice, as if selling something at market.

"No good woman has such a teat."

Soon the Governor and the men of the jury were gathered closely around Goody Gilbert. She could feel their heat and smell their odors, of smoke and rum and decay, above her own. She could not see them, and was glad of it. Lydia rose up out of herself then, and felt nothing. She saw herself below as a poppet with two heads. The one underneath her skirts was the beastlier of the two.

She remembered when she had been taken away to jail.

She had just washed and dressed herself, and since the weather was turning cold, she had stayed close to the hearth that morning playing with her little grand daughter Elinor. She recalled thinking how Thomas had gone away only a few weeks before Elinor had been born, and he had not yet returned, nor had Lydia had any letter from him, and the child was now seven months old. So much had happened in those seven months' time. Lydia wanted very much for Thomas to come home again, for she was weary of living at her son in law's house, and wished to return to her own house and to live life the way she had been used to it.

She had Elinor upon her knee, playing with her and singing,

"Ride a cock horse,

To Banbury Cross,

To see a fine lady

Upon a white horse..."

When there came a loud rapping upon the door, and, from without,

Lydia could hear the voices of at least two men. They were voices she did not recognize.

Sarah had been stuffing sausages, and her hands were covered with grease and blood. Lydia picked the child up on the crook of her arm and went to open the door. Even before opening it she had a foreboding feeling that they were not bringing good tidings.

There stood two crude men, both dressed as wandering shepherds —unclean and unkempt. The one with a full dark beard spoke. He said,

"Missus Lydia Gilbert, are ye?"

He had not a tooth in his mouth.

"Yes I am she."

"Perhaps ye should put the baby down," he said.

As she was ready to question him why, Sarah appeared beside her and took Elinor from her arms into her own. Lydia's daughter took in the sight of those two fellows on her doorstep without looking directly at them.

Then the beardless one produced a piece of hemp rope from his pocket, and before she knew what was happening he had bound both of her hands very tightly behind her at the wrists.

Lydia looked at her daughter, and then not at her, but at her grand daughter, who was watching with great dark eyes.

Sarah appeared calm and not surprised at what the bearded man said,

"Yer going to jail, lady, until your trial."

"Why?" Sarah asked them, now alarmed.

"What has she done? You cannot take her away like this for nothing!"

"Talk to the Governor," said the bearded one.

"The Governor!" she said.

And then her face changed, as they both remembered what Nicolas had told them a fortnight earlier—the newly elected governor was Magistrate Allyn.

"Allyn!" she said.

She looked not at Lydia nor at the men, but at nothing, and then at her child, who continued to stare fixedly at the bearded man.

"Never mind," said Lydia.

She did not wish to make her grand daughter frightened, nor to leave her so suddenly and in distress. She preferred to leave there quietly, and as if she were merely stepping out unexpectedly for bread.

"Then the trial must be for this afternoon," said Lydia.

"And I am certain to be back by evening."

The men said nothing, but pushed her out the door. She had not even had time to put on her cloak. She walked between these men, her hands bound, along to the road, where all who peered out could see her. Flurries of snow began to fall.

From behind she heard Sarah close the door tight. Lydia did not turn.

The jail in Windsor was a cold cellar behind the meetinghouse. She had only known it to be used twice previously, but she thought there were other times it held prisoners that she had not known of. One time she knew Samuel Redknap's brother, a thief of chickens, had been thereheld, and another time there was Peter Grigson the Quaker. Lydia wondered now, how cold would that place be?

Her wrists were bound too tightly. The rope was burning into her left one, and after a short while, before they had even reached the jail, her left hand was prickling and numbed.

These large men had long strides and Lydia had to walk very quickly, as both of them pushed her along with their hands upon her shoulders.

As they approached the meetinghouse she saw, coming along the road in the opposite direction toward them, Susannah Fuller the thornback, with some loaves under her arms and her hands deep in the pockets of her cloak. She did not greet Lydia, nor even let her eyes meet Lydia's, but she crossed over to the other side and kept her head down. She would surely tell Wrastle of seeing Goody Gilbert thus— bound and driven in the cold to jail. Every soul in town would soon know, and some would feel themselves emptily vindicated, and some would be outraged.

She had known of the existence of the jail, but she had never seen it.

It was far worse than she had imagined.

When the bearded man opened the heavy wooden door, her eyes could see nothing, but her nose, and perhaps even her whole skin, could smell the terrible stench of deteriorating human excrements. It was so strong that it made her eyes burn. The men pushed her in before them, and she stumbled on the first few steps and almost lost her balance and fell down. They shut the door behind her and she heard one of them fumbling with the key in the iron lock, and then he locked it, and they went away.

She was left alone. It was not as cold as she had feared. With her shod feet she felt her way to the bottom of the steps, where it was cool, but not so cold as outside. She stood still, afraid to walk around, for she could see nothing, but she knew the place was very dirty and she did not wish to dirty her shoes.

Since she had not been told how long she was to stay there, nor why she had been brought there, she could only guess that she was awaiting trial for that afternoon. That should be at two or three hours past noon, and since she had been taken a few hours before noon, she thought she would not have long to wait in this fetid place.

There was nothing to do but stand still in the dark, breathing as lightly as she dared, for the stench was disgraceful. She forced herself to think uplifting thoughts. For although one's natural inclination, when left alone in such a place for several hours and under unexplained happenstance, might be to grow bitter and angered at the unjustness one is suffering, Lydia knew that to allow her mind to become stirred up and full of ire would only add to her anguish. Her thoughts, at least, were still her own to control.

She pictured the baby, Elinor, in her mind, seeing her as if she were seeing portraits of her in many various scenes starting from the day of her birth the previous April. She had come into this world so small and red and naked, squalling even before she'd finished being born, and with a tiny barrel chest and a shock of dark hair, her skin tender like a mouse's skin, and everything so perfectly contained therein.

Sarah was well and joyful.

Lydia only occasionally assisted as a midwife; for her daughter she did.

Nicholas had told Sarah he would assist her, but Lydia thought that she did not like this prospect, and so her pains began unexpectedly while Nicholas was absent, and the baby came quickly, before his return. Lydia had helped in delivering numerous babies previous, and it was always a joy when all went well. With her own daughter it was a blessed exaltation.

She pictured her grand daughter cleaned and swaddled, suckling contentedly at Sarah's breast, and she could think of the smells of her new skin and the milk and the clean linen. For some moments the fetid odor of that place seemed to fade away, and her nostrils filled with the conjured sweet essence of a newborn baby.

She saw baby Elinor sleeping in her cradle that Thomas had made many years earlier for Sarah and Lydia's other babies. Sometimes a tiny baby smile flitted across her lips, as she dreamed infant dreams. Sometimes her eyes opened half way, but she slept on thus, for her eyes rolled up and Lydia saw only white at the slits.

Lydia saw her the first time Sarah brought her outside, in May, to be christened. It was a beautiful spring day, and Sarah was well gratified by the wishes of many townspeople who admired the child, and Lydia, too, was proud.

For a good long while she lost herself in these pleasing and happy thoughts, but she was not so lost that she did not hear the beating of the drum for three hours past noon, and, again, at six hours past.

Then her heart became heavy as she knew there was to be no trial that day, but that she must spend the night in that wretched place.

Some time after six hours, she heard one of the men returning and putting the key into the door lock, and she grew happy like a little dog whose master returns. The door was opened at the top of the stairs, and a chill and a weak light from the brightness of the snow shone upon those dismal steps. She saw two rats run down.

The man threw down a loaf of bread, as if she were a sow in a pen. Then he placed a bucket of water just inside the door. He stood at the doorway. It was the bearded one, and with his gruff voice he said,

"Come here."

She did not go to him for she was afraid. He waited some moments, and when he saw that she would not come he repeated,

"Come here. I'll cut yer ropes."

Indeed, both of her hands and wrists had become so numb that she had forgotten them. She moved toward him and she spoke, saying,

"How long am I to stay here?"

He did not answer, but turned her around roughly and cut the rope with a knife and then pushed her again down the steps. This time she fell upon her hands. As she lifted herself he was locking the door.

She rubbed her unfeeling hands on her skirt and searched for the loaf. It was not fresh, but she was hungry and she ate it. Then she felt her way slowly with her feet, to the top of the steps and drank two ladles full of water. She was still hungry, but could not hope to receive more food before tomorrow.

Knowing she had many more hours of waiting ahead, Lydia could no longer think pleasant thoughts. She could not sleep standing up like a horse, she thought, but neither would she lie down among the rats and excrement.

She wondered if this punishment had been contrived by the Devil. Did she deserve it? Was God displeased with her? She had sinned by fornicating in her mind, and she had murdered a baby and her mother as well, and perhaps it was even true that she had cursed her neighbors with years of misfortune by looking upon them with an evil eye, for she had never wished them well. How could she have continued to encourage Reliance in reading heretical materials, instead of guiding her to the best of her abilities on the path that God wished all women to follow—that of being subservient to men in all their daily toil and thought? By God, she thought, she must surely have wished Henry Stiles' death upon him, for she was not sad when he failed to return that evening. If she had not agreed, with the devil in her heart, to take him into her house and care for him, he would still likely be alive, and toothless. Perhaps she had sinned in not allowing Magistrate—Governor—Allyn to use her body for his pleasure, for he was a powerful and important man and should be served.

Had she been wrong to exchange her old brown pocket for the silver glove William used to keep his money in? Perhaps she should not have been so selfish as to take it back, and then use it upon the visitors' baby. Nicholas was right to burn it, for that thing was a tool of Satan's workings, and putting it upon her hand had made her a servant to the dark forces. She was evil, and deserved to be in jail.

Thinking in this way Lydia soon felt ruined and helpless. She wept for a long while and begged God to save her soul. When there was no more weeping left inside of her, she finally sat down upon the step, and with her head against the wall, fell asleep.

With enough strength and time, and her natural good nature Lydia thought she could have forgotten this terrible episode—the jail and the trial and now the torture—but she believed that she hadn't time for forgetting.

The men around her watched while the Searcher pricked at her, and then she heard a great gasp from one of them and a cry came from another of them.

She wondered what they were pretending to see between her legs. Would they have the townspeople believe that she was made differently from their own wives and mothers? Theirs was but a show, and, if such a thing were possible, a way to humiliate her more.

Her petticoats and skirt were taken back down to cover her legs, but she could not look up and meet the eyes of any one for her humiliation was so great.

Now the jury must deliberate and make their judgments.

Was she a witch or not a witch? Who was she—this woman who was to be either condemned or pardoned? Did she deserve to die? Must she necessarily be put to death so that her threatening human form would not disturb others? That woman was once called Lydia Gilbert, but the woman at the front of the meetinghouse was not she, and she knew not who she was nor where she had gone. What remained sitting upon the chair with limbs tied behind its back was nothing more than a beast imbued with an invented evil, the horrible nightmare of a man's imaginings, and they called it by the name that sorry woman had used, Lydia Gilbert. Seeing what it was, she believed it deserved to die. But she did not know how to extricate herself from it.

There was a tension of waiting in the meetinghouse for some long minutes. None of the townspeople spoke. The sound of a low sibilant whisper came from the jury in the front corner. She stared at the floorboards, and heard the creaking of the benches, and some coughing, and the swinging of a child's feet against the bench board, and a slapped scolding.

Governor Allyn asked for the jury's consensus.

There was the crackling of paper changing hands.

Governor Allyn moved close to her. He stated the indictment.

"By verdict of the jury, five to one, Lydia Gilbert, thou art here indicted by the name of Lydia Gilbert that not having the fear of God before thine eyes thou hast of late years or still dust give entertainment to Satan the great enemy of God and mankind, and that by his help thou hast killed the body of Henry Stiles, besides other witchcrafts, for which according to the law of God and the established law of this commonwealth, thou deservest to die."

CHAPTER TWENTY-SEVEN

AT THE END of Judge Allyn's pronunciation of the verdict, all the withheld tension circulating amongst the people in the courthouse was suddenly released into what seemed a great explosion of yelling, hollering and whooping voices.

Lydia was not surprised by the verdict, for, even if the majority of the men on the jury had found her not guilty, she knew that the judge's decision presided over that of the jury, and she knew that Judge Allyn was determined to take her body, if not carnally, then mortally.

She was not surprised, but, upon hearing Judge Allyn say so clearly, "According to the law of God and the established law of this commonwealth, thou deservest to die", and especially those condemning words, "thou deservest to die", Lydia felt her last remaining energy and the tiny flicker of hope drain away from her. Already the extreme humiliation she had endured these last weeks, which had become ever more intense, right up to these last few minutes, in which she was stripped of her final bits of integrity, a part of her knew that, even if she were to go on living she could not stay here, in Windsor, among the people who had sat and watched the destruction of her humanness.

If the verdict had been banishment, she thought she could go to live in Boston with her sister. Her daughters could visit her there. And Thomas? Would he ever return?

She had been sitting with her face down, and now she stood, and looked out at the terrifying horde before her.

There, at the doorway, she saw her husband. He seemed taller than she had remembered, but perhaps this was an illusion, since she felt herself so much smaller than she had previously been. He was strong and well dressed in a blue singlet underneath his open greatcoat, and he wore a black hat. His steps were fast and sure as he made his way through the crowd.

There was her husband!

Lydia could not tell if he were real, or a trick played by her own mind. Was he some other man who resembled Thomas? Was she only remembering him from another time, long ago?

She looked down again, at her filthy skirt, and felt with her tongue the spaces where the teeth were missing from her mouth. Was this real, or was it a dream? Her hands were so numb and cold she could no longer feel them. She kicked the heel of one shod foot against the toe of the other, but felt only dullness.

Thomas was standing in front of her now. She saw his feet in waxed shoes, and his long strong legs. She smelled his familiar scent of cinnamon. She was afraid to look up, afraid to show him her face, afraid that it would not be him. She knew she looked hideous. She did not want to see the look of disgust and horror in his eyes, if it be him, and if it were not him, she did not want to see who it was.

"Lydia—" he spoke, quietly.

The sound of his voice was like a banquet to her.

She looked up, into his kind, familiar face. His eyes looked into hers.

"Thomas!" she cried out.

Her husband—when had he come back?

He stood before her, and Lydia looked fully upon him. He did not shift his gaze away in fear or disgust, but looked upon his wife with the love and intelligence she had always known in him.

She rushed two steps to him, and although she could not touch him with her bound arms, he encircled her in warm embrace with his strong steady ones. He stroked her hairless head, and for a moment it seemed that all was well again.

Together they stood before the townspeople, he so great and tall, and Lydia so shrunken that she suddenly felt herself as defenseless as a baby. She felt as if her husband were God, for he was the only hope that remained to save her from this nightmare.

From behind her someone suddenly pulled Lydia forcefully away from her husband. It was the Searcher. She held Lydia back, roughly at the elbows. She held her, and kicked at her legs behind with heavy shoes.

Lydia was weak, and she wept now for she wished to be embraced by her husband and never to be let go again. But she had not the strength to escape the Searcher's grip.

Thomas approached the Judge, and spoke,

"I petition for my good wife Lydia's innocence, and would urge you, Governor Allyn, to use your judicious and pious considerations in seeing plainly the wily subtleties of my wife's accusers. I do not question your duty, Governor, in discovering and detecting witches and the practitioners of witchcraft in the colony of Connecticut, but in the case of my good wife Lydia, unfair accusations, attributable to the envious ill-wishes of a few neighbors and townspeople, do not make a case against her. It would be difficult to find a lady more godly and innocent of evil intent than my wife Lydia Gilbert. I wish that the Lord would have directed you in your judgment, Governor Allyn."

The buzzing ruckus had died down somewhat, as people strained to hear what former Magistrate Gilbert was saying.

He turned toward the audience, and then briefly toward Lydia. Again he met her eyes with his, and that gave her strength and composure. She no longer felt the pinching, nor the tight grasp of the Searcher, nor her kicks, nor quite so much the dislocation and tiredness.

"Could you call for order, Will?" she heard Thomas say aside to Judge Allyn.

"The verdict has already been made," Judge Allyn said.

With her husband present, Lydia felt herself filled with a great hatred for Will Allyn.

"I ask you again to call for order in the courtroom," Thomas said.

Grudgingly, Judge Allyn slammed the Bible down upon the oak wood, and called out loudly for order.

This was achieved after some moments, and, when Thomas had got the attention of all present, he spoke clearly, saying,

"I petition, on behalf of my wife, Lydia Gilbert, judged guilty in trial by jury of practicing witchcraft, for Benefit of Clergy."

Everyone was silent.

Lydia knew that Benefit of Clergy could be requested in the Commonwealth by those found guilty after a secular trial, as long as the guilty person was literate enough to read from the Bible, and had not been condemned previously. It was a way to avoid harsh sentences, for it meant that she would be re-tried before a court of clergymen, whose punishments were more merciful.

Lydia remembered now that Anne Hutchinson had asked for a trial by Clergy after being found guilty in the secular court for heresy. She had not thought to ask for it for herself. She had not thought about it at all. She had been unthinking, unable to see any way to save herself from Governor Allyn's preposterous antagonism. But Thomas had come back, and he had thought of it! She would live, after all. Perhaps she would be banished, but she would live.

CHAPTER TWENTY-EIGHT

WHEN THOMAS GILBERT finally returned from England it was the grimmest time of year.

The brook was iced over and the ground frozen hard. He arrived at his holdings in the early part of the afternoon with a post rider and found no one about the place. Where was William? He expected to find him outdoors working. But he was nowhere to be seen, nor was he in the barn, when he stuck his head in for a quick look.

He went to the house, and saw that fresh water had been hauled, and both barrels outside the door were full.

Inside, the house was cold, for no fire was lit, nor had been for some time. Where was Lydia? Where were his daughters?

He found his letter to Lydia, still sealed in its envelope, on the Welsh cabinet. Had she not read it? He had written to her as soon as he was able, at the end of the spring, and he had not had any word back from her. Where was she?

He left his bag in the cold bedchamber, and went toward the barn to saddle his horse. He would ride into town, to Nicholas Carver's house, where Elizabeth dwelt. She had birthed her child in April, after he had left. He had had word from Peter Stiles that it was a girl.

Because of his absence from the election in October, and also because his term was over, Thomas was no longer a magistrate. In his place were Masters Peter Stiles and Nathaniel White as magistrates, and Master Allyn as Governor, to replace Hopkins, who remained in England. Thomas had received two letters from Peter Stiles during his absence. Apart from the news of the birth of a healthy grand daughter, he'd had no word of his family.

Lydia's horse, Aisley, was not in the barn. Thomas quickly curried Talevent, who showed his pleasure at his master's return by rubbing his head affectionately against his legs. He found the saddle and fittings in their place, and in good order, and the stable was clean, so he knew that William had not been away long.

When he rode off it was already beginning to get dark out. He carried a lantern in one hand, and entered the woods at a trot.

Upon his arrival into the town of Windsor it seemed peculiarly empty of life, and Thomas noticed that crafter's shops such as the wheelwright and the cooper on the edge of town were closed and dark.

The only thing he could think was that it was a funeral day, and he wondered who had died.

He walked his horse onto the main street, where the weekly market was held, and saw, ahead of him in the dim light, many tied horses and oxen on both sides of the street, and a crowd of people all around the steps, where the meetinghouse was.

Some of the wall sconces had been lit inside, he could see as he approached the building, and the meetinghouse was packed full of many people. Just as he was preparing to dismount at a vacant hitching post, the people inside the meetinghouse let out a great cry and shouting, full of both huzzahs and bahs. He wondered what this was all about? Could it be a trial? Certainly he would find his wife and daughters there.

Gilbert hitched his horse, and then sauntered up to the meetinghouse steps wearing his greatcoat and new black hat, as if he'd been gone only a fortnight, instead of the better part of a year.

Before the entrance were some rough housing boys, and he recognized one of these as the apothecary's son, John.

Thomas smiled and said hello, but the boy only glared at him and turned away.

Right at the doorway, Thomas met Samuel Bellringer.

"Goodman Bellringer. It's my pleasure to be back home and to see you again."

He shook the man's somewhat reluctant hand and embraced him.

The two men looked each other over.

Samuel was hesitant to speak.

Thomas peered at him a moment longer. Then he said,

"What's going on, good man? What's happened here?"

Samuel Bellringer could not look Thomas Gilbert in the eyes when he told him that his wife was on trial for witchcraft.

"What? Why? You're gaming with me!"

"No, Master Gilbert, tis no game. Judge Allyn has just given the jury's verdict. She's been found guilty."

Gilbert's face turned crimson red with anger and confusion.

He asked,

"What is her sentence?"

Goodman Bellringer hung his head. He could hardly speak the word, for his voice cracked with sorrow.

"Death."

"Empty-hearted malignancy!"

He entered the courthouse, which was stifling and warm with so many noisy bodies. All day he had been traveling, and the sudden heat and noise in the room was unsettling. He stood at the back, by the door, for some moments, taking in the sensations bombarding him simultaneously from every direction. For such a homecoming he was not prepared.

He searched the front of the courtroom for Lydia, but did not see her.

He saw Allyn sitting behind the podium, turned halfway around to parley with the jurymen. There were altogether too many women seated and standing on the left side of the courthouse for him to make out or distinguish any of his daughters.

His eyes returned again to the front of the courtroom. There was a small sad looking little waif, sitting on a chair with its hairless head turned down. He kept his gaze pinned upon this strange being, and, eventually it looked up, in his direction. Could that be Lydia? He looked some more, until he was quite certain it was indeed his wife.

Seeing what had become of her in the eight or nine months he'd been away, Thomas became infuriated. He began to make his way to the front of the courthouse, using the adrenaline of his anger to think pointedly all the way, what to say, and how best to say it.

Lydia was remembering the last time she had seen Thomas, the hours before he had left her, so many months ago.

Spring had begun to come again, and it seemed to make Thomas unquiet, for he became quite restless at night, tossing about and turning, and twisting the bedclothes so that neither could Lydia have a good night's rest, but was often wakened due to being uncovered and cold, or else from a kick or an unmeant jab from one of his feet, knees or elbows, or else from the movement of the mattress below her, which seemed almost to be the earth quaking.

In all of their years together she could not remember him being so tormented at night, and she wondered why, and she questioned him about it. But he was in a closed mind, and would not come up with an answer she believed, but said only that the responsibility of his Magisterial duties was a heavy load of late as there were disagreements among the representative men concerning the new Navigation Acts, but perhaps he also was concerned about other, personal matters, for she knew he had been suffering some pain while passing water, though he did not tell her this, nor either would he let her treat it. She supposed that to admit to having a physical ailment would be akin to him admitting he was not invincible.

Due to this lack of restful sleep, in his waking hours, Thomas sometimes spoke testily and was more than the usual litigious. Lydia could not say that she, too, was not suffering in some ways from tiredness.

One evening, after having cleaned and put away the trenchers and spoons, and brushed up the crumbs from the board and the floor below, Lydia sat down by herself at the cleared board with the pack of cards.

Reliance had retired early to her attic room, to her books, and Elizabeth was in town for the night, at Sarah and Nicholas's house. There was a full moon overhead, and it had been many months since Lydia had played at reading the cards.

Thomas was late in the barn with William, discussing what needed to be done during his absence, for he would be leaving on the morrow to Boston with some other Magistrates, and should be away about ten days or a fortnight.

Lydia shuffled the deck thrice, and very slowly lay the cards in one of the arrangements her grandmother had taught her, paying careful attention in particular to the last four, and above all the final one. The fourth to last card she turned over to place in the left hand position was the fifteenth, represented by the Devil. She did not like this, and it worried her, for it meant that forces of perversion and hatred should hinder her during the next months. She told herself that it was only a game and meant nothing. She was certain that she played at it only as a divertissement and it could tell her nothing of her future. She tried to allay her own fears in this way.

She lay the third to last card in the position of the right foot. It was the five of clubs. The meaning of this one, coming after the fifteenth, was that she should submit to the forces of the devil, and that she should live fearfully. She did not like this reading a whit, in fact it was one of the worst she had ever lain, but she would have continued on anyway, in order to know the outcome, if, at the moment she was getting ready to turn the second to last card, Thomas had not come bursting into the room.

He disapproved of her playing at cards, and when he saw them on the board, as he was in a foul and terrible humor, he brushed them to the floor with his hand, and said, without looking at his wife,

"Lydia, with all of the things you could be doing at this moment, why are you now idly gaming?"

"What is it you wish me to do?"

Lydia said these words calmly as she bent to gather the cards from the floor, and place them back into their wrapper.

"Need you to ask?" he uttered.

He then left the house again, slamming the door behind him.

Lydia was left shaken by his brusqueness and could only attribute it to his state of nerves, but she thought that his treatment of her was unjust. She had spent a good part of these past two days washing and mending his undergarments and other sundry items he would need to take with him to Boston, in addition to doing all of her regular chores in the house and barn and garden, which were neither few nor light. She had done all he'd asked of her and many other things he'd not asked but which she knew he'd want to have done, and by the evening after supper, she believed it was not wrong to take a half an hour's time for her own quiet gaming and pleasure.

Having placed the wrapped cards away again in their hiding place Lydia now stood idle before the hearth, not knowing what she was supposed to do, but believing that, as long as she appeared to be at work, her husband, when he saw her, would not be displeased.

She found the besom broom and began to slowly sweep once more the previously swept floor.

Thomas again entered the house, and she kept her back to him, sweeping.

He spoke not one word to her, but went to the chamber where they slept; a sign perhaps that it was time to retire. Since he would be away for a while, Lydia had thought that they might pass the night in loving embrace.

She put away the broom and went to the bedchamber, where she found Thomas beneath the quilt, his body turned toward the wall.

She had not brought the betty lamp, but could see the shape of his body by the moonlight coming in at the window. By this pallid blue light Lydia removed her shoes and skirt and bodice and petticoats and stockings, and lay her own body on the bed beneath the quilt, beside Thomas, wearing, as she did each night, only her chemise and drawers.

After some few moments of lying still upon her back she understood, by his breathing, that her husband was deep asleep, and this offended her somewhat as a wife, for she believed he did not think enough of the love between them to renew it again before his departure. Instead he had been so concerned with his own preparations that he had forgotten her.

Never mind. Lydia turned her body with her back toward his, and shortly fell asleep.

When she awoke at dawn Thomas was all ready out of the bed. She dressed quickly but found him not within the house.

Neither was he in the barn. William told her he had already left, riding to Magistrate Allyn's to initiate the trip with him on horseback to Boston.

She found no written letter he left behind.

In the state of mind he was in she supposed her husband had not purposefully intended to neglect her, but whether it was his intent or not, Lydia felt most surely neglected, and the memory of those past days and of his restlessness and irritability did not make her unhappy about his departure.

So much had changed during these long months of his absence, but now at last Thomas had returned from England! There was hope. He would take her back home, or take her away with him somewhere, and they would live as they had before, and this nightmare could be forgotten.

"Her felony is too serious, Gilbert," Judge Allyn said.

"It is an unclergyable offense."

"Show me where in the Code such a thing is stated, Governor Allyn," Thomas said.

"Or she shall be granted Benefit of Clergy!"

While her husband was speaking to him, the Governor had kept his eyes withdrawn and downward.

For some moments more Thomas remained before Judge Allyn, waiting for his response.

Judge Allyn took a monocle from his pocket and held it up to his right eye. Hunching over to lean close, he turned over several pages of a pamphlet in front of him on the podium.

After some moments, he removed the monocle, cleared his throat, and said,

"According to Exodus 22. 18; Leviticus 20. 27, and Deuteronomy 18 10, 1L, if any person be a witch, he or she shall be put to death."

"Because witchcraft is a capital crime," Thomas agreed.

"But, according to Deuteronomy 19; 16, 18, 19, if any person rise up by false witness—"

Thomas turned and looked directly at Elizabeth Wescott sitting near the front of the left side.

"Wittingly and of purpose to take away any man's life, that person shall be put to death."

Thomas spoke eloquently as he moved his gaze to settle upon the faces of several other people in the audience, for, besides the Wescotts he could not think who would have testified against his wife.

"The witnesses are not being tried," Judge Allyn said.

"Your wife has had a fair trial. We have heard from several single witnesses, all of them of competent age, of sound understanding, and of good reputation—"

Thomas smirked at the judge's last words, but made no comment.

"All having been witness to the case in question, their testimonies shall be accounted sufficient proof, though they did not together see, or hear, and so witness to the same individual and particular act, in reference to the felony of practicing witchcraft. Without testimony from at least three witnesses, no person shall be put to death, but the men of the jury will attest to the authenticity of each witness's testimony against Lydia Gilbert."

"If my wife, Lydia Gilbert, be a witch further evidence against her would be proved by the inability to recite psalms from the Bible, for such a book should repel powers governed over by Satan."

Thomas spoke with great composure, and had the attention of everyone in the courtroom.

"I say her offense is unclergyable," Governor Allyn persisted.

"Let God be her judge," Thomas said.

"The verdict has been made. She shall be put to death."

Lydia had gotten down upon her knees in front of the wooden stool, and remained thus, with her head lowered as if in prayer.

"Let God be her judge!" Thomas repeated.

He grabbed the Bible from the podium.

"Very well then, Gilbert! This court shall make an outstanding exception, and grant your wife Lydia, who has been found guilty of the capital crime of witchcraft by jury vote of five to one, the unprecedented opportunity for Benefit of Clergy."

Thomas carried the Bible to Lydia, but, having her hands bound, she was unable to take it.

"Unbind her hands!" Thomas said to the Searcher, who stood close behind.

"Tis not for me to do," she said, barely looking at him.

Judge Allyn called for one of the jailers.

The large man approached Lydia with a knife, and, going around behind her, pulled her to her feet with the rope that bound her wrists, and quickly cut the rope.

Lydia's hands had been bound so long that they had turned pale white and were numb and unfeeling. She shook them at her sides. The jailer pushed her down again to her knees.

The Searcher moved to stand more closely behind her.

Thomas had watched the jailer's rough treatment of his wife in anguished silence.

She was kneeling before him, clasping and unclasping her hands, low at her sides, her head down-turned. When she looked up at him, he handed her the heavy black covered book with two hands.

She took it. Now she must read Psalm fifty-one without fault, but this would not be difficult for her, for she had memorized nearly all of the psalms by heart and had repeated them many times during her weeks in jail.

Lydia opened the Bible, and found Psalm fifty-one.

Holding the Bible in front of her with both hands, she bowed her head over it and read,

"Psalm fifty-one.

"To him that excelleth. A Psalm of David, when the prophet Nathan came unto him, after he had gone in to Bathsheba. Have mercy upon me, oh God, according to thy loving kindness:

According to the multitude of thy compassions put away mine iniquities."

"What?" called out Judge Allyn.

"She speaks too low. Let her voice be heard by all, so that we might know if she is literate, or merely recites. Every word must be correct."

Without having lifted her head, Lydia continued reading, louder now, and more slowly.

"Wash me thoroughly from mine iniquity, and cleanse me from my sin."

"Did she say sin or skin?" Judge Allyn commented, looking around at the townspeople for laughs.

Some of the men guffawed and a few women snickered.

One woman near the front commented loudly,

"God knows she could used a bath!"

And this brought a short burst of laughter from the jurymen.

Thomas stood facing the audience, and looked at them sternly and without remorse.

Lydia continued,

"For I know mine iniquities: and my sin is ever before me.

"Against thee, against thee only have I sinned, and done evil in thy sight:"

As she read, Lydia thought of how she had betrayed Thomas by being too intimate with Wrastle Fuller, and for this she was truly sorry.

She went on,

"That thou mayest be just when thou speakest, and pure when thou judgest.

"Behold, I was born in iniquity; and in sin hath my mother conceived me.

"Behold, thou lovest truth in the inward affections: therefore thou hast taught me wisdom in the secret part—"

At these words, Judge Allyn let out a very loud false gasp of horror. Lydia realized she had mistakenly read the word "part" instead of "heart", and felt a sudden terror that this small error would mean her death. She dared not look up or away from the words printed in the book she held before her.

And then she heard Judge Allyn snicker, and realized that he had not noticed her mistake, but, at the words "secret part" was only making a vulgar reminder to the audience and the jury of the recent view they had all had of Lydia's secret parts.

Behind her, the Searcher nodded her head in agreement and crossed her fingers over her heart.

Many in the audience gasped or made disturbing groans.

Lydia, greatly relieved, spoke as loudly as she could, struggling to be heard over everyone else. She was nearly yelling.

"Purge me with hyssop, and I shall be clean! Wash me and I shall be whiter than snow!"

"Amen!" shouted Judge Allyn raucously.

The audience burst into laughter.

Lydia shouted,

"Make me to hear joy and gladness, that the bones which thou hast broken, may rejoice!"

She smiled without lifting her head as she shouted these words, for indeed she was hearing sounds of joy and gladness, and she believed her salvation was near.

"Hide thy face from my sins, and put away all mine iniquities!

"Create in me a clean heart, oh God; and renew a right spirit within me!

"Cast me not away from thy presence; and take not thine holy spirit from me!"

The townspeople were now making so much noise that Lydia knew her voice could not be heard above it. Still, she went on shouting her prayer,

"Restore to me the joy of thy salvation; and establish me with thy free spirit!

"Then shall I teach thy ways unto the wicked; and sinners shall be converted unto thee!

"Deliver me from blood, oh God, which art the God of my salvation; and my tongue shall sing joyfully with thy righteousness!

"Open thou my lips, Oh Lord, and my mouth shall shew forth thy praise!

"For thou desirest no sacrifice; though I would give it: thou delightest not in burnt offering!"

"What?" Judge Allyn interrupted.

"I did not hear. I believe you made a mistake. Repeat verse fifteen, Goodwife."

"She made no mistake," Thomas said.

The audience quieted somewhat to hear the exchange between these former colleagues.

"Must I remind you who is in charge of this court, Master—Goodman—Gilbert? She shall repeat verse fifteen."

Everyone seemed to be listening now as Lydia shouted out,

"Open thou my lips, Oh Lord, and my mouth shall shew forth thy praise!"

To one of the jurymen Judge Allyn said,

"Her nether lips!"

Both of the men laughed loudly.

Now Lydia was unsure whether to continue where she had left off, or from verse fifteen. She hesitated.

"Proceed!" said the Governor, still laughing.

"For thou desirest no sacrifice; though I would give it: thou delightest not in burnt offering."

Judge Allyn said nothing, and seemed not to even be listening to her. Still without looking up, Lydia continued reading loudly.

"The sacrifices of God are a contrite spirit: a contrite and a broken heart, Oh God thou wilt not despise.

"Be favorable unto Zion for thy good pleasure: build the walls of Jerusalem.

"Then shalt thou accept ye sacrifices of righteousness, even the burnt offering and oblation: then shall they offer young bullocks upon thine altar."

Lydia had finished reading the psalm, but she dared not look up. It seemed that almost no one was listening to her, save Thomas.

Then she heard Judge Allyn's voice.

"Repeat verse nineteen, Goodwife Gilbert."

"Then thou shalt be pleased with the sacrifices of righteousness, with burnt offerings and oblations: then they will offer young bullocks upon thine altar."

"Repeat it once again, just the last part."

She hesitated. Had she made a mistake in her reading of it? She looked over the words carefully once again, although she knew them well by heart.

"Then they will offer young bullocks upon thine altar."

"Young what? I did not hear what you said, Goodwife. There is quite a bit of noise in the court room."

Without his Bible to use as a gavel, Judge Allyn could only use his voice to obtain order and quiet in the court.

Thomas turned and looked at Lydia kneeling on the floor.

She knew he was looking at her but she did not meet his eyes, for she felt that this was her one last chance at salvation and she dared not do anything out of place. She kept her head bowed in prayer.

"Order!" the judge yelled.

"Silence! Order!"

Once the rumor had died down sufficiently, Governor Allyn said, cockily,

"Goodwife Gilbert, what is it that will be offered upon the altar of the Lord?"

"Then they will offer young bullocks upon thine altar," she repeated.

What had she read wrong? She could find no mistake in her reading. Her eyesight grew bleary from staring at the page.

"Young what?" Allyn said again, as if in a nightmare.

"Then they will offer young bullocks upon thine altar."

Tears were clouding her vision now.

"You need not repeat the entire phrase. I only asked for one word."

She was silent a moment. Then she understood that he wanted her to say the word "bullocks", as in "testicles" before the audience, so they would laugh at her and she would be further humiliated.

"Bullocks," she said, without lifting her head.

As predicted, many people burst out laughing at the sound of this bawdy word coming from her praying lips.

Thomas waited patiently in his perturbation, until the laughter had died down somewhat. He then turned to the Governor, and in a resounding voice said,

"She has successfully read psalm fifty one. Her case shall pass to the clergy court."

These words were spoken so clearly and with such authority that many of the townspeople, and even some of the men of the jury, believed they had been pronounced by Judge Allyn. The courtroom became quite silent.

Judge Allyn gave Thomas Gilbert a fierce look.

"She has not passed the test yet, Gilbert. It would be easy enough for her to have memorized psalm fifty-one, which we have all heard so often times spoken, by heart. For Benefit of Clergy, the witch must prove she is capable of reading the words as written in the Bible. She must read the lesser-known psalm eighty-eight. Every word must be exacting. I would ask some one of the learned men of the jury to govern her reading of it by tracking the words in his own Book."

There was some commotion amongst the jurymen as they decided which of them should silently read along with Lydia in the Bible.

The sallow-skinned man stood and said to Judge Allyn,

"I will govern the witch's reading if I might be provided with a Bible."

"Reverend Stiles," Governor Allyn called to him.

"Could you kindly lend Master Rishworth a Bible?"

Reverend Stiles stood and said,

"I would, except that Lydia Gilbert has my Bible, the same one that you previously were using to gain order, Governor."

"Have you only one?" the Judge said, disapprovingly.

"Goodwife Gilbert holds the Geneva Bible. That is the one we are all familiar with and the one I use at meetings."

"Have you no other copy, Reverend?"

"Here I have but the King James version."

He took a black covered book from the bench behind him.

"Let Master Rishworth have it."

"But it differs in its wording, Governor Allyn."

"Is it not the word of God?"

Reverend Stiles looked in silent perplexity at the Judge.

"Is not the Bible the word of God, Reverend?"

Thomas interjected, "I think the Reverend is saying that the newer translation differs slightly in some places in its choice of wording. Master Rishworth could not be too exacting, for he would be reading from a different version of the text than would my wife."

"You will be seated, Goodman Gilbert!" Judge Allyn shouted at him.

He had yelled with such force that his dentures nearly slipped out of his mouth. No one dared laugh.

Thomas did not move.

Judge Allyn lowered his head and pushed his wooden teeth back into place.

"Be seated! Or you shall be dragged out of the courthouse!"

Thomas had not been seated before, so he strode not far into the sea of townspeople, where he stopped and turned to again face Judge Allyn.

"Give the Bible to Master Rishworth, Reverend," said Allyn.

"I shall return to my abode for another copy of the Geneva Bible," said the Reverend.

"No! I order that you shall give that Bible you now hold in your hands to Master Rishworth!"

"What will it prove?" Reverend Stiles said, not too loudly.

"The words are not identical from one book to the other."

"Bring the Bible!"

Reverend Stiles brought the Bible to Master Rishworth. He handed it to him, and said,

"You must not be too exacting. The wording will differ. Tis the meaning which is the same."

Master Rishworth stood up to accept the King James Bible from the Reverend. He nodded his head in accordance, and sat down again.

Reverend Stiles returned to his seat, giving Thomas a worried look on the way.

"Goody Gilbert, you are to begin reading Psalm eighty-eight," Judge Allyn said.

Lydia had already found the place in the Book, but she waited some moments until, by listening to the turning of the pages, and then the ceasing of that sound, she believed Master Rishworth had found the psalm, too.

The courthouse was silent. She began reading.

"Psalm eighty-eight. A song or psalm of Herman the Ezrahite to give instruction, committed to the sons of Korah for him that excelleth upon Mahalath Leonnoth.

"Oh Lord God of my salvation, I cry day and night before thee.

"Let my prayer enter into thy presence—"

"She has erred in her recitation!" Master Rishworth cried out.

He stood and read,

"Let my prayer come before thee: incline thine ear unto my cry! Those are the words written here!"

"Let my prayer come before thee," Lydia repeated.

"Incline thine ear unto my cry,

"For my soul is filled with evils: and my life draweth near to the grave."

"No! No! The witch cannot read! She says all the words wrong. It should be, For my soul is full of troubles: and my life draweth nigh unto the grave!" said Rishworth.

Suddenly Lydia stood up and turned around to face Master Rishworth.

"We are reading from different versions. As the Reverend explained, the words will not match exactly, but the meanings are the same."

"You have broken prayer!" Judge Allyn shouted at her.

"You shall not receive Benefit of Clergy!

"Take her away! The witch will be hung tomorrow at noon!"

There was a chaotic uproar of shouting and movement of the townspeople in the courtroom

Lydia dropped down to her knees and continued reading,

"I am counted with them that go down into the pit: I am as a man without strength: Free among the dead, like the slain that lie in the grave, whom thou rememberest no more: and they are cut off from thy hand. Thou hast laid me in the lowest pit, in darkness, in the deeps. Thine indignation lieth upon me, and thou hast vexed me with all thy waves."

Thomas pushed through the few delirious people in front of him to reach his wife.

"Jailers! Take her away!" shouted the Judge.

"Thou hast put away mine acquaintance far from me; and made me to be abhorred by them: I am shut up, and I cannot come forth," Lydia continued, murmuring quickly now.

One of the jailers fought off Thomas while the other grabbed Lydia by her wrists.

"Mine eye is sorrowful through mine affliction. Lord, I call daily upon thee. I stretch out mine hands unto thee."

As she read these words the Bible dropped to the floor. Lydia stayed in a kneeling position, and her arms were stretched upward. She was being dragged along the floor.

She continued quietly reciting the psalm though memory.

"Wilt thou shew a miracle to the dead? Shall the dead arise and praise thee? Shall thy loving kindness be declared in the grave? Or thy faithfulness in destruction?"

Thomas came after the jailer who was crudely dragging Lydia out of the courthouse. He jumped upon his back, and, notwithstanding the jailer's greater size and strength, in his rage the older man knocked him to the floor. Lydia was free, her hands were unbound.

She did not move, but stayed on her knees, her eyes still on the floor. It seemed as if she were unaware of the chaos all around her. She continued praying,

"Lord, why doest thou reject my soul, and hidest thy face from me? I am afflicted and at the point of death…thine indignations go over me, and thy fear hath cut me off."

"Lydia!" Thomas cried out to her, but he himself was being tackled and pinned down by several young townsmen. The two jailers seized Lydia and bound her hands once again behind her back with strong rope.

She was passive and seemed oblivious to what they did to her.

She was escorted by the jailers out of the torch lit courthouse amidst the riot of jeering and shouting people, into the cold darkness of the November evening.

Still, she continued her recitation, inaudible to all but herself.

"They came round about me daily like water; they compassed me about together. My lovers and friends hast thou put away from me, and mine acquaintances hid themselves."

The boys gathered around the steps outside the meetinghouse showered Lydia with handfuls of pea gravel. The jailers held her there for some moments so she could experience the full effect of its sting upon her bowed head.

CHAPTER TWENTY-NINE

ONE OF THE jailers, holding a torch, unlocked the familiar oaken door and, stepping in before her, shoved William down the steps. Then he came back out and his fellow thrust Lydia in. The heavy door was slammed shut and locked behind her.

She had forgotten that William was in the jail.

"Darkness!" she called out softly.

The sound of the jangling keys and the jailers' guffawing laughter slowly disappeared outside.

"Missus Gilbert," she heard William's voice from several steps down.

"I've alighted in dung. You must forgive my stench."

Lydia laughed aloud.

"I can no longer see, for darkness encloses me. And neither can I sense your stench, William, for the fetor of this place is already so hideous that it covers any other stink."

She could hear him slowly making his way up the stone steps. His ankles were shackled, and she thought his wrists must also be tied.

"For the better, lady," he called to her.

"On my own I could not think of it as being better. I am glad for your company."

"If my company makes the stink seem less, I am grateful for your compliment."

Because of her passivity, the jailer had not thrust her into the jail with too much force, and Lydia had tripped down only two or three steps, where she remained, standing against the wall.

William's face now touched her shoe as he had inched his way up, like a worm, from several steps below.

"Oh! Is that you, or a rat?"

"Tis me, I believe. I beg your pardon."

He moved up another step, and struggled to get to his feet without losing his balance.

Now he stood in front of her. She could feel the warmth emanating from his body.

"What will become of you?" she asked him.

"I know not. Perhaps I will be tried. Perhaps banished."

"How would Thomas manage without you?"

The big man did not answer right away. They had not seen his master since March. And Reliance had said she was going to go to the college at New Haven. Who would feed the animals? Would the neighbors take everything, take over the house and land as well?

He was silent for some time.

"Did you know he came back?" she said softly.

They were standing so close that he could feel her breath when she sighed. When she had spoken those words he at first did not believe them, but thought she had gone a bit mad. But, in the silent moments that followed, although he could not see her face, he felt the relief mixed with anguish mixed with hopeless joy emanating from her, and he knew it was true.

"When, lady? I left the holdings after noon, and there was no one about."

"I know not. He must have come after noon, then, today. He was at court. He wore a new hat and looked very well."

"I am glad to hear it."

"Reliance will be glad to have him back home. But how will they manage without you?"

He did not tell her that Reliance would soon be leaving.

"Your husband will easily find a new, and much younger, servant. Indentured men are arriving every week in Boston."

"Any way, William, who's to say you will not be back there in a few days' time? You may well be given a much lesser punishment than I."

"What about you, lady?" William said.

"I shall hang in the morning."

Although he was not surprised by her words, he knew no way to respond to them. He was silent. He remembered the time she had embraced him at the board, after dinner. He would like to return her embrace now, but he could not. His arms were tied.

In his silence she felt his desire to comfort her.

"We shall spend these, my last living hours, together, William. Had I a lamp and my cards I would read to you your future."

"May be better you do not, in case there is none of that either."

She ignored his pessimism.

"Or, had I a book...a great book of diverting stories, I would read to you, and we could forget ourselves," she said.

"Lady, of stories I have a great many inside my head, as I am sure you do, too. And we need no lamp to read them with."

"Stay close to me, William. You are warm. Let us sit down against the wall," she said.

With some difficulty they sat, he one step below her, their bodies so close that her hurt shoulder was pressed against his hip.

She leaned her head upon his arm, and after some moments, perhaps because they were engulfed in darkness, she spoke boldly, saying,

"Have you never had a dear friend, William? Someone you loved in body and soul?"

William thought of Saint Barthes. Did he dare speak of the friendship he had shared with this man to Master Gilbert's wife?

"Lydia, you know I have never married because I did not ever feel the need for it."

"Because you prefer those of your same sex," she said, without moving or stiffening, or seeming to pass any negative judgment upon him.

He was surprised by the ease of her words, and it gave him courage to tell her more.

"In my youth I had a young woman, but it was an unsatisfying relation and caused me to suffer loneliness so I soon quit her."

Lydia made no comment, but he felt her willing for more, so he continued.

"I had reached the age of sixty-three years without having consummate relations with a woman, and I had not desire for it."

"William, what is your age now?"

"Sixty-seven, lady. Aged!"

"Ageless!" she said.

"Tell me about your men friends."

"Not in the plural, Lydia. There was a French fellow. He was the first, and, although there were a few others after, I think he was the only true one."

"Tell me about him. Tell me your story, William."

"Very well. Let's think. I met him after Yule in 1651. I had gone on foot to Hartford, before dawn. The sky was clear and there was about an inch of snow on the ground.

"Your husband was away for business, and he had offered me the use of Talevent, but I preferred to walk. I liked to watch the sun rise on the right on my way, and to see it go down again on my right when I returned.

"In the pockets of my great coat, you know, I always carried with me two baked potatoes to keep my hands warm, and then I ate them when I arrived in Hartford.

"I went to procure some items for you, I don't recall what, perhaps sealing wax and a packet of needles. These tasks complete, I went about finding acquaintances to parley with, and, at midday, I dined with two fellows at White's Ordinary."

"Are there many taverns in Hartford?"

"There's White's, and there is Greenleaf's. And there is Ruggles."

"Have you been to all of them, William?"

"Only White's and Greenleaf's. But my preference is for White's."

Lydia remembered what Elizabeth Wescott had testified under oath —that her son had seen William going into White's with a lynx, and the place was frequented by devils and witches.

"What about Ruggles?" she said.

"Never been there. It's on the other side of town. Mostly for Dutchmen."

"Go on with the story, William. Sorry."

"White's was crowded that day and my companions and I found our places at a table near the hearth next to some French seamen. They were dressed in uniforms, and were officers of high rank. They were four older men like myself. I sat beside the one to whom the others were in charge."

"Tell me about their uniforms. Are they grey? And with golden epaulets?"

"No, they are blue. The epaulets, red. And with gold colored fringe."

"Singlet or doublet?"

"Doublet, I believe. Buttons of brass."

"How lovely! Do continue."

"I sat down beside the Frenchman, and he turned to me and said,

"Good day, and bienvenu, monsieur. I am Lieutenant Jacques Saint Barthes of the fifth Maritime division of the French Naval Militia."

"I looked him over carefully. His fingernails were well trimmed. I took his hand in my own and I said,

"Good Day. I am William Farnsworth from Windsor.

"He and his men had all most finished their stew, but I thought they would stay on afterwards to smoke, or drink."

"What was the stew they were eating?" Lydia asked.

"I do not remember," William said.

"Ah, yes, I think it was of venison, with lardoons and turnips.

"He had finished eating, and he fixed his attention upon me, and, while I waited for my own dish to come, we conversed. Sometimes he stumbled in his speech, or was at wont for a word or phrase. For this he used his hands to much advantage."

"His hands with the clean fingernails. Were they fine hands, or gross?"

"His hands were those of a very fine gentleman, and calculating in their movements, like a clockmaker's.

"He kept his eyes upon me whilst I spoke, but I noticed that they roved about the room whilst he himself spoke. Sometimes he stopped in mid phrase and looked at me with a nakedness that made the blood rush to my face."

William paused for a moment. Had he spoken indelicately?

Lydia bent her knees up close to her chest and leant them against William's hip.

He went on,

"The food, the venison and roots, tasted good, but my attention was not on it. Did my companions remain with me? I know not. Nor do I remember who else was at White's that midday. The Frenchman told me he was from Lille, and had been in the Navy since the age of fourteen. He spoke of a wife in France, and of two grown children and many grandchildren.

"Midday passed into afternoon. We smoked a pipe, drank of ale, and talked. The way he pronounced words was foreign, but not unpleasant.

"Being with him that day I had a strange sensation. It was as if, until that time, I'd taken my breaths through a piece of straw, and then, of a sudden, my mouth and nose were open wide and I was inhaling barrels full of air."

He paused, remembering the feeling.

Lydia caught her breath. Was she crying? No.

"My companions grew impatient and wanted to leave. St. Barthes and I agreed upon another meeting for the following week.

"For six and one half days I tended the animals, the house, the fields, and carried out all of my duties as usual, but, at night, when I lay my old body down to sleep the long years of work and toil fell away, and I was filled with expectation for what was to come."

He was speaking to her more heartfully than he had ever done before. It was as if he were talking to himself, but aloud.

He could hear her breathing beside him, deep and measured. She was waiting for more.

"When Monday arrived, I left the house before dawn. The sky was clouded, but the moon, near its fullest, could be seen in the northwestern sky before me as I trod on. Twas cold and I feared there would be snow, and the flurries started as I was entering town.

"The weather grew worse and the snow fell steadily, I quickly finished my commissions and went to White's, though twas only half past ten by the church tower bells. Ordinary service had not begun, but the keeper's boy brought me bread and sausage, which I ate by the hearth in the empty room. Each time I heard the floorboards creak I looked to see if it was St. Barthes, but he did not come.

"Through the tavern glass I saw the snow piling higher on the road and on the roofs, and I could not wait there any longer. I left word with the boy to inform the Frenchman to remand our meeting for the following week.

"Shortly past the hour of eleven. I put my greatcoat and hat on, and left the Ordinary for home.

"All the way the snow continued to fall. By the time I reached home it was as high as my knee and coming down faster.

"All that night snow fell. It kept on through the next day and night, and until the morning of the third day. Do you remember that storm?"

"Yes," Lydia said.

"The snow got so deep that, had you not shoveled around the house and barn doors continuously, we would not have been able get out, and the animals would have starved. I was worried about Thomas. He was in Mystic."

"And when he returned he said the worst of the storm had not reached Mystic, as I recall."

"Go on, William," Lydia said.

"After the storm ended, you probably remember that the weather became much colder. The deep snow stayed, and I could manage only the necessary chores of feeding the beasts, and milking the cows. I brought buckets of snow to melt by the hearth, and uncovered wood from the pile to burn. Other than these things there was nothing to do, and we all stayed indoors by the hearth, for the better part of a week.

"By the next Monday the air was less chilling but more snow fell, so I went no where. For one thing or another I was not able to get to Hartford again for several more weeks, until Shrovetide."

"Thomas returned then, too," Lydia said.

She pressed the side of her face closer into William's strong arm.

"By then my memory of the Frenchman had become like a dream. I remembered his essence, but could not recall a single particular. I did not think I would see him again.

"I went about my duties that morning in Hartford, and met again with companions I had not seen for over a month. The roads and trails were muddy, and all looked gray, but I was glad to be out of doors again and in divers company.

"At noon I went to White's Ordinary for dinner, and without forethought, I saw, sitting at the table near the hearth with some of his men, St. Barthes.

"My limbs, trunk, and face grew warm and red from the heat in the room when he turned and looked at me. He gestured to me for me and my fellows to join his party.

"When I sat by him I felt as a young boy with his father, or of something else I could not name.

"Since our first meeting it seemed mere minutes had passed, and the time we spent together that day in the ordinary stayed in my mind for long after. We conversed—he of his recent voyages, and I of my daily life in Windsor. He was unlike any man I had known previous.

"I stayed on until afternoon, and before I left, we made an appointment to meet again."

Lydia shifted her face against William's arm.

"You only conversed!"

"The first times, yes," William said.

He was unsure how much detail of his relation with Saint Barthes he should tell her. He only wished not to cause her consternation, but to provide her with a pleasant entertainment in telling her this episode which he had never before told to anyone.

"But there was sentiment between you and he."

"Yes. Much."

"Did you never wish to embrace, or to kiss him?"

"Yes, lady," William said.

"But it came as a surprise to me, for I had never wished it with anyone before, and neither did I need to wish it between the Frenchman and myself. It happened quite naturally."

William thought back to that day, seeing in the dark before him the details of expression on Saint Barthes' face, as if he were there in the jail with him, illuminated by sunlight.

"That was a splendid day!" William said.

He smiled as he spoke, and Lydia could hear the smile in his voice, and it made her feel glad.

"Spring was ready on the breeze—I could smell it coming in," he said.

"We met on the green—he was waiting for me. He linked his elbow into mine and we walked together, conversing like two brothers separated for many years.

"The sun on my bare head was warm and the town, from the other side of the green, looked small and far away. It seemed we were players in a different world altogether.

"And then something caused me to act as I had never done previous."

William paused for a moment, waiting for some sign from Lydia that he should go on.

"What?" she whispered eagerly.

William had his eyes closed and was reliving the scene as he spoke.

"I turned to him, and placed my hands on his shoulders. We had stopped walking. I drew him closer to me. We stood face to face. I felt his breath on my skin. It was scented with fennel.

"Without considering what I was doing, I kissed him full on the mouth.

"He held my body to his own, and when the kiss had finished I knew that would not be the only expression of our sentiment."

Lydia was silent. She would like to have known what were the other expressions of their sentiment, but she dared not ask William such an indelicate question.

William wondered if his words had been worrisome to her. Perhaps he should not have told her about the kiss.

"After that first time St. Barthes and I met regularly for the better part of the year, whenever on my weekly jaunts to Hartford, he too happened to be there."

"And then what?" Lydia asked.

"Did he return to his wife in France?"

"Oh, no. I don't think so. No. I think he returned to his maker. In October of that year his ship was lost at sea. I saw him no more. Otherwise, I believe our meetings would be going on still."

"Perhaps his ship was taken by pirates," Lydia said.

"And he joined ranks with them."

"Perhaps," William said.

"But in any case I know I shall not see him again."

"You loved him well," she said.

"Indeed," said he.

They sat together in silence for some long minutes.

When Lydia began again to notice the stench of excrement all around her, and to think on the horrible thing that awaited her the next morning, she spoke, saying,

"William, that was a beautiful story, but I didn't much like the ending. Have you no other story to tell me, one that ends well?"

He thought for a while. He sensed her desperation, and did not want to leave her too long in silence.

"Yes, here's one.

"I told you that I once had a lady friend, many years ago. Twas when I was young—nineteen years of age or so. Her name was Joan Chesley. She was a neighbor's daughter, back in Whitechapel. She said she had fancied me for years before she was courageous enough to speak to me.

"Every day I passed by her house on my way to work, and again on my way back home."

"For my husband?" Lydia asked.

"Your husband was only an infant then, and we hadn't yet met. It was when I was working as a tavern servant."

"And you lived with your family in Whitechapel."

"No, it was after the Great Plague. My family was dead, and I had found work as a tavern servant."

"Go on," Lydia said.

"Joan Chesley lived with her mother and sisters in a hovel nearby. She was a few years my elder, a spinster.

"One day on my way to the tavern she walked along with me, and invited me for dinner at her home the following Sunday.

"I accepted the invitation gladly, and looked forward to it all week. My life at that time was made up only of long hard workdays and long lonely Sundays.

"What did she look like, this Joan? Was she pretty?" Lydia asked.

William was silent a moment, thinking back.

"Yes. I suppose she was pretty."

"Was she stout or thin? Light or dark?"

"About your height, Lydia, but with rather more meat on her bones. Her hair was brown, I believe."

"Like mine...was?"

"Darker, almost black."

"Was she sallow, or ruddy, or pale?"

In his mind, the picture William had of Joan Chesley was indefinite. He had not thought of her much over the many passing years, but when he did, he thought of her as a female presence more than as an individual.

"Her skin was white as milk," he invented.

"And her eyes were green and merry. She had a sprightly smile and a dimple in one cheek, and a marvelous gladsome laugh. Her hands were fine, and she worked as an embroiderer.

"She had had many admirers, but none of them had struck her fancy.

"All the rest of that week, she accompanied me on my walk to the tavern in the morning, talking and laughing, and keeping me company. In her I believed I had found a friend, and, when Sunday finally arrived, I put on a clean blouse, and presented myself at her family's hovel at noon.

"Joan and her two sisters and their mother made quite a fuss over me. Her father had died in the plague, and neither of the younger sisters had yet a suitor, so they were welcoming of male company."

"What were the sisters' names? Do you remember?"

He did not. In truth he was not sure if there had been two of them or three. But he said,

"Mary. And Catherine. And the mother was called Magdalen.

"They had prepared a grand dinner. There were two roast ducks, and carrots, and bitter greens. There was sack to drink, and apricocks. I was embarrassed at first by so much fine food, but the mother—Magdalen—must have seen my embarrassment, and she told me that her brother had come down from the north country with a brace of ducks he had shot, and given her these two.

"Because of my work I was fortunate, in that I always had good left over food to eat. But I knew that most of my neighbors were lucky if they ever ate anything but porridge most of the year."

"You met her in the fall," Lydia said.

"Yes. Twas the end of October, 1606.

"The family was kind and very pleasant to be with, and, after that first dinner, they invited me back every Sunday. We ate like kings in that hovel, and the sisters were plump and merry. My employer usually gifted me something on Saturday nights—a piece of bacon, or some extra turnips, or, on more than one occasion a pineapple—and I brought these along to the Chesleys. They almost always had game or wild birds from the uncle, and I wondered why they did not also go to the north country to live, since he must have been very fond of his sister to make these frequent visits. Magdalen said she had always lived in her hovel and was comfortable there. She said she would just as soon move to the New World as to the north country.

"Joan continued walking with me to work each morning during the week, and it wasn't long before I realized that neighbors and other people noticed us, and thought we were betrothed!

"I began to think that Joan, too, considered me to be her future spouse. I knew this was the proper way these sort of things happened, yet there was something not right, and I knew not what. For I found pleasure in her company and considered her a dear friend, but when she put her hand in mine, after dinner when we all sat together at the little table in that hovel, I thought I could never give her more than simple friendship, more like a brother than a husband.

"The autumn turned into winter, and the days were short and dark and miserably damp cold. A sadness came over me, and, although I continued walking with Joan in the mornings, and going to her house on Sundays, there was no longer any joy in it for me. Joan sensed this and grew worrisome, which irritated me, for I could not explain to her the reasons for my sadness, as I myself knew them not."

"As Yule approached I left earlier in the morning, and walked a

different way, so I would not pass by Joan's house. I made excuses not
to come for Sunday dinners, two or three times, and then she invited
me no more.

"The few times I saw her after that, or her sisters or mother, they
pretended not to see me, and I likewise them.

"I sought employment in the countryside, and was assumed by
Master Gilbert's cousin, who owned a great deal of land and an estate. I
started as a servant, but soon became their jack-of-all-trades. To
Whitechapel I returned very infrequently—perhaps once or twice in a
year. I lost track of Joan Chesley and her family for many years."

"This is a sad tale, William. Joan truly loved you. Was not her
friendship with you important?" Lydia said.

She lifted her head from his arm.

He could not see her, and he imagined her as she had always been
—with thick hair, and intelligent eyes, her body finely made but not
skeletal.

For her part, she was glad he had not borne witness to the
Searcher's public assault upon her body.

"I was greatly saddened, and became quite solitary. Twas useless
for me to lead her along in a way that could never end where she was
headed. These were sentiments I could not understand in myself at the
time, but, looking back upon it now, I acted judiciously."

"And you know not whatever became of her?"

"I do know," said William.

"I shall tell you now.

"Some years afterward, perhaps three or maybe four, I went back
to Whitechapel, and there in the marketplace I met again her mother
Magdalen.

"She was finely dressed, and was purchasing oysters from the
fishmonger. I saw her from far off, and deliberately walked toward her,
watching her. I thought that, as I got close, if she were to see me she
would pretend she had not, and I, too, would avert my gaze from her.

To my surprise, when she looked over and saw me she smiled, and, having finished her transactions with the fishmonger, approached me.

"William!" she said.

"Upon her ears she wore sparkling jewels, and these lit up her face like a star. I could hardly believe how lovely she had become, for rather than ageing, she seemed to have become more youthful."

William was silent a moment. Then he went on.

"She greeted me warmly. I asked her about Joan, and she told me that, shortly after I had left for the countryside, Joan had been assumed by the Guild of Royal Embroiderers. It was through her fine handiwork that, according to Magdalen, Joan met a lord, who took a great fancy to her. This Lord eventually married her. Joan Chesley became a fine lady living on an estate north of London. One of her sisters went to live with her, but the younger sister and the mother stayed in their hovel, although they were, by then, very well-off, and could afford to eat well every day of the week."

"Did she love the lord, or was it a marriage of convenience?" Lydia asked.

"Her mother said she loved him. She had already one infant, and was expecting another. Only later on, it occurred to me that this Lord must be the same person as the uncle from the north country."

"She had put him off, for you."

"I think not, lady. I think he bought her."

"Then she loved him not. But perhaps, with time, she learned to. What is love, anyway?"

William was silent.

"Did you never see her again?" Lydia asked.

"Never. Twas not many years after that I went to work for Master Thomas. And then, as you know, I came indentured to him at the same time you did."

"Well, I am glad Joan Chesley found a way to feed herself and her family so well," Lydia said.

"But certainly she has not forgotten you even now."

"As neither I have forgotten her," William said.

"Sometimes tis the memory of a person that lives on longer than his physical presence in another's life."

"Do you believe my soul will go to hell?" Lydia asked him.

He thought about this for some time. Several minutes passed. He was unsure what she wanted to hear, and he knew not how to answer. Finally he said,

"Your soul will be set free."

CHAPTER THIRTY

LYDIA AND WILLIAM both heard the drumbeats coming from the meetinghouse's empty bell tower, marking the hour as eight.

Since she had been brought back to the jail past six o'clock, Lydia knew she had missed the evening's stale loaf and water, and would not eat again until morning, if then. But she wished not to think of the morning.

"Are you hungry?" she asked William.

"Not much," he said.

She knew this could not be true, for he was a big man and hardworking, and had probably only had some bread and cheese for noon dinner.

"They threw me a stale loaf of bread before they brought you back in," he said.

"But you have not eaten."

"Sarah brought me a splendid mitchin at noon. I am still satisfied from it."

They were quiet for a few minutes, and then Lydia said,

"I will tell you about her wedding, since you were not present."

"I will listen gladly," said he.

"Do you remember—she was married at noon in the month of May. The sweet locust trees were in bloom, and their white blossoms, under the warm sun as we passed through the woods on the way to town, emanated such a perfume that it made all of us pleasantly light headed and excited.

"Thomas rode Talevent, with Sarah. She was dressed in a new periwinkle blue bodice and skirt she and I had sewn, and rode pillion behind him. The tips of her shoes were polished with beeswax, and they shone from under an edge of crocheted lace on her petticoat, at the hem of her skirt. She wore a new straw bonnet decorated with white and pink ribbands.

"I thought she looked very pretty but a little bit sad. Maybe this was because she would be leaving her childhood behind. I knew not the reason for she has never confided in me as Elizabeth or Judith Stiles' daughter Mercy do.

"I rode Aisley, while Elizabeth and Reliance walked.

"We all wanted you to come, but you stayed behind at home, for you said you had much work to do in that season."

"Well, and I have never liked weddings much," said William.

"Then shall I not recount it?" Lydia said.

"I do like to hear you recite. And please tell me about Sarah's wedding. I should have gone."

"Nicholas Carver…" Lydia started, but her voice broke.

She turned her face into William's sleeve, and breathed deeply.

Then she began again.

"He had come to our holdings the day previous with his wagon and ponies, and he and Thomas had loaded the trunk on, the same one I'd brought with me from England so many years before. It was filled with Sarah's personal belongings, and the bed linens and quilts we'd made for her over the last few years. He had brought the trunk to his abode in town, where the two of them would be living henceforth. You have never been there, but his house is well furnished, and includes a small barn for his horses. He has many cooking implements and trenchers and spoons that he brought with him from England, and now he also has a wife to make use of these things, for previously, and like many single men, he was in the habit of taking all of his meals at the Ordinary.

"He told me before he married Sarah that he had had Judith Stiles' Mohegan girl come to sweep and dust his house once each week, but as a married man he would have no more need of her.

"Thomas thought that Sarah had made a fine match with Surgeon Carver. I was unsure. I could not sense deep love between them. I knew that Sarah was ready to start her own family. And I told myself then that sometimes tis better that a marriage be not too fraught with emotion, for so being can make daily life less placid. I thought she would learn to love him.

"For my part it was not that way. I was twenty two years old when I met Thomas, and when I met you, as well, William. From the start I had great respect for him. Respect is a strange feeling when accompanied by love. I think there is a measure of fear in it. Perhaps because he was seven years older than I, when I understood, by his looks and words, his love for me, I was thrilled but fearful as well, for I saw him as a great and important man and myself as little more than a girl.

"You were so kind and gentle," William said.

"Master Thomas was smitten by you."

"Had he other ladies before me?"

"There were two or three, chosen for him by his mother. He didn't care much for any of them. He was involved with his studies, and then started in the shipping business. He had little time to waste on idle courting for sport."

"But he found time to court me," Lydia said.

"Our courtship only lasted a few months. I wasn't surprised as he told me in the spring that he would be leaving with Reverend Warham's group in June, to voyage to the New World. How excited I was! Rebecca had already told me she would be marrying her suitor, Michael Trye, and leaving with Warham's group. I was so thrilled when he asked me would I come with him as his wife!"

William listened to the sound of Lydia's voice in the dark. He knew she was reliving her memories of more than twenty years ago. Her voice had not changed, and he imagined her now as she had been then.

"My sister and I were married to our husbands the same day, and five days afterward we set sail for Boston.

"I was not prepared for such a long voyage. I had been so excited by the whole idea of it that I had not given any thought to the duration of the trip. That voyage lasted two months. By the end of it I wanted nothing more to do with ships. We were fortunate, though, weren't we, that it was smooth sailing overall and without incident. The crowded conditions on board were neither as clean nor as private as I would have wished, although I am certain that where you slept, twas worse. Nevertheless both Rebecca and I were got with child before we arrived in the new land.

"Rebecca and Michael settled in Boston, where he had already a cousin and a position as Statesman. We all stayed on for some days with them, you remember. Thomas had planned to go on to Dorchester, Connecticut. He said it was a new village, and in need of another magistrate. I imagined it would be all new like Boston, but lacking the port, for I had no other idea. He bought the horses—Paisley and Uncle Mac. We rode along with the post rider all that long journey from Boston to Dorchester. It seemed unending. I was suffering from unwellness in my stomach because of the child, twas August by then. I rode pillion behind Thomas, and you made that journey on foot, Uncle Mac carried our belongings, I did not much enjoy this part of the journey. I had been told by people whom we met in Boston of the savage indigenous tribes, and of vicious wild animals—lynx and wolves and bears, and I was rather fearful. Truthfully, as we passed by a good many large groupings of Pequot, and sometimes scattered individuals walking along the way, and they never gave us any trouble, but seemed to be peaceful and with a great deal of knowledge concerning living well in such a vast and uncivilized land, I wondered why people believed them to be savage."

"There had been some trouble previously," William said.

"Over territory."

"At the time I did not know about that. I only saw that they were peaceful, and in good health."

"Then when we finally arrived at this outpost town called Dorchester, now Windsor, I was glad to be done traveling, but dismayed to see that it was nothing like Boston."

"There was not much here then," William said.

"Just a few thatched roof houses, and the old meeting house."

"And we stayed at first with Reverend Stiles and Judith. Judith Stiles is a few years older than myself but she was still childless then. I took an immediate liking to her, and it pleased me much to have found a friend so soon in this place.

"We stayed with the Stiles several months. You were there at the start, too, but then you started staying out at the holdings. once you had the barn built.

"Finally, by the following spring, you and Thomas and a few other good men had put the roof on our house. Thomas brought me to see it for the first time and I was astounded by the amount of acreage. There was so much wilderness all around the house. Thomas told me he had purchased ten acres of land holdings. When we moved in to the new house I was very full and near my time of deliverance.

"After not even two weeks there my pains began one morning. I was alone, for Thomas had so much work to do, and was looking at ships to buy, and was often away over night. I knew not what to do.

"Then you went for Katherine Harris, the old midwife. If you hadn't been there I would have had to do it alone, and that is not always easy, especially the first time, when one has no prior experience."

"I am sure you would have been fine," William said.

"It was a great comfort to have midwife Harris with me. And your presence has always brought me solace."

She turned her face and pressed it into his arm.

He said nothing, but she felt his kindheartedness, as if he were gently stroking her nonexistent hair, in the darkness.

"I was safely delivered of my daughter Sarah before evening fell.

The very next day, the twenty-first of April, Judith Stiles came to pay me a visit, and brought with her a letter from Rebecca, telling the glad news that my sister had, seven days previous, brought an infant boy into the world. She had named him Elliot in memory of our deceased father.

"And now Sarah is twenty two years old herself. So many years have passed by, William. All the times I made the same trip into town, whether on horseback or on foot, so many times, and each time I traveled through the same woods and along the same edge of White's field and followed the same Pequot trails along the brook, my eyes always saw something new. It hardly seems so many years could have passed since the birth of my first child.

"And we traveled again that same way to bring Sarah into town for her wedding to Nicholas Carver. She had grown into a woman. Where did those years go?

"Sometimes when I think back on the past it is as real to me as the present moment. I cannot believe that time is a natural element, but only an invention of man to measure what resists measurement. Twould be akin to trying to measure a bird's song."

"I hear there is such an instrument," William said.

"Oh? What's the name of it?"

It took a few moments for William to reply.

"A cantascope, I believe."

She knew by the tone of his voice that he was jesting.

"I'll resume telling you about Sarah's wedding.

"We arrived into town and made our way, at a walk, to the meeting house."

"Was it the new one yet?"

"Yes, it had just been finished, a few months before.

"I believe that all the towns' people were present. Most of them were already seated or standing inside, though there were a number of boy children playing in the street under the watchful eyes of six or seven men, who were, in the meantime, entertaining themselves with a smoking pipe and conversation and such.

"It was crowded, but not as crowded as it was today! And, of course the atmosphere was divers. There was an air of happy excitement, and everyone was on their best behavior. Windsor has had its share of weddings, but these are so often unions of desperation between widows and widowers or old bachelors and girls already with child, and are usually performed by the Magistrate rather than the Reverend.

"I was so pleased with Sarah. I was proud, too, to be her mother. She carried herself well, and no one could find fault with her.

"Inside the meeting house Reliance and I took our places on the left side at the front. Thomas walked with Sarah to the altar where Reverend Stiles was standing, and Elizabeth, who was testimony for her sister, came behind her."

"I remember nothing of your wedding to Master Thomas. Was I present?" William said.

"No. You weren't there. Thomas and I, and likewise Rebecca and Michael Trye, were not married in a public ceremony, as Sarah and Nicholas were. Since we adhered not to the principles of the Church of England, we could not be married in church. Twas Reverend Warham who performed the ceremony secretly. He held the Bible in his two hands, in the house of my brother in law in Yardley."

"The Bible," William said.

Lydia did not know how to take William's comment. They had never discussed matters of the spirit, and she did not know his beliefs.

"I give not much credence to such things," she said.

"Having spent my earliest years in my father the Printer's shop. A book is not a magical thing in itself—tis only the words therein that can have an effect on a man. And then only if he knows how to read and to reason. The power resides not in the object of a book, but in a man's mind, and following that, the actions of a man. Perhaps tis fear of the mindful power we possess that makes men want to put this power into objects such as books, or into animals or invented creatures."

"Well put," William said.

"Where was I? Sarah's wedding to…him."

"The double-crosser," William said.

Lydia laughed lowly.

"My thoughts wandered as Reverend Stiles performed the matrimonial service. I contemplated the dinner we would soon be enjoying at the Stiles' house, for Elizabeth and I had helped in its preparation the day previous, and there were many good dishes and I was hungry.

"In anticipation of this meal, and especially thinking on the escalloped oysters and the warm salt risen bread, I smiled and tenderly embraced my double-crossing son-in-law. I gave him and my daughter my blessing for a fruitful marriage.

"At dinner there were my daughters and my husband, and the double crosser,"

"Judas!" William said.

"Ha! There was Judas, and his brother Amos, and the Reverend and Judith Stiles and their daughter Mercy, and the Reverend's cousin."

"The Reverend's cousin?" William said.

"James Stiles," Lydia spat.

"The venomous malignancy," William said.

Lydia had never heard him use such words, and was shocked. Calling names like these could earn a person time in the stocks, or in jail. But, after all, they were only words.

"Well, we had placed a cloth on the large board, and the Stiles had many chairs. I was seated between Thomas and the Reverend, with James—the venomous malignancy—facing me. Of this arrangement I was not very pleased, for I knew even then that he held a grudge against me, and believed me to have been responsible for Henry's demise. But since we were seated such and I desired not to be, nor to cause others to be, uncomfortable, I regarded him anew, and hoped that he would do the same toward me.

"In fact, he conversed finely, entertaining us at table with a tale of some Massachusetts Wampanoags who captured a whale from a dugout canoe. He told us, although he had not born witness to this particular event, that he had seen with his own eyes the skillful way these Indians used the harpoon, and they were indeed known to be excellent whalers.

"For some moments I much enjoyed imagining the Indians in their ocean going canoe and the enormity of the whale beside them. I was lost in this delightful vision as Thomas spoke at some length of the great whale migrations along the coast from the Maine territory to Rhode Island.

"We ate of the various dishes. And then James—the malignant venom—spoke again, and his words were not welcome ones.

"Whilst looking directly at me, he said, "If my brother Henry were alive, and with us here today, I would call on him to write these tales down with ink on parchment, and we could make a book of them."

"Shortly after Henry's death, Judith Stiles had informed me that his brother blamed me for it. At the time I had forgiven him, thinking his confusion in reasoning was due to wrongly placed grief. If he now still held to this erratic conviction, then there must be some deeper motive for it, but at that time I knew not what.

"Alas," said he, still not taking his eyes off me.

"Henry was the victim of a maliciously directed happenstance by someone seated now at this board."

"I could hardly understand the meaning behind his words. The case was closed, and Tommy Allyn's father had paid the penalty. The only thing that was clear to me was that he wished to destroy the happy sentiment of the occasion. And I thought he would certainly do it if he continued in such a tone. But, as he had made an accusation, I felt I must defend myself. I was about to speak, when Thomas said,

"Let bygones be bygones, Stiles. We all deeply regret the incident that took your brother's life, but let us not now dwell on sad memories, but rather enjoy the felicitude of the present."

"Aye," spoke the Reverend, lifting his glass.

"I was relieved that my husband had spoken for me, and that our dinner could continue pleasingly. But because the subject of Henry Stiles' accident had been brought up again, my mind again conjured memories of that unfortunate event, and this was a damper to my mood.

"After we'd finished eating and drinking our fill, and the men had gone to the other room to smoke, and we had put away and cleaned what needed cleaning, Reliance and Elizabeth took Aisley and rode home. We had left you alone with the animals to care for and there was the water to fetch.

"Thomas and I stayed a while longer. I conversed with Judith outside in the sunshine by the stable, whilst on the wood hewn step Sarah sat and let young Mercy take down her hair and comb it with a horn comb, and rub some oil into it until it shone like golden hay under the sun.

"Judith told me of a foreign man she and her husband had visited while they had been in London. This man kept a monkey in his house. She said it resembled in some ways a small man and in some ways a squirrel. She told how the animal climbed upon the cupboards and broke many pottery dishes and some fine glassware whilst she was there, and terrified her with its high pitched screaming and chattering noises, and she could not imagine why the gentleman, who was from the continent of India, would keep such a creature inside his house. She said he also smoked sweet smelling herbs and seeds from a large decorated pipe that sat on the table like a vase, and could be smoked by two or three people at the same time, but neither she nor her husband had tried it.

"Before taking our leave of the Stiles' house, Mercy served to us rum punch and banbury cakes she had made, and sugared ginger, and then it was time to accompany the newly married couple back to Nic— the traitor's—house.

"The poisonous canker!" said William.

"Thomas and I walked with them the short distance over to the next lane, and then we each embraced our daughter and the venomous traitor good evening. By that time the sun was very low, so we returned to the Stiles' barn for Talevent and started towards home."

Lydia's voice had begun trailing off at times in the middle of sentences, and William knew she must be very tired. He heard her breathing become deeper. He thought she had fallen asleep.

And then she said,

"Thomas's jerkin smelled of tobacco and wood smoke... his hair used to be brown, but now tis grey and smells of bayberry soap... he washed himself with it I made it for him. The evening was chilling. My body was close to his and I wrapped my arms around him...and I leant the side of my face against his strong shoulder."

She snuggled closer to William's arm. She was quiet. Then he heard her snore, once, and she woke up again.

"Talevent is walking fast down hill towards the brook, to the west the sky is colored in stripes of many hues, and across this flagrant background, there flies a flock of geese...they are returning from their winter homes, to the northern provinces, the north country. They are honking and honking, like a flock of sheep. But the geese have no need of a shepherd nor money, they trade off amongst themselves to lead the group. Each bird is a leader, they all know the flock's destination,each takes a share of the blunt wind, and does his part to bring the whole group home safely."

"Are you chilly, Lydia?" William asked her.

"Thomas asked me if I were chilly," she spoke, as if in a trance.

"Your beard is regrowing, Thomas.

"Kiss my hand, one tip at a time. I fed him honey on my fingers. I put my hands into his pockets. Into his breech pockets. And now I must sleep."

Lydia's eyes had been closed for a while, as she saw again her memories of happier times. Now, as she drifted into sleep, she felt herself being carried along on the back of Thomas's horse. She let the movement carry her along like a child, safe on the back of a strong animal and against the back of a great man. It brought her an immense sensation of warmth and security to be led forward in time thus.

CHAPTER THIRTY-ONE

WILLIAM WAS THINKING of Reliance, of the secret work she had done for Deggory Phillips, and of her going to teach at the college in New Haven. He wondered if he should tell Lydia of these things. He had promised Reliance he would tell no one of her work for Phillips, but Lydia was her own mother, and she had not now long to live.

He wondered if Lydia's knowing that Reliance had done transcriptions for magistrates and governors, in the name of her old tutor, would bring peace or gladness to her heart. He did not know. He could not tell her of Reliance's position at the college if he did not first tell her of the transcriptions. And perhaps she would rather not know of that stealthy work, for she might then wonder, as he already did, if Reliance had not known something beforehand of Allyn's methods to secure the Governorship of the colony for himself. There was turpitude in the girl's reserve.

He would think on it overnight. Perhaps he would tell Lydia at least a part of it in the morning.

Lydia was dreaming that Allyn, still a magistrate, came home late with Thomas. It was after dark, and, not having supped, Thomas asked Lydia to lay the table for them and bring them food to eat.

Sarah was there, and she lay the table while the men removed their hats, cloaks and gloves, and then warmed themselves standing by the fire. She noticed something different about Magistrate Allyn, and when he opened his mouth to say something to Thomas, she saw that he had no teeth.

She asked them if their horses had been seen to, and Thomas replied that William had brought Talevent to the barn, but that

Magistrate Allyn had no horse—he had ridden pilion behind, like a lady.

She was worried about a book. She did not want Magistrate Allyn to see it, for she was afraid he would steal it. When she thought he was not looking, she picked the book up from the sideboard, thinking she would hide it under the Bible. It was

a beautiful crimson leather bound book, tooled in gold foil, called "Discourse on Method", written by the heretical author Descartes.

Sarah had brought out a cheese and bread, and tankards of ale, and two roast ducks and placed them on the board.

The men sat down to eat, and Lydia saw that she had left the book there, and that Magistrate Allyn had it in his two hands, and was spotting the crimson leather with his greasy fingerprints. Thomas noticed this but said nothing.

Lydia felt powerless and wished her husband would take the book from him.

Then Sarah appeared again, with a big bowl of salad. Elizabeth followed with a tureen of rich milky chowder. Lydia was hungry and wished to eat, but she was not allowed to sit at the table with the men. She could only watch, mutely, as they ate.

The men spoke at great length of the weather, tobacco, and Stuyvesant, who had ceded most of his lands at the House of Hope, renaming Manhatten Island New Amsterdam. All the time they spoke, Magistrate Allyn was eating and eating. She heard the sound of him crunching the duck's bones in jaws, and saw that, when he opened his toothless mouth to put in more food, he had fierce molars and canine teeth like a marten. She heard also the sound of his spoon scraping against the side of the pewter tureen, there was no more chowder in it, he was eating all the food, and leaving her none.

Thomas asked for more ale and Sarah brought it. Their conversation was turning to Ludlow's Code of Laws. Sarah filled Master Allyn's tankard first, but as she did so she turned not her eyes toward his. He was gazing upon her throat and her lips. Lydia wanted to smite him a great blow, but she could not move from where she stood in the corner of the room.

Thomas lifted his tankard and said,

"To the continued health of Lydia and our daughters!"

"Aye!" Magistrate Allyn declared.

He lifted Descartes book high above his head and threw it into the fire.

And then Lydia was mixing a deck of cards. When she spread them face up upon the table she saw that these were strange cards indeed. Rather than pictures, or common symbols such as cups or hearts, each card was covered with illegible writing. There were no designs. The only way to read the writing was to look at the cards in reflection. Lydia tried to read them using her silver spoon as a mirror, but she could only make out some of the words.

"Knowledge and learning harm your way placing undesired restrictions upon you."

She read the words aloud but they made no sense. But this was what the card said, and so she thought it must be true. She lifted the next one, and looked at its reflection in the spoon and read as follows: "Strength leads to independence in a shrewd and well established man. Faulty judgment, or immoral actions overcome by creativity, will power and control. Lack of spiritual comfort."

When she finished reading this card Lydia saw that Reliance was sitting across the table from her.

Her daughter whispered, "That is your own spread, mother."

She could not decide whether to believe what the cards said.

She feared the cards said that Thomas would soon die, because of her immoral action.

She collected the cards from the table and gave them to Reliance, saying,

"You will need these more than I."

Reliance then threw the deck into the fire.

Lydia cried. She had brought the cards from England. They had belonged to her grandmother.

Then she heard again Magistrate Allyn's voice.

"It is forbidden in the Code of Laws to play cards, and games used for divining. This is a sign of witchcraft."

"Ludlow's code," she heard Thomas's voice through a closed door.

And Allyn's voice replied, "A pretty bosom, yet too saucy in her speech. But a woman can all ways be made silent by putting a rag in her mouth and a sack over her head,"

"I wouldn't be so certain," Thomas said.

Lydia was sitting in the high backed chair by the fire, but she was not warm enough. She drew her shawl around her and stared into the embers, and trembled with cold. She wanted to put on another log, but the wood was finished.

Lydia woke up in the dark, thinking at first that she was in her bed at home beside Thomas, and that she had better get another quilt.

She could not get up. Then she realized she was in jail, and it was William beside her. And she remembered that she was to be hung in the morning, in just a few hours.

She wanted to escape from this place, but she knew now that her only escape could be death.

And then she suddenly thought of Thomas's old dear friend James Higgins. He had died unexpectedly a few days before she'd been taken away to jail. A rushing of memories of him came pouring into her mind, and she was certain his spirit was with her now.

She remembered one evening when Thomas had returned home from town with him. It was dark, but not so late, and, while William took care of their horses in the stable, she'd made a good supper out of a big trout with pumpkin sauce and turnips and buns and conserve of sage, and gingerbread, and strong bitter ale to drink. And there was freshly churned butter, and a cheese, and macaroons, and dried apricocks.

James Higgins had been her husband's longest friend still living, as they had known each other since they were boys in England, and had remained close friends throughout their youth, sharing many ideas and passions, and both were of the Reverend Wareham's group. James had traveled with them to New England. She wondered if Thomas had heard of his death.

Lydia believed her husband and Mr. Higgins had shared some deep sameness that had not changed over time, for certainly their stations in life were different. James Higgins had suffered some misfortune upon his arrival in the colonies, and his young wife, Anne, who was with child during the voyage, took ill and soon died, along with the child she carried. James was sad and bereft for many months and it seemed to Lydia that he was all ways at her house, and some times she did not like him there. She thought he looked upon her as if she were his own wife in a different body, and he treated her newly born child as if it were his own. She thought that she needed not two husbands, for one was sometimes too many then. Lydia did not mention this sentiment to Thomas, for he felt sorry for his friend and tried to cheer him in the evenings with songs and gaming and drink.

James Higgins had never gotten over his love for his dead wife. Although he was handsome and kind, and had had several possibilities, he had never remarried. He was not voted to be a magistrate, but was instead a secretary at court, for he was a superior scribe, and he was patient, and listened well.

That evening, the last time he'd come as a visitor in their home, James Higgins had sat in Lydia's high backed chair, and Thomas in his usual one, and William and she had the low Brewster chairs, and the girls shared the wood bench. With the room lit by the great hearth and two betty lamps on the Welsh cabinet they were quite cosy, and did not feel the chill from outdoors, but ate their fill and were merry, and all seemed well then.

James Higgins had red hair and beard, and conversed freely, and

Lydia was glad to have him as a guest, as long as he was not in mourning for his wife.

Once they had finished the last of the gingerbread and the dried apricocks, William and the girls and Lydia cleared away the trenchers and everything except the men's two pewter tankards, and Lydia folded down the leaves of the drawing table and put another trunk on the fire. For now they would smoke a pipe and drink more ale, and speak of politics or whatever other subject they deemed important. William went to his room, and so did Elizabeth and Reliance. Lydia stayed up, seated by the hearth behind the door, in the small room, and would wait until James Higgins left before going to bed. She had taken up her knitting in the dim light next to the fading hearth.

She was tired, and a bit sleepy from a long day out of doors in the chill air, but she heard the men's words from the other room and they kept her awake. They were talking about Cromwell's Rump Parliament.

Thomas said, "Now I've heard that the Rumps are soon to be no more, for Cromwell has decided to dissolve his parliament. He managed to incorporate Scotland into the English Commonwealth, but the Irish have proved to be too feisty for Ironsides. Now he is planning an Act of Settlement, which will take most of the Irish lands away from the Irish."

"Oh?" said Master Higgins.

"And what do the Irish have to say about that?"

"No one is asking them, of course," Thomas said.

"Thousands of Irishmen have been forced to forfeit their lands and are then exiled out to armies in Poland, I've heard. They've had no say in the matter. Cromwell gives them a choice—to Connaught or to Hell, and if they won't choose either of these, it's to one of the Continental armies."

"Well, in the name of economic expansion, the Commonwealth will be more powerful with Scotland and Ireland adjoined, especially considering the force of England's naval power," said Master Higgins.

Thomas interrupted, "And Cromwell and the Adventurers will surely benefit economically—"

Said Master Higgins, "Cromwell needs to do something about settling the nation before expanding too far outward, though, or he risks collapse. Everything as it is remains undecided—is England going to be a republic? Or return to being a monarchy? Or, as some have suggested, a limited monarchy? And what is happening with the Fifth Monarchist Movement. Have you any word on this, Thomas?"

Lydia had listened only casually to the men's conversation, for politics was a subject that did not interest her greatly. She paid more heed to the relation between those involved in it.

"Ah, what rubbish!" Thomas had said.

"The Fifth Monarchist Movement hasn't any chance at all."

He was tamping the pipe.

"What's in it, Tom?"

"What? Oh, the radical lunatics, Simpson and Feake, who believe in violence for overthrowing everything as we knew it in England. Ironically, they think to be followers of the Biblical prophecy for the fifth kingdom of Christ, which can only occur after their "saints" have been in power for a thousand years. They are pressing for the "saints" to take over once the Rumps dissolve."

"What daftness!" James guffawed, and then Lydia heard him take a long draw from the clay pipe.

"Of course you've heard how Cromwell has outlawed Catholicism in Ireland?"

"Something. What's that about? Does he expect the entire world to adopt Puritanism?"

"It seems so, Higgins. He's made celebrating their Catholic Mass illegal and punishable by death. He's killing priests left and right, and those he does not kill are sent to prison camp on the Isle of Inisbofin, where they live on crumbs of bread and sea water, and are given forty lashes for worshipping their own catholic God."

"Frankly I'd like to see Ludlow in power together with Cromwell," James said.

"Notwithstanding his part in having the King beheaded, I find his idea of separation of church and state appealing."

"At least since the Uniformity Act, it would have seemed England was on the right path."

"Well, not if you stop to consider how the Rumps started out by enforcing strict observance of Sundays," James said.

"And the Adultery Act. And the Blasphemy Act."

There was a moment in which neither man spoke. Lydia heard them smoking, and one of them lifted his tankard and then put it down again.

"We're fortunate, anyway, in Connecticut, under our Fundamental Orders, that a man needn't obtain church membership in order to vote."

"'Tis true," James said, exhaling.

"At least theoretically."

In their silence Lydia could hear all of the things neither one of them dared say—how church membership and attendance ought to have naught to do with any matter besides one's individual spiritual beliefs, which can and do vary greatly from one Christian man to another, and that Quakers and Baptists should not be persecuted, and that, despite the colony's original purpose of being a place to worship freely and unfettered by any government tithe, Connecticut, and even more so, the Commonwealth of Massachusetts, was becoming more bound in unnecessary moral law than could have been foreseen by those who came before them, thirty years previous.

There were many ways in which the colonists paid no heed at all to the English Commonwealth and its laws—for if a Magistrate, highly positioned, were to break an English law, who would fine him or jail him or hang him? Many of England's laws were therefore disregarded by the most highly placed of the colonies' men, though enforced sometimes by those very same men upon citizens of lower social standing, for the sake of convenience. It was all together too easy, she had thought then, for this sort of thing to happen when there are dishonest and corrupt men amongst the good ones.

She remembered in strangely slow detail how she had turned her needle then to knit another row, and heard Thomas say to his friend almost those same words she had been thinking one moment previous.

"I won't name any names," said he, "But amongst the deputies and magistrates there are a good too many who should have remained in England, for it seems their only reason for being is to amass ever more power and wealth for themselves, regarding no higher principle, and being wholly unscrupulous in their pursuit of such power and wealth. A clever but greedy man can find ways to milk even a heifer, but it does her harm and is not in the best interests of anyone with a long view."

"Well said, my man," James declared.

Then their conversation moved away from politics, and on to more personal matters—namely, those of James, who, it seemed, had begun courting Widow Goodenough. She had been his neighbor before her husband died the previous spring, and was living with her sister and her brother-in-law in Hartford, so James Higgins traveled all that distance to court her on Sundays.

He had traveled there to see her many times, he had said, and next time, if his plans carried out well, he intended to ask her to marry him.

Lydia had never known her, although she had seen her in church meeting the previous year, coming with her youngest daughter. As it turned out, poor James Higgins died before the marriage was performed.

"I am happy for you," Thomas had told his friend.

"Indeed, this is very good news, James. Tis not right for man to be alone."

James then spoke at length about the Widow Goodenough, especially about her culinary skills, and in particular detail her mince pies, which, he said, could not be bested. The crusts were flakey, flavorful and golden-brown, and the filling contained such a harmonious bouquet of autumn flavors from the orchard, farm, and spice rack, added to it a touch of rum, and Barbados sugar, and a special hidden ingredient she would tell to no one.

Lydia had listened carefully to the ingredients he'd mentioned for the pie filling. At the time she had wished to question James more carefully—or rather, question Widow Goodenough—but this was impossible, for even though Thomas knew she was listening to the conversation from the other side of the door, and he did not mind her doing this, she must pretend she was not, it was not a wife's right.

She heard Thomas yawn, and knew that soon he would be sending his dear old friend on his way home for the last time.

CHAPTER THIRTY-TWO

LYDIA AWOKE AT dawn when she heard the key unlocking the heavy door.

The jailers brought no bread.

One of them pushed William down the steps while the other pulled her to her feet and dragged her out of the jail. The other jailer came out and slammed and locked the door again behind him.

She had not had time to say farewell to William. What would become of him?

The morning air was frosty cold. It bit into her skin and took her breath away as the two big men pulled her along by her armpits.

They were taking her to Blackbird Pond. That was where the hangman's oak was. It was on the north side of Windsor. She had passed by it only twice in all the years she'd lived here. It was an isolated, desolate site, with no houses around. The pond itself was murky and deep, and no good for bathing. In the summer the pond swarmed with biting insects. Someone cared for the cleared place and the tree, for the hangman's oak was strong, and stood alone. She had seen it from afar those two times she had passed by on horseback, and it made her shudder. It was tall with one strong horizontal branch about eight feet off the ground.

The jailers wore ragged greatcoats, and gloves, and knit caps pulled down over their ears. They walked fast and talked and joked with each other, as if she were not there, or as if she were a dog and could not understand them.

"Twill snow today," said one.

"Look at the grey clouds over there."

"We're headed into them, mate," said the other.

"It's not often we get to see a hanging."

"The last was in the spring of fifty-two. The sodomizer."

"Twas an adulterer."

"Same thing, Wiggin. Any was it's stuck, s'better not to be caught at it."

"Tis not the deed but being caught at it that earns the final banishment."

Lydia was cold, and her nose was running, but she had no way of wiping it. Her eyes teared in the frosty air, and all of her bones ached, but she walked as fast as she was able, trying to keep up to the pace of the jailers, so she would not be dragged. Her left shoulder still hurt very much.

"I must shit," said one of the jailers.

The other one said,

"Go ahead, then. I will hold her myself. She has little strength."

He stopped and grabbed her from behind, in both armpits.

The other one walked several paces off, took down his breeches and squatted in the old snow at the side of the road.

The one holding her let the fingers of one of his hands open out onto her breast. She stiffened.

"What a stink!" he called out.

"Ah, but my comfort is revived!" the other laughed.

His huge hand was upon her. She turned her head and grimaced at him over her shoulder.

"God ugly cursed trull!" he said.

"Your body will soon enough be without breath!"

He moved his fingers back to her armpit.

The squatting jailer stood again. Before re buttoning his breeches he briefly wagged his penis toward Lydia. She looked away, expressionless.

He took his place again at her left and the two of them walked on, faster than before.

The sun rose weakly to their right, covered in grey clouds. They walked for quite a while, and she slipped several times and had to be dragged along.

As they drew closer to Blackbird Pond, she could hear the noise of the gathering crowd, and saw several people hurrying on their way to watch the coming spectacle.

They were assembling to watch her die, but in her emptiness and degradation she thought she had already died.

Even though the ground was frozen, Lydia believed she could smell the rank odor of the brackish pond.

People were gathered all around the hangman's tree. She could see the noose rope dangling from the oak tree's strong branch.

The jailers dragged her through the crowd. She heard the peoples' jeering voices, but she could distinguish no particular voice, nor word, and her eyes were watering so that all of their faces were blurred together.

Then she saw that a wooden box had been placed under the branch.

The jailers walked her to behind the box and lifted her onto it.

One of them placed the noose around her neck. It was tight, and it ringed the flesh of her neck with its roughness.

Suddenly she could not remember how she had got there.

She felt unreal, and all of the events leading up to that moment had no meaning.

She tried to focus her eyes upon some of the faces among the crowd of townspeople. Surely among them there must be someone she had treated and healed not so many months before. She had helped so many, there must be some few of them here to help her now.

She stared out at the faces, and being no longer one of them, no longer human, she knew that not one of them would look at her in the eyes. They were afraid. They were afraid of the evilness that would vanish with her body's death. But she thought, if anyone had dared to look at her he would not have seen a fearful witch, only a broken woman full of sorrow and forgiveness for them all.

Traveling outside of her body she went to Thomas, who had been pushed away from her at the last. She thought how she had not even been allowed to clasp his hand once more, after so many months apart. He was working now, trying to occupy those hard working hands, if not his mind, and she tried to give him comfort, for he had given her only happiness, and she hoped for him to continue on without regret or too much sorrow.

To each of her daughters, none present, she went in turn. To Sarah she wished strength and courage, for she lacked in these at times. To Elizabeth, most like her in character, she gave an embrace full of the soft stuff of her previous presence, and for some moments mother and daughter were again together, and she knew Elizabeth felt her with her. And to Reliance, with her thoughtful and patient temperament, she hoped for a more comprehending race of men, if not now, perhaps a thousand years hence.

Her good mother, long dead.

Her stillborn son.

William, who had been her final comfort.

Judith.

Wrastle.

The hangman stepped behind the box and her bowels constricted, and her heart seemed to leap into her throat. She did not close her eyes, but kept them open and fixed on Governor Allyn, who stood before her in the crowd.

The box was pushed away and she hung.

The Governor believed in himself even as she went out of her body and to him. She was full of goodness and hope and he sensed her close to him, but he did not uncross his arms from his chest, and he did not open his heart.

The world darkened and closed.

The townspeople were quiet, then agitated, and they began to speak, quietly at first, and then ever more loudly. Their words gathered together like great clashing storm clouds, and she could make no sense of them, for they had become unintelligible noise.

Impressions of light and music passed over her in soft waves as she moved away, over the crowd, and out to sea with the wind.

About the Author

Suzanne Ress grew up mainly on the U.S. east coast, and perfected her writing skills at The Johns Hopkins University in Baltimore. For many years she has been living on a small farm in the foothills of the Italian Alps. She has written both fiction and non fiction for a variety of publications. This is her third novel.